I0780282

HONEY POT

THE SPIES WHO LOVED HER
BOOK 8

KATRINA JACKSON

Copyright © 2024 by Katrina Jackson

All rights reserved.

No part of this book may be reproduced in any form or by any electronic or mechanical means, including information storage and retrieval systems, without written permission from the author, except for the use of brief quotations in a book review.

This is a work of fiction. Any resemblance to actual persons, living or dead, or actual events is purely coincidental.

Statement on Artificial Intelligence: There has been no AI used in the creation of this book or cover. The publisher also does not consent to have this book fed into any AI generator.

Editor: A.K. Edits

Cover photographer: Jeferson Gomes

Cover designer: Katrina Jackson

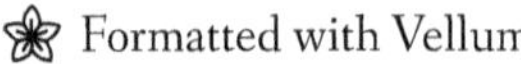 Formatted with Vellum

CONTENT WARNINGS

Physical violence
Shooting deaths
Allusions to domestic violence
Stabbing

Chanté

+

Asif

PROLOGUE

"That looks sexy on you."

Asif was standing at a jewelry counter, trying on a gold link bracelet with small diamonds embedded around the chain. It wasn't really his style, but he could imagine it around Chanté's ankle. Every time she siphoned a significant sum from his bank account, she reminded him that her favorite accessory would always be expensive and shiny, and this anklet fit the bill. But that potential theft was a thought for another life — another code name. In this identity, he turned slowly at the sound of the woman speaking to him.

Sonja Bershov was beautiful. Tall, nearly six feet, dark brown skin, a soft pout to her lips, and big, expressive brown eyes. Unfortunately, in all the surveillance images he'd seen and taken of her, the only expression she seemed to emote was despair.

"You think so?" he asked, lifting his arm to show off the bracelet on his wrist.

For the first time in the two days he'd been tailing her,

Sonja smiled in a way that seemed to indicate a genuine emotion, accentuating how unhappy she'd seemed just a few moments ago when he walked into the jeweler and also how gorgeous she was.

"I love men who wear jewelry," she said.

"Really?"

"Really. I think more women think like I do, but men's egos are so fragile."

Asif smiled. "I agree. Your accent is lovely. Where is it from?"

She smiled softly, the sadness radiating off her in waves. "Irkutsk," she said.

Asif's face lit up. "Russia? Really?"

"Really," she said again. "I don't look it. My father moved there for work and brought my mother to join him just a few months before I was born."

"Where did they migrate from?"

"The States. I believe they were from Maryland."

He shrugged. "I've never been to the States. Have you?"

Her smile wobbled. "No," she replied sadly.

Asif learned a lot about her in that simple sentence, even though he already knew much of what she wouldn't say, certainly not to a stranger.

"I've never been to Russia either," he laughed. "There's so much of the world I've never seen."

She turned fully toward him and let her gaze wander slowly down his body. "Really? You seem quite worldly to me."

Asif mirrored her stance and posed. "You think so?" he laughed.

"Where are you from?" she asked.

"Melbourne."

There were Agency spies far better at mimicking accents, but Asif was no slouch. Over the years he'd managed to hone his accent acquisition to a couple of weeks, but even after all this time, he still felt a frisson of anxiety about those first words he said to a target. He couldn't run from the fear that he'd be outed as a fraud or the dire consequences that would come from that. But Asif had always loved living on the edge.

"What brings you to Paris?" she asked, inching closer.

"The same things that bring most people to Paris," he said noncommittally, inching along the glass display case toward her as well.

"And what is that?"

He raised his eyebrows and she glanced at the men behind the counter. That was all it took to get them to scatter.

When he'd read the mission brief, the agents who'd compiled it had put a proverbial question mark next to Sonja's name. She was technically tangential to the target of their investigation, but for the last three years, wherever their target traveled, Sonja was by his side. No one knew exactly what she knew or how deep her involvement went, but one thing that look cemented for Asif was that Sonja Bershov was far from innocent.

"Continue," she said. "I doubt you mean croissants."

He laughed softly. "I don't. I came here to close a deal with Françoise Allard."

Mentioning this name was a gamble. Sixteen hours ago, Carlisle and his team had kidnapped Françoise Allard from her home and transported her to a secure and confidential location. They were currently pumping her for information on a sex trafficking ring The Agency believed was feeding

Eastern European girls and women into the American market and Black and brown girls into the European market — the worst kind of trans-Atlantic exchange. Capturing Allard was phase one of who knew how many. The goal was to sever those trafficking routes and arrest as many people as possible. It was just the sort of iceberg job Asif had come to specialize in over the course of his career. Easier to lose himself in work if the work never stopped.

"And did you?"

"I did. I believe your boss experienced the fruit of that labor just last night."

She didn't recognize him, but last night, he'd spent four hours in a private gentleman's club watching as Sonja sat next to their target with a blank, bored look on her face, as if the debauchery around her were happening in another universe — one far away from her.

Her eyes lit up. "This was no accident, then?" she asked.

Exposing himself this way was risky, but anyone could look at his personnel files and see how much he loved taking risks. Well, actually, no one but the Director of The Agency had ever seen his personnel file, but his reckless reputation certainly preceded him. "I might not be worldly, but I never let anything stand to chance."

She considered him for a moment before a slow smile spread across her face. "How can I help you..."

He offered his hand to her. "Yusuf Mahmoud," he said. "And I believe we can help one another."

Chanté

+

Asif

ONE
LONDON

CHANTÉ HAD ALWAYS BELIEVED that the easiest way to deal with anxiety was to pretend it away. It wasn't permanent or peer-reviewed, but self-delusion was a kind of self-care in her book. It had saved her more times than she could remember.

Often, the delusion would manifest as a cute mantra that got her out of bed, an overactive imagination that helped her forget a squalid group home, or sometimes it amounted to a good, firm strut down a good stretch of sidewalk, a deserted hallway, whatever. If Chanté needed a cute little mood boost, all she had to do was put one foot in front of the other, let her heels hit the floor — or pavement — with purpose, and in a few steps, she felt like Naomi Campbell's short cousin without fail. Caleb *and* Kenny sometimes made fun of her, but their teasing didn't undercut the success of her methods.

Chanté's stomach started doing flips as soon as her train pulled into Brixton Station. She'd hoped to hold it together a little bit longer, but she couldn't, so she pivoted, strutting straight off the train onto the platform. She was a little restless on the escalator up to the street, but once her heels hit Brixton Road, she turned right and made the busy midday street her runway. The trick was to not care what anyone thought of her, and Chanté had managed that feat years ago. All she cared about now was money, orgasms, and Asif, and at least two of those things never disappointed her.

She strutted for a few blocks, checking the directions on her phone. Google told her to turn left at the A203 and she dashed across the street, heels clicking loudly on the pavement, just before the light turned red. An older Black man waiting at the bus stop smiled at her encouragingly. She bounced onto the curb and gave him a little twirl before twiddling her fingers in a grateful wave and going on about her way, taking that little boost to her mood as she eased up the road.

Two days ago, she'd been in Japan running ops for Kenny while he was in Singapore with Maya. It had been a great time, and Chanté had primed her credit card for some premium content on Maya's ChatBot page, but of course, Asif's hardheaded ass fucked her plans up, so now she was here.

"Turn left, and your destination will be on the right," her phone's navigation announced.

Chanté stopped at the corner and took a deep breath to take in her surroundings. She wasn't that far from Brixton Road, but the pedestrian traffic had lessened as she moved into a cute little neighborhood with slightly curving roads, alleys jutting off in angles, and tall attached Victorians in various states of gentrification towering above her. It was something out of a cute little romcom, but Chanté's stomach was full of dread.

The secure email from The Agency Director inviting her

here had been short and to the point. A date. An address. A time. A name.

If there had been any other name at the bottom of that message, she would have stayed in Tokyo and suggested Maya and Kenny turn on Maya's streaming camera, but for Asif, she'd do damn near anything. Kenny called it an obsession, and he might have been right, but Asif was *her* obsession, and if he disappeared from the face of the earth, it would be with her. Period. That's why, in the ten years she'd known him — if *known* was really the best way to describe their acquaintance — she'd had to build a surveillance system to keep track of him so sophisticated, the CIA sometimes piggybacked on her servers without realizing it. And sure, those glimpses of access to CIA information was lucrative, but they weren't the point. The point was to make sure she knew where Asif was at all times, and for the first time in years, she didn't. That was unacceptable. But those were her motivations. She'd come to London to find out what The Agency had on their agenda.

She looked both ways — left to right before she remembered where she was — before she stepped off the curb to cross the street.

"You have arrived at your destination," her phone said before she turned it off and shoved it into her bag.

She was standing in front of a nondescript four-story townhome on the corner, hardly distinguishable from many of the other properties on the street. It was so nondescript she had to check the address twice. This wasn't exactly the kind of house she'd expected for the director of one of the most clandestine spy outfits, but to be fair, Monica and Lane lived in a suburban home in New Jersey, of all places. And technically, the first time she'd met the Director, they'd been in a building at a Midwestern public university that should have been condemned at least a decade before, so this location was an upgrade.

"I can leave," she whispered to herself. And she could. If Chanté wanted, she could turn around and walk back to Brixton Station. In a couple of hours, she could be checking into an egregiously expensive hotel in Mayfair. By the time the sun set, she could be letting some pasty but obscenely wealthy accountant buy her drinks while she massaged his dick under the table with her toes. In a week's time, Chanté could have convinced that man — or someone richer — to fly her across the continent with only the vague promise of how tight and wet she was. In a month, she could forget Asif.

She'd run this line of thought through to the end dozens of times, and the fantasy always fell apart at that lie. It wouldn't matter if she ran from him for one month, one year, or five years, Chanté couldn't forget Asif if she tried, and she wasn't interested in trying. No matter where she was in the world and no matter who was buying her expensive lingerie, her heart would always beat to the cadence of Asif's laughter.

"Fuck it," she said louder than before and started up the steps.

The button was encased in an elaborate doorbell plate, but when Chanté moved her finger over the bell, she could feel the smooth, slightly warm, familiar fiberglass that screamed scanner. "Clever," she whispered under her breath, smiling as the machine scanned her fingerprint. Once it was done, she bent down to get a better look at the lovely little piece of technology. Technically, Chanté didn't have a permanent address, but one day, she might be ready to settle down — whatever that meant. If that time ever came, she thought a doorbell like this should be near the top of her housewarming registry.

She stood, clasped her hands behind her back, and put a serene smile on her face. There wasn't much she could do but wait, and so she did. The brisk walk from the station had left all of Chanté's exposed skin warm and the nerves that dogged her through Brixton had burned away finally. It took only a few moments before she heard a lock whir, then a few more seconds before the door opened with an elegant antique creak. Chanté redoubled her smile when the face of a kindly older South Asian gentleman with honey-brown skin, thick salt and pepper eyebrows, and a striped apron covering his front appeared inside the doorway.

"Hello," he said softly. His voice was gentle and low. His smile was warm and welcoming, even as his eyebrows bunched in confusion.

"Hello," Chanté trilled back, lifting onto the balls of her feet as she spoke — a habit when she was nervous.

"May I help you?" he asked.

"Oh," Chanté said. "What?"

"Amin, is that my student?" a deep but feminine voice called from behind him, deeper in the house.

Chanté watched as the man's confusion melted away and he smiled knowingly. He turned toward the voice.

"Ah, I forgot you said one of your students was popping by." Chanté watched his profile, watched as the smile on his face shifted into something more familiar — something drenched in love. He turned back to her and pulled the door open further. "Come in, please."

Chanté nodded politely and stepped inside. The house was warm and a little stuffy, but the air in here was beautifully citrus-scented.

Amin closed the door and turned to her. "Please," he said, pointing at the shoes lined up at the front door.

"Oh, yes. Of course," she said quickly. She had to bend down to unzip her heeled boots before toeing them off and placing them neatly against the wall. Amin pulled some slippers from behind a small cabinet and placed them on the floor at her feet. He walked down the hall and stopped just in front of the woman Chanté was here to see.

The woman standing in front of her looked to be barely above five feet tall. She wore a bold sapphire salwar kameez and bare feet. Her wrists were adorned with gold bangles, and there were small gold hoops hanging from her earlobes. Her hair was pulled back in a long braid that hung over her left shoulder. At first glance, she looked like someone's sweet Pakistani mother, and Amin had looked at her as if she were made of porcelain, but all Chanté could see was power. It was the strength of the color of her clothing, the fierceness in her eyes, and the gentleness of her smile. The ease with which she moved through this moment — the way she lied effortlessly to a man she clearly loved deeply. Chanté had met many agents in her time running freelance tech support, but Maryam was the only person who inspired equal parts awe and fear.

Chanté watched with slow, steady breaths as the woman reached out to smooth a hand over her husband's arm, looking lovingly up at him. "We'll meet in my office, shohar. But we should not be long," she said in her whisky voice.

Those words made Chanté's stomach clench again. She didn't know if that was good or bad, but she understood that it wasn't up for debate.

Amin nodded. "Shall I bring you some tea?" he asked in

a voice that was as eager to please as Kenny ever sounded when he talked to Maya.

Maryam turned to Chanté, and they made eye contact for the first time. Her stomach froze in fear.

"Would you like some tea, my dear?" the woman asked solicitously. "My husband makes the loveliest jasmine tea. It's his own blend."

Chanté was nodding before she could muster the wherewithal to speak. Her throat was dry, and if she didn't have such thick thighs, her knees might have knocked together. She didn't want tea, but she could see that saying no wasn't an option. "Y-yes. I would love that."

Maryam turned back to her husband and reached up to pat his cheek. "Yes, please, my love."

He bent forward and placed a kiss on her lips, and she closed her eyes to accept it, a sweet gesture that was also the biggest show of dominance yet. This was a woman so secure in her power, she didn't worry about inviting Chanté into her home. She didn't worry about letting Chanté see her husband's devotion to her. She didn't worry about taking her eyes from Chanté for even a moment because they both knew she didn't become the head of The Agency without putting in the work.

Maryam made Monica's career look like child's play. And if she wanted Chanté to be afraid, she would be.

She was.

Chanté

+

Asif

TWO

AMIN PADDED down the hallway and turned out of view, leaving them alone.

Maryam stared at her with a sense of calm on her face.

"This isn't what I imagined," Chanté admitted nervously.

"No?" she asked curiously. "What did you expect?"

Chanté shrugged. "I-I don't know. I guess something like an underground office building like you see in movies." She laughed nervously, but then frowned. "Although I guess Monica and Lane's office is in their house too. Is that a thing you guys do by design? What are your taxes like?"

Maryam smiled at her but didn't answer her question. It was a subtle shift, but Chanté noticed it — the slight hardening of her eyes and the subtle downturn at the corners of her mouth. It wasn't anger, just an indication that small talk was over.

"We both know why you came here," Maryam said gently. "And we both know you would have come from clear across the world for this."

"Technically, I did," Chanté said, forcing herself to laugh, hoping it would cut the tension between them. The woman's smile didn't budge, nor did she join Chanté in her mirth. Chanté cleared her throat and swallowed nervously.

"That you did. Then let us not waste any more time. Follow me," the woman said, turning on the ball of her bare foot.

"Waste time?" Chanté said, shocked. She'd been on a red-eye from Tokyo as soon as literally possible, as discreetly as possible.

She turned into the rest of the house and the smell of roasting spices and herbs filled the air, making the house seem warmer and cozier by the step. They moved down a long hallway that seemed to cut through the entire main floor of their home. She could hear Amin whistling from the kitchen ahead of them.

The woman's steps slowed, and she turned to Chanté, beckoning her forward.

Chanté shuffled in her slippered feet until they were side by side. The woman wound her left arm around Chanté's right. "You may call me Maryam," she whispered.

"Isn't that your name?" Chanté asked in confusion. She'd never known the woman to go by any other, and the surprising realization that it could have been a cover made her brain kick into the next gear. What in the world had she let Asif get her into?

Maryam laughed softly and patted Chanté's arm. "The answer is as much yes as no. When you live a life like mine, you find that some questions are easier to answer than others, and yet easy might still be far too complicated to comprehend."

"Um...okay," Chanté replied to that riddle because what was she supposed to say to that? "Do I need another name?"

The woman pressed her lips together and cocked her head to the right. Her gaze drifted off in consideration. Chanté hadn't expected that response and found it surprisingly endearing. "I guess that is up to you. But there is no rush. We have other, more important things to discuss, you and I."

Chanté nodded, but dread cut through her gut. "Is he—" The rest of that sentence got lodged in her throat.

Maryam cut her off with a raised finger. "Wait until we get to my office," she said in a tone that sounded like a soft request, even though it very clearly wasn't.

Chanté's eyes went wide and she nodded quickly, pressing her lips shut dramatically, but in her mind, she rejected the possibility that Asif was anything but fine. Refused to believe it. Wherever he was, he was healthy and safe, and when she found him — which she would — she'd let him know she would no longer be allowing him to pull these disappearing acts. She was putting her foot down.

Maryam and Amin's home was something out of *Architectural Digest*. She led Chanté through a sitting room and everywhere she looked, she saw dark wood furniture decorated with beautiful carvings. The heavy furniture was softened by plush throw covers and beautiful abstract paintings in warm colors — browns, oranges, deep reds and creams. "Wow," she breathed, looking everywhere, even the ceiling. "This can't be a safe house," Chanté said.

Maryam laughed, but that was it.

The sound of Amin's whistling grew louder as the kitchen neared. The space was even more amazing than the sitting room, with a wall of windows that looked out onto a garden — a garden that still seemed lush in the middle of winter. The walls were a soft cream and captured every ray of light shining through the window, even though it was a typical gray London day outside. There was a fireplace on the far side of the room surrounded by built-in bookshelves, carefully curated to accentuate the color palette of the rest of the house. It was a chef's wet dream. Chanté wasn't a chef, but she could appreciate the beauty, nonetheless.

This was clearly Amin's space. He was rushing around the kitchen, exerting far more energy than most people used to cook a full-blown meal, let alone to make a couple of mugs of tea.

"Would you ladies like some pastries?" he asked excitedly. "Or a charcuterie board?"

Maryam laughed. "You and your charcuterie boards," she sighed softly. Lovingly.

"I went to the market this morning and bought some lovely cured meat. I spent a bloody fortune, and someone besides us should enjoy it."

"Are you a vegetarian?" Maryam asked Chanté.

Amin's attention moved to her, and he frowned sadly. "I hadn't thought of that," he whispered, as if it was an unforgivable oversight.

He lifted his eyebrows expectantly, and it pulled at Chanté's heartstrings. She'd been too flustered at the front door to think about it, but there was something about the earnest openness that made her certain that whatever Amin did, he didn't work for The Agency. She could sense his kindness in the same way she could sense the latent danger in his wife. The thought of disappointing either of them made her chest constrict.

She shook her head quickly. "I'm not. I'd love a charcuterie board."

He punched the air happily and turned to the surprisingly large refrigerator, humming to himself while pulling out one package wrapped in butcher paper after another.

"You've just made his day," Maryam whispered, pulling her through the room.

She led Chanté into a small office at the far back of the house. It looked like it belonged to a librarian or writer, not a spy. The walls were covered in dark wood paneling, and an intricately woven circular rug in the middle of the floor brought all the disparate colors around the rest of the room together in one fell swoop. Maryam's office was so gorgeous and well-designed that it took Chanté at least a full two minutes to wonder where the woman hid her guns.

"Have a seat, Chanté," she said lightly, gesturing toward a banker's chair on one side of the desk as she walked around to the other.

Chanté wasn't in any more danger now than in the kitchen, but something about her invitation to sit activated her fight-or-flight instinct, and she froze.

Maryam eased into her chair with a chuckle. "If I wanted to harm you, I could have done so a dozen times before this moment."

For some reason, that eased Chanté's distress. She exhaled loudly. "Oh my god, I was thinking that." She settled into the chair, holding her purse in her lap.

"How long have you worked for me, Chanté?" Maryam asked.

Chanté gulped. "Almost eight years," she said dutifully.

She'd met Maryam near the end of her first year in an accelerated master's program that didn't hold her interest but kept her in Cleveland and close to Kenny. She'd been craving stability and holding onto a small flame of hope for the same man who seemed determined to extinguish it. Meeting Maryam had given her something to take her mind off him and inadvertently brought him back into her life.

"In that time, you've been an invaluable asset to our organization," Maryam said.

"Thanks," Chanté trilled. "I like the money."

Maryam chuckled. "I am certain you do, but we both know the money isn't why you continue to work for us."

Chanté raised her right eyebrow. "It's not? That's news to me. Do you know how much y'all pay me?"

"I do, actually, and that's how I am certain."

Chanté shook her head at this confusing conversation.

"Three months ago, I met with a colleague of mine. You might know them, Juniper Barker."

Chanté was even more confused. "Who?"

Maryam smiled. "They're the head of AtomX Information Systems."

Chanté squinted at her for a few more seconds before those words clicked. "Oh! That spy agency masquerading as a tech startup. I don't know if I ever met Juniper, but that place is wild."

"They tried to recruit you."

Chanté nodded and sat back in her chair. "They did. Nice people. *Great* budget. I've never been wined and dined so well." She cringed and started to correct herself. "By a company." She cringed again. "Legitimately."

Maryam laughed softly. "They were willing to pay you very well. Nearly thirty percent more than we pay you."

Chanté shook her head. "Not everybody."

"Right, you give Monica a shocking discount."

Chanté shrugged. "I like her. And Kierra has a—" She cleared her throat. "Kierra's a peach."

"As I've been told. But you turned AtomX down?"

She shrugged again. "I mean, yeah. They started talking about a 401(k) and tenure bonuses and quarterly retreats and a salary!" Chanté hadn't meant to raise her voice, but just remembering that job discussion still made her anxious. "They wanted me to move to Seattle and go into an office at least three days a week. Why the fuck would I ever do that?"

It was Maryam's turn to shrug, but hers was slow, measured, and elegant. "Maybe you want to settle down."

"I don't know, maybe. We'll see. I'm not in a rush."

"Or maybe you're waiting for something. Or someone," she offered with another elegant shrug.

Chanté froze again; this time, her fight-or-flight wasn't activated on her own behalf but Asif's. Her face fell, and her mouth went dry as a lump formed in her throat. "He's fine," she said definitively.

Maryam raised her eyes. "Have you spoken to him?" she asked.

That question made her eyes sting with tears she refused to let fall. This was one of her most sensitive wounds, and the one everyone always seemed to poke inadvertently. It wasn't as direct, but it was the way everyone learned to speak to her without saying Asif's name, or they said it quickly as if they were pulling off a Band-Aid. When it came to Asif, almost everyone treated Chanté with kid gloves.

Everyone except him.

"No," Chanté admitted.

"Neither have we." Maryam sat up straight in her chair and was just about to get to business when there was a soft knock at the door.

Maryam put both hands on her empty desk. "Come in, my dear," she called in a voice Chanté now understood was soft for her husband. She hadn't been soft with Chanté.

Amin pushed the door open and wheeled in a trolley. "I come bearing treats," he called adorably.

Maryam smiled in genuine excitement and gave Chanté a sharp look to let her know she should be doing the same.

Chanté put on her best smile and clapped happily.

For the next five minutes, both women gave Amin their full attention as he served their tea and gave them shockingly detailed descriptions of each item on the charcuterie board he'd whipped up. Chanté tried to pay as close attention as she could just in case Maryam decided to quiz her on it at gunpoint, but she could hardly focus on the Italian salami as she tried to figure out when someone might have spoken to Asif last. Her mind was whirring like a fan without a belt.

When they were alone again, Maryam picked up their conversation as if there had been no interruption.

"Three weeks ago, we sent Asif to Paris for what should have been a quick reconnaissance trip. It should have taken no more than two days."

Chanté felt like her heart was pounding at the base of her throat, and she pressed her lips shut, worried she might throw up if she tried to speak.

"Our last communication with him was just before he'd planned to make contact with our target."

"Wh-what'd his backup have to say?" she whispered.

Maryam just stared at Chanté until she got it.

"Why do you keep letting that trifling motherfucker go out in the field *alone*?" she screeched.

Maryam raised a finger to her mouth. Chanté nodded, but she was so pissed, she was starting to sweat.

"He is surprisingly resourceful," the woman replied in a droll tone.

"Not that resourceful," she muttered, unable to keep the judgment from her voice.

It came and went in an instant; a steely look shot through Maryam's face — eyes squinted closed and mouth tightened into a straight line — but Chanté saw it. The danger had come and gone faster than Chanté's reflexes could respond.

"Our agents are not children," Maryam said in a measured, even light tone. "We train them well, and they know the dangers of life in the field. Agents like Asif have a particular knack for doing what others cannot. Will not. It makes them very valuable."

Chanté's heart stopped for a millisecond at the 'dangers.' "If they know the..." She hesitated and had to breathe through her nose to calm her nerves enough to continue. "If they know the dangers, then why am I here?"

Maryam's smile was almost cold. "Many reasons," she whispered. "Regardless of what you might think of us — me — we are not in the habit of wasting millions of dollars of training without trying. If I thought it would work, it would be Monica and Lane in your seat, but Russia is not the kind of country where I feel comfortable sending a team. It might just as easily backfire as anything."

"Okay, so you don't need a team — just send Monica. Or Kenny."

Maryam laughed softly. "If I sent Kenny, I would worry that he might let Asif die for his own pleasure."

"He wouldn't do that," Chanté whispered fiercely, and she wished she hadn't because she could tell by the shrewd tilt of Maryam's eyebrows that she'd betrayed herself in that admission. What she'd betrayed, Chanté might never know, but it was something.

"I can always call Monica, Lane, Kenneth, or any of the other dozens of professionals in our employ, but I'm sending you."

"Why?"

"Oh, that's an easy answer," Maryam replied, the words filtering from her mouth with a ghost of a giggle. "I trust Asif implicitly with the intelligence I need. I want someone searching for my agent who wants to bring him home, not the data."

"Oh," Chanté said, knowing she had no retort to that. "My rates—"

Maryam cut her off by raising a hand in the air. She bent over to open one of the drawers. The manila folder she slapped on the desk was fat with papers neatly collated with paperclips.

"What's this?" Chanté asked.

"Your fee for this mission."

"Uh...what part of this is supposed to be my vibe? Server backdoors for the stock market? I'll take it and I'll make magic. Off-shore account information for a billionaire with more money than sense or morals? I'll have a website for a reputable charity organization and plans for the redistribution of their wealth in less than a week. But paper? Please. Who's gonna carry all that around?"

When Chanté was done speaking, Maryam turned the file around and pushed it across the desk toward her.

From this angle, Chanté could read the name typed on the front of the folder.

Bakri, Asif.

"Asif's last name is Bakri? Do you know how long I've

been looking for that?" Chanté asked, lunging toward the desk.

Maryam quickly pulled the folder back to her. "I can only imagine. Just as you can only imagine all that lives in this file."

"I—" Chanté was speechless.

The Agency kept their personnel files under lock and key. Chanté knew because she'd gone in search of Asif's as soon as she'd realized they worked for the same entity. She'd spent a wild thirty-six hours hacking into The Agency's system to get his personnel folder, only to open a digital file with five years' worth of *New York Times* crossword puzzles. She could say a lot of things about The Agency, but she couldn't accuse them of not having a sense of humor.

"The whole file?" she asked.

"Everything. His family history, training, mission briefs, *financial assets.*"

The way Maryam said those last two words made her think the woman knew Chanté's creative...economic relationship with Asif, but that wasn't the most important thing right now. Chanté lifted her eyes to hers. "So, if I find Asif, you'll give me his file?"

"I cannot *give* you his file, no, but I promise to tell you all the things you've ever wanted to know about him."

Chanté was so desperate for that, she was out of breath.

"But you must find him alive, Chanté. You must find him quickly. Can you do that?"

It was Chanté's turn to give the other woman a shrewd look. "Would you have invited me here if you thought I couldn't?"

"No," Maryam said with a smile. "I can have a plane ready for you by tonight. All we need is a location."

Chanté's eyes moved to the file again before she met Maryam's gaze. "The information and forty thousand."

Maryam's smile was immediate. "I will approve that."

Chanté beamed and then remembered. "Should I get another name?" she asked.

Maryam nodded. "It might be prudent."

"Any suggestions?" Chanté squeaked.

The woman's eyes focused on Chanté's face with a serious concentration.

"Beti," Maryam said, but Chanté heard, "Betty."

"I look like a Betty to you? Seriously!?"

Chanté

+

Asif

THREE

CLEVELAND.

Eight years ago...

"BREAK A LEG!" Ms. Francine called after Chanté as she darted down the front steps and onto the curb. "Hardheaded," the bus driver sighed. If the older woman felt any real annoyance at Chanté's refusal to use the back door, it wasn't enough to harm their relationship. "Your next bus'll be here in fifteen minutes. Don't miss it 'cause there won't be another for thirty minutes after that."

"I remember, Ms. Francine," Chanté said with a playful roll of her eyes. Chanté had mapped the bus route from her apartment to her new club more than a dozen times before today and didn't need Ms. Francine's advice. She also technically didn't need to catch Ms. Francine's bus at all since there was a faster crosstown express, but catching up with her favorite bus driver before work had been a part of her routine since she started working at The Petal, and she wasn't ready to give that up. Not yet.

"Now I won't see you tonight, but I wanna hear everything next time we cross paths," the bus driver called.

"Definitely. Drive safe!" Chanté called as the door slid closed. The familiar sound of the air pressure lifting as Ms. Francine released the brake was her friend's only goodbye. Once Ms. Francine's bus disappeared into traffic, Chanté reached into her backpack for her headphones and slid them over her ears.

Chanté had a playlist full of songs she was auditioning for the stage, everything from independent R&B to sad white boys with acoustic guitars to heavy metal. She put as much thought into her music as her outfits — even more so because finding new music was free, and if the music hit, it could paper over the fact that most of her clothes were hand-embellished. Sure, most of her customers didn't give a shit what she wore just as long as she took it off, but Chanté cared about it all.

First up on her playlist tonight was from a new Australian artist she'd found on someone's Tumblr page. Kimbra's "Good Intent" was a little quirky, fun, and playful — not the typical kind of vibe at the Black clubs, but she'd been working on the choreography for a full two weeks and knew it was good. The customers at The Petal were used to her taking chances with her music, and even if they didn't always like it, they trusted her to make it worth their while. She'd thought about playing it safe, but that wasn't Chanté's style, and if she'd wanted to do that, she would have just stayed where she was, not just at The Petal but in Detroit.

Almost as soon as she'd arrived in Cleveland, she'd started planning to leave. The only thing that had kept her there was all her scholarship money and Kenny. After graduation, Caleb had started pressuring her to move closer to him, but her best friend had a chronic inability to sit still, so neither knew what her moving closer would have actually meant, and surprisingly, somehow Cleveland had started to feel like home. It was enough like Detroit to feel comfortable and still far enough away that she never had to worry about running into her parents. So, when Kenny decided to stick around for a master's degree in leadership — whatever the fuck that was — Chanté followed his lead, even though her mentor Dr. Charbonneau thought she was too good for the program — his program — and made sure to note that in her letter of recommendation. Technically, the world was kind of Chanté's oyster. She could have gotten a halfway decent coding gig in Silicon Valley during her junior year and lived better than anyone in her family had managed in two generations, but the idea of coding all day, every day made her want to pluck her eyes out. Also, she made damn good money stripping on the side a few days a week, so if she was going to do anything, it was strip, which is exactly what she was doing while she took a couple more years to figure out what she wanted to do with her life.

She spotted her bus down the street just as the song ended. She pulled out her phone to replay it as her routine restarted in her head.

Chanté wouldn't have thought of herself as a creature of habit because, to be honest, she hadn't had the privilege of habits as a child. Her parents had made sure her life was so chaotic that something as simple as being certain of where she would lay her head from week to week or month to month was practically a pipe dream. And now that she'd achieved that goal, she was surprisingly loath to let it go, and that had included The Petal. She would have happily stayed there, but the place had been going downhill fast since their majority owner Mia Malkova went ghost a couple of years ago. Saraiya had tried to keep the club afloat in her absence, but there was only so much she could do with a building literally crumbling — like everything else in East Cleveland — stiff competition, and obvious members of the Russian mafia stopping by, looking for Mia and scaring away customers. It had been a slow descent for Chanté, but when her favorite dancer Joi left, the place hadn't felt the same. Even her friend Angie had been encouraging Chanté to leave while putting in for waitressing jobs to make her own escape.

Still, Chanté would have stayed through all that and more because The Petal felt as much like home as the shabby apartment she shared with Kenny. Chanté could always make money, but it was the people that mattered to her. Then a couple months ago, Angie got a job as a bartender in an upscale bar downtown, and Chanté finally understood that the end had come.

The Petal closed for good a month ago. Chanté couldn't help but feel like a part of her had closed with it because The Petal was where she'd met Asif. Thinking about him hurt, even now. She climbed onto her next bus, giving the bus driver a bright smile and an audible hello. The man grunted, barely looking in her direction — nothing like Ms. Francine — but her first ride on Ms. Francine's route had been rough too, so Chanté didn't worry about that. There was always next time. She made her way to the back of the bus and plopped down in a hard plastic seat.

She switched to a new song, something slow and moody. She didn't recognize it, and she didn't bother looking it up because she'd made the mistake of thinking about Asif and now she couldn't think of anything else. She fished her phone from her bag, closed the Spotify app, and opened her text messages. She had to scroll and scroll and scroll until she found his name. Asif hadn't texted her since before he'd disappeared from her life, and even now, she thought about him every day.

She wondered where he was.

Who he was with.

If he thought about her.

She knew she should hope that his memory would fade over time, but her heart refused to accept it, so here she was, two years later, with vivid memories of a man she barely knew. It's not how she'd thought she'd waste her twenties, but it seemed harmless overall.

What wasn't harmless was the hours Chanté had spent in the far, shadowy reaches of the internet looking for him and coming up empty. Maybe if she'd ever asked his last name. Maybe if she'd gotten his fingerprints — or been in a position to get his fingerprints. Maybe, maybe, maybe.

Chanté had lived a hard life in such a short period of time, chaotic and devoid of the kind of basic care most people got to take for granted. She'd had the kind of childhood that made the concept of love nothing more than that. She didn't need a therapist to tell her she was searching for someone who would fill the void her parents left — that was obvious. What she needed was for someone to explain why those few moments she'd shared with Asif felt more real than most of her childhood.

What she wanted was for someone to promise her that wherever he was, he would come back.

And maybe that was why she couldn't leave Cleveland yet.

Chanté

+

Asif

FOUR
SAINT PETERSBURG

WHEN HE WAS STRESSED, Asif dreamed about Chanté.

When he was tired, Asif dreamed about Chanté.

When he was angry, Asif dreamed about Chanté.

And so on to infinity.

It had been a decade, and Chanté could still make him wake up from a dead sleep, covered in sweat with a dick so hard it ached. He'd convinced himself years ago that the power she had over him would fade with time, and maybe it would have if he hadn't sought her out as often as he could bear. Sometimes, all he needed was a few hours, and he could make the joy he felt from her presence last months. He was still riding high on the fumes from their last mission together, but every day without her made him increasingly weary.

And so, of course, he dreamed about her on stage. Nothing boosted his mood quite like Chanté in a skintight bodysuit... No, he'd been having a particularly annoying couple of weeks, so now she was wearing a cute pair of silver bikini bottoms with nothing on top. There was a spotlight in the middle of a stage and everything outside the arc of that spotlight was black, as if his brain had given up on creating anything beyond what really mattered.

Not as if, it had. All that mattered was Chanté and so that was all he could see. She was holding onto the pole with one hand and walking in an endless circle. Her silver spiked platform heels were impossibly tall, and she placed every step carefully — heel to toe — to accentuate the curve of each calf and the soft dimples on the back of her legs. When she turned away, Asif watched her muscles move under her skin. She turned to look at him over her shoulder and Asif's heart raced — in his dream and in reality. At the last minute, she gently placed her arm over her breasts, hiding her nipples from his gaze. For now.

There could be more after this, or this could be the dream, and Asif could never be disappointed. It was dangerous to dream during missions, but no amount of training had ever been able to stop his mind and heart from seeking out Chanté. Somehow, he'd been having wet dreams about Chanté for a decade. He'd spent more time with her in his imagination than in the real world. That imbalance in their time together was entirely his fault, but it didn't make it sting less, and it couldn't stop his mind from returning to Chanté repeatedly. Asif knew this was just his brain working through the futility of his sacrifice, and he didn't care. If the only place he could have her *and* keep her safe was his imagination, then he would live with it. He was already keeping himself from being with her; he couldn't bring himself to police his imagination any more than he already had been for all these years.

Few agents needed to sacrifice the way Asif did. Monica and Lane didn't, even Kenny didn't, but they weren't Asif.

He'd spent a lifetime emulating his mother, and when he followed her into The Agency, it only heightened that adolescent desire to be a good son and an even better reflection of her legacy. If he could be half the agent she was, he would have succeeded beyond his wildest dreams. That desire was more than the gripping fear he felt at realizing that he wasn't alone in his bed dreaming about Chanté.

"Someone's having a good morning," Sonja whispered into his ear.

It would have been natural to startle awake, but this wasn't the first time Sonja had broken into his hotel room. Asif blinked his eyes open and pretended to yawn, using these small moments to orient himself in this room, this mission. This identity. He reminded himself of where he was, what he was doing, and what he was *supposed* to be doing. He reminded himself that Yusuf Mahmoud had been playing a cat and mouse game with Sonja for days. He didn't know how it would end, but the ultimate goal had been to facilitate a deal that would bring him millions of dollars and set her free. He reminded himself that of all he'd learned about her in their short acquaintance, it was that Sonja was skittish, and without concrete evidence that she could be deadly, it was best to assume she was. Once he pulled the threads of his consciousness into the mission, he sat up in bed.

"I wish I could remember," he said, turning to Sonja with a smile.

She was laid out on his bed, her head propped up on her palm. "At least you can dream," she said with a shrug.

"You can't dream?"

"I cannot," she said mournfully, sitting up with an elegant grace.

"I'm sorry."

She shrugged. "I cannot change what is. But if I could dream, I would probably have nightmares, so this is a blessing."

Asif laughed. "That's not a bad way of looking at it."

"I know."

"Is there a reason you broke into my hotel room?" he asked. "Again."

"I knocked this time, but you didn't answer." She pouted prettily.

"I was asleep."

"As I discovered. But now, you are awake, and I would like to invite you to brunch."

"I don't eat breakfast," Asif said. "You know that."

"I said brunch, and I think you don't eat enough. Russian winters are brutal. You must make sure to sustain yourself with nutrients."

Asif shook his head. "Coffee's all I need. Is there something else going on?"

It was an educated guess, but one based on hard work. It didn't take a rocket scientist to realize that Sonja hated her life. He'd approached her because of her close relationship with Raphael Verinac, a French trafficker masquerading as a member of the aimless European elite who populated his clientele. The few times Asif had seen Sonja smile in his presence, her thinly veiled displeasure was written all over her face. Only people who didn't care to see it could miss her frustration, and thus far, Raphael and all the men who surrounded him were blissfully unaware. Asif distinguished himself through the thinnest veneer of interest and watched as Sonja opened up to him like a dying plant set out in the rain.

"He has a lunch scheduled with an associate later."

"Okay?" As a spy, Asif cared very much to know who that associate would be, but as a businessman, it hardly mattered. For the last two weeks, he'd been working to build Verinac's trust and broker a deal that would ostensibly make them both a lot of money. In reality, once the wire transfer went through, Raphael would be on a one-way ticket to a supermax prison, Sonja would be set free, and Asif would be onto the next mission.

Sonja chewed on her bottom lip and dropped her eyes. She plucked at the expensive cotton, her internal battle evident on her furrowed brow. Asif's patience was endless. The quiet gave him time to fully wake up. It allowed him to glance around the room and verify they were alone — that no one was hiding somewhere with a scope aimed at his head. That nothing, as far as he could see, was out of place.

When she finally looked up, her mouth was set in a plush frown. "He has an Israeli contact who came into town last night. They're brokering an arms deal that might preclude the one you've been negotiating."

"Why? There are far too many weapons in the world. Plenty to go around," Asif said breezily.

Her frown deepened. "Unfortunately true, but the Israeli has a seemingly unlimited budget. I can't be certain, but if the deal with the Israeli goes through, Raphael might have to postpone your deal or cancel it altogether."

"That's unacceptable," Asif said.

"I know."

"If he postpones my deal, I will have to postpone yours. And if he cancels it…"

"I understand. There's no need to threaten me."

Asif moved his hand to cover hers on the bed. "It's not a threat, just business."

She gave him a wry laugh. "You all say that."

He squeezed her hand. "So, brunch?" he asked, jogging her attention back to the matter at hand.

She looked at him again, nodding once. "If you come to his penthouse in two hours, you can disrupt their meeting."

He nodded. "Thank you."

She pushed up from the bed. "I'm not doing this for you," she said. "I'm doing this for me."

He smiled at her. "As you should."

Sonja turned and looked around Asif's room as if seeing it for the first time. She moved to a dresser on the other side of the bed, near the short hallway that led to the door. He'd placed a few belongings atop it — a bottle of cologne, a brush, an old watch he wore everyday — some knickknacks to hold his cover together, things he could gather in a hurry. She ran her hand over each item, musing at each or at the sad state of her life.

"Wear something sexy," she said before turning and walking from his room without another word.

"Don't I always?" he called after her with a casual smile in his voice, even though his face was set in a grim stare.

He listened for the sound of his door snicking closed and then waited for a few still moments more. Once he was certain he was as alone as he could reasonably be, he jumped out of bed. His first stop was the door, where he opened the door stop — something he'd done the night before — and twisted the lock closed. He still didn't know how Sonja kept breaking into his room, but he was impressed by it. The relative lack of privacy kept him on his toes and alive; that was all that mattered.

Next, he moved to the dresser. He inspected the knick-knacks Sonja had touched and the floor around it. He didn't know what he was looking for, but he knew he'd recognize it when he saw it. When he'd confirmed there was nothing out of place, he pulled a drawer from the center of the dresser out as far as it would go and moved his hand underneath, making sure the emergency cell phone he'd taped in the corner was there. There was no way of knowing exactly how long Sonja had been in his room before he woke up, so he did a quick and dirty sweep of the area, looking for bugs, cameras, anything that might indicate that his cover was blown.

He gave himself five minutes to get it done, timing himself for his own safety and as a general reflection of his distaste at being woken up in such a way. This building had once been a mansion or a palace before the Soviet regime and had only recently been renovated into a luxury hotel targeting a foreign market. There seemed to be endless places where one could hide a bug. Still, Asif did what he could. Probably the most important of the early lessons Asif learned in The Agency was that nothing he would do in this job was foolproof; all he could do was make sure he wasn't the fool who got in his own way.

When his sweep was done, he walked into the surprisingly cavernous bathroom — the only part of the room he truly enjoyed. He turned on the shower and stripped off his pajama pants while looking at his reflection in a mirror so big it took up half the wall. He didn't think there was anything exceptional about his own reflection, but maybe that was part of his cover. Yusuf was an unassuming businessman who didn't have to worry about the petty aspects of life — a schedule, time, meals, his own appearance. It was the best kind of cover as far as Asif was concerned — inconsequential but mysterious. Yusuf was intriguing enough to catch Raphael's attention, but not bold enough to hold it for long. Even the accent had become nearly second nature, signaling that he'd sunk deep enough into his cover that success and danger were assured in equal measures.

But when he looked into his own eyes, his mind immediately conjured Chanté. When he closed them, the darkness brought his dream back again. Chanté was still slowly circling her pole, but this time, when her front came into view, she uncovered her breasts. He couldn't remember the last time he'd seen her naked, but he could remember the first. He reached down and grasped his dick, grunting when his cool fingers wrapped around the base. His skin was hot to the touch. He wanted to stroke himself — so desperate for a release he could taste it — but he breathed through the need. Slow, deep breaths that calmed his racing pulse but did nothing to fill the hunger in his gut.

There was only one woman who could do that.

Chanté

+

Asif

FIVE

AN HOUR LATER, Asif was showered and dressed. He checked his tactical gear, light as they were under the circumstances — cell phone in his back pocket, a SIM card with important numbers in the lining of his left shoe, and a pen-sized taser tucked into his breast pocket. It wasn't a gun or an earbud with a direct feed to tactical support, but it was something. He stopped at the dresser, sprayed himself with the cologne, and wrapped the old watch around his right wrist before walking from his hotel room.

In the lobby, he had the concierge call a car. The small boutique hotel in the heart of the Golden Circle was either a logistical nightmare or the next best thing to a safe house as he could acquire on such short notice. The small staff was regular enough that Asif had managed to learn everyone's names and faces, making it far easier to spot a new face in the crowd. Every morning, while he waited for his car to arrive, he scanned the room covered in rich wood, marble, and gilded fixtures, looking for someone who didn't belong.

Someone like him.

The concierge, Artyom, was his anchor. Each day, he slipped the man a wad of cash as a precaution, hoping that if anything out of the ordinary happened, he'd at least give Asif a few minutes' head start. It was a long shot but worth the discretionary funds. Unfortunately, Artyom, for all his attention, hadn't managed to stop Sonja getting into his room thus far, which was a conundrum Asif still hadn't figured out how to handle. His eyes scanned the room as he recognized the staff behind the front desk, a luggage attendant stepping from the elevator and wheeling his cart back into place, even the janitor mopping in the far corner. Everything was as it should be, and still, Asif knew he wasn't safe.

"Mr. Mahmoud," Artyom called to him, gesturing toward the door with a smile.

Asif nodded and slid a folded bill into the other man's hand as he passed. Artyom pulled the door open for him to walk through. Asif clutched his heavy coat close at his neck, hating how often he seemed to find himself in such cold weather, then hating himself for choosing this even when he didn't have to. He'd grown up mostly in Chicago, but the cold of Saint Petersburg in the late morning was the kind of cold that made him seriously consider quitting his job for the long seconds it took to stroll across the sidewalk. The front door attendant was standing at the back of a black car with the door open, and all Asif could do was hope that this car had better heat than the one he'd traveled in yesterday.

Asif walked quickly toward the car without thinking because if he thought about the absurdity of his life, he'd crumble. If he thought about the fact that he'd chosen this life, he'd start to wonder about his mental health. If he thought about the fact that he chose this life over Chanté, he wouldn't have to wonder.

"Spasiba," he muttered to the man, slipping him a few bills as well before sliding into the backseat of the car.

The driver confirmed the destination Asif told the concierge and Asif nodded silently but didn't speak. The man looked forward and started to pull off into traffic.

Asif had been at this hotel for almost two weeks. In a few days, he'd need to leave this location, either to another hotel or, preferably, out of the country. Two weeks was pushing the bounds of his safety and he knew it, but relocating somewhere else in the city was daunting. This was why people like Monica and Lane traveled with Kierra in tow, but their situation was a luxury Asif couldn't afford. Wouldn't agree to. He turned to look out of the window toward the hotel just as the door attendant sprang into action. Asif's eyes shifted to a man in a long, puffy jacket walking into the building. It wasn't a moment worthy of special attention except that when he pushed the hood from his head, Asif squinted at the sliver of the man's face he saw and swore he recognized it.

That was either good news or a terrible sign of what was to come.

Asif sighed in resignation and sat back in his seat. He'd find out soon enough.

ASIF AND SONJA HAD A SURPRISINGLY PLEASANT MEAL in Raphael's penthouse at the outer edge of the Petrogradsky District. Since he'd been in Russia, he'd wasted so many hours of his life in this penthouse at Raphael's various stuffy cocktail hours, competing with most of the other guests desperate for just a few moments of the powerful man's attention. Sonja had helped to put him in front of her boss at the beginning, but for the past week or so, Asif had been doing the heavy lifting to broker a deal. He was a day or two, at most, from succeeding, but only if the Israeli contact didn't get in his way.

He and Sonja waited for Raphael to arrive, chatting about nothing of consequence because talking about the business that brought him here would have been a death sentence. Asif had done his best to surreptitiously case the home during those same cocktail hours and had discovered just enough cameras and microphones to let Sonja steer the conversation to fashion and weather, nothing more. Thankfully, Asif was from the Midwest and the latter, at least, was comfortable territory.

They were just discussing the likelihood of a storm in the next few days when the front door opened.

Normally cool, Asif noticed Sonja's back stiffen. Her fingers clutched the knife next to her empty plate.

Asif took a deep breath and placed his hand on the table. He said her name and she jumped as if his whisper had been as loud as a gunshot. They locked eyes and he took in a deep breath through his nose, holding it until Sonja followed suit. They exhaled together just as the sound of Raphael's voice boomed around the cavernous room.

Sonja sprang into action, pasting a beautiful, seductive smile on her face. "Oh, lovely, you're home."

Asif heard shoes skidding on the floor, but he reached for his water glass rather than shift toward the sound. Just as the men turned into the dining room, Asif took a slow sip and relaxed in his seat.

Sonja stood slowly from her chair. She was wearing a

shirt dress with dark green leaves over a crisp white backing. The room was decorated in the excess characteristic of a Russian oligarch, but Sonja brought a touch of class to the room that, frankly, it didn't deserve.

"I thought you would be out," Raphael said guiltily, as if Sonja was his wife and he was caught at the door with his mistress.

Asif still wasn't certain about the nature of their relationship, which was almost as interesting as Raphael's illicit contacts across Central Europe. But only one of those was his business.

"I was out earlier but came back for brunch with Yusuf."

"Brunch with—"

Sonja sighed dramatically and crossed her arms in front of her. "I told you about it. You never listen to me."

"I do," Raphael said quickly, rushing into the room. "But you know I am always so busy, many things slip my mind."

Asif tilted his head to the side to track his progress toward Sonja, taking a single second to glance at the man standing just inside the room.

Joseph Herman.

He'd never met the man, but his reputation preceded him like a warning shot before a deadly shootout. It didn't bode well that he was here; not for Asif, not for Sonja, not for anyone.

"You always say that," Sonja pouted.

"Because it's true," Raphael said. "I hate to leave you behind, but how else can I make sure we live such a beautiful life?"

The man was as believable as he was honest, but Sonja didn't show anyone her true reactions. If she seemed happy, Asif knew she was sad. If she seemed distracted, she was hanging on every word said. If she seemed loyal, she was anything but.

She turned to Raphael and rolled her eyes before grabbing the man about his chin. Raphael Verinac was allegedly the son of a reclusive billionaire who'd decamped to the Netherlands decades ago. Asif couldn't remember the man's name because it was a lie anyway. Raphael was a con artist. He'd gotten his start as a low-level financier with more ambition than ethics and a fuck ton of luck. Just before agents of the Swiss Stock Exchange had been able to concretely uncover his insider trading, the man had quit his job and gone underground. He was charming and smart, but a terrible liar.

Sonja was a natural.

"Are you done with work?" she purred.

Raphael's unnaturally tan face flushed. "Just one more meeting, my dear, and then I'm all yours."

"You and your credit card?"

Raphael wrapped his arms around her waist. "At your service."

She smiled at him, and Asif set his glass on the table. He knocked his knife with the glass, pulling all the attention toward him.

He picked up the knife and laughed nervously. "Sorry, mate."

Raphael looked at Asif like he was trying to place his face, a surprisingly comforting move. "Yusuf," he said after a while. "How was brunch?"

"Wonderful. Your hospitality is impeccable even when you're not here."

Flattery always brought a smile to Raphael's face. "Ah, this is my associate, Joseph Herman."

Asif was surprised to be introduced to the man under his real name rather than one of his many aliases. In Asif's line of work, identities were like fast fashion — disposable and cheap — but to use Herman's real name said something about how Raphael felt about Asif, or maybe Sonja.

Joseph was an unassuming man — forgettable even. However, Asif had seen INTERPOL's file on Herman. He knew what the man had done. What he'd gotten away with. He and Sonja turned toward the other man, both feigning surprise at his presence. Asif turned in his chair, but still, he didn't stand. Under normal circumstances, he never would have remained seated, but Yusuf was too casual to shuffle to his feet to shake anyone besides Raphael's hand. Yusuf bent his arm over the back of the chair and took the man in with bored interest. Yusuf was thinking about a stiff drink.

"Joseph, this is my dear friend, Sonja, and her dear friend, Yusuf."

'Dear friend' was doing an incredible amount of work in both of those descriptions, but Raphael at least believed them, which seemed to set Joseph at a kind of ease.

"It's lovely to meet you," Sonja said softly.

Asif nodded and pulled a smile onto his lips. Joseph's response was similarly curt before he turned his attention to Raphael.

"Maybe we should talk later," Joseph said in a thick French accent.

"Oh no, come, let's go to my office."

Joseph shook his head. "No, your..."— he shifted his head toward Sonja — "dear friend has clearly missed you, and our business can wait."

Raphael's eyes shot up. "It can?" His voice was far less playful in this moment.

"It can wait for a short while. Do you have plans tonight?"

"No," Raphael said.

Sonja sighed testily.

Joseph smiled. "I have booked a table to see a performance at one of my favorite burlesque clubs. There's room for you," he said, then turned to Asif. "And you as well." He set his attention back on Raphael. "We can speak there."

"Of course," Raphael replied, his light tone returning.

"I'll message you with a location and time," Joseph said, already turning toward the door. They watched him go.

"I hope we didn't scare him away," Asif said in a serious tone.

"Oh, no," Raphael replied with a lightness that didn't meet his eyes. It might have worried him on another man's face, but Raphael's only genuine expression seemed to be greed. "Not at all. Not at all. He is always so serious. Now, what did you have to eat? I find myself a bit hungry."

Sonja reached for the bell set just beyond her plate. The ring bounced around the room, and the sound of rushing steps galloped toward them.

"Sit," Sonja said, walking from Raphael's grasp to pull out his chair at the head of the table. "Please, sit."

Raphael smiled at her seeming submission and lowered himself like a king into the chair. Her eyes skittered to Asif's for a brief moment before she looked away.

One of the housekeepers spoke in soft Russian and Sonja called back, her voice much stronger, also in Russian. Even though he understood she'd grown up in Russia to American parents, every time she spoke in Russian, Asif's brain wanted to stutter to a halt and pick apart the puzzle of her life. But he was here to get information on Raphael; the enigma of Sonja's background didn't matter. He hoped.

"Sonja and I were discussing spring dresses," Asif said to Raphael. "I was telling her how lovely I thought she'd look in red."

"I tell her that every day," Raphael gasped before launching into his vision for Sonja's spring attire. The man talked about her like she was a pretty doll he could maneuver and dress up however he liked. It wasn't just demeaning, it made Asif's skin crawl. He'd never seen anything directly that made him worry for Sonja's safety, but he still found it hard not to recoil at the man's warm voice and dead-eyed gaze.

He would never fault Sonja for betraying the man.

Chanté

+

Asif

"UGH, THIS LIGHTING IS TERRIBLE," Chanté muttered to herself while blending her foundation with practiced bounces of her makeup sponge over her cheeks. "And is the heating even on?" She was still speaking to herself, even though she was technically in a room full of people.

The Glass Menagerie wasn't the best or worst club she'd ever danced at. Hell, this one wasn't even the first Glass Menagerie. Under normal circumstances, this club wouldn't be on her radar at all. Chanté had been crisscrossing the world under lucrative featured residencies at some of the best exotic dancing and burlesque clubs in the world, and she'd never heard of this place. The only reason she was even here was because the program she used to cross-reference what little she knew of Asif's target, the country, and the man's unpredictability chose this club as the most likely location to stumble upon a man dead set on not being found.

But if the math was wrong, she would fly to wherever the fuck Caleb was and kick his ass for his shoddy code.

Besides the fact that the residency fee was well below

Chanté's average, the other dancers were, objectively, annoying as shit. From the moment she'd arrived at the club, the only person who hadn't been an asshole to her was the owner — although he clearly wanted to fuck her, so she wasn't that excited about his solicitous attention. Everyone else, especially the dancers, had been giving her the cold shoulder. Granted, the building was cold itself, so maybe they didn't have any other option.

A shockingly pale and timid girl appeared in the mirror behind Chanté's reflection. She froze, widening her eyes, and waited to see how the other woman would respond to her because she believed in matching energy in all professional situations. Their reflections existed in a blank-faced standoff before the girl hazarded a tentative smile, tucking her long jet-black hair behind her ears.

Chanté smiled brightly back and swiveled on her stool. "Yes?"

"Eh...eh..." The girl swallowed nervously and brightened her smile, but she didn't keep speaking.

"Is it time for me to go work the room?" Chanté asked kindly.

The girl nodded.

"Now?"

The girl shook her head quickly and held her hand up, palm facing Chanté.

"Five minutes?" Chanté asked.

"Da. Da." The girl tried to mimic what she said and Chanté immediately understood the problem here.

"Are you learning English?" she asked, and the girl nodded back. "I understand. I only speak very little of a few languages, but I think it's like dancing. You comprehend more than you can do until you're ready to take a chance."

Chanté tried to speak clearly and slow enough for the girl to understand without being condescending. The girl listened closely as Chanté spoke, her brows furrowing in concentration, before nodding and smiling excitedly for the first time.

She took a slow, deep breath and licked her lips before contorting them in a way that was clearly still new for her. "Thank you," she said with a thick Russian accent, obviously.

"You're welcome. Four minutes?"

The girl looked at the watch on her wrist and nodded. "Y-yes."

"What's your name?" Chanté asked.

"Inessa," she said, blushing.

"Very pretty," Chanté said before turning back to her mirror. She watched the girl walk away, standing a little straighter, Chanté thought. On the other side of the mirror, she saw a girl with the most perfect blond hair pulled back into a bun sneering at her. Chanté wiped the smile from her face and glared at the woman's reflection until she sheepishly looked away. This wasn't a unique experience in her line of work, but it was disheartening. Chanté liked people and *loved* dancers; it hurt her heart to have to bottle that up. But the mood of this changing room wasn't her doing, so she bent forward to line her lips in a deep brown carefully before swiping her stickiest gloss across her mouth.

She stood from her stool and untied the belt of her silk robe. Slowly. By the time she'd hung it on the hook next to her vanity, every eye in the changing room was on her. As she deserved.

A decade in the game wasn't much to some people, but in a place like this, it was like a century. Chanté had packed clubs in Atlanta, Miami, Mexico City, and Tokyo. She didn't give a shit what anyone in this cold ass shack in Saint Petersburg thought of her because she was a fucking star.

They'd figure that out by the end of the night.

ASIF HAD WANTED TO GO BACK TO HIS HOTEL FOR A NAP but stuck close to Sonja, even if only so he could provide a buffer between her and Raphael. He tried to talk business with the man, but he dodged the topic artfully, a worrying development. Apparently, Sonja had been right to warn him about the Israeli deal.

Arms dealers were tricky. Either they hoarded their stash of weapons like a dragon with its gold, or they made deals with anyone and everyone, desperate for more money even if they had to defraud a criminal to get it. Technically, neither strategy was better than the other and, in Asif's estimation, usually just decided when and how their business dealings came to an often-bloody end. Raphael was of the former persuasion, apparently, which meant that Asif would likely have to start looking for a new almost safe house tomorrow morning.

By the time they arrived at The Glass Menagerie just after sunset, Asif was weary of this day, this mission, himself. He didn't have a home of his own, but in the back of Raphael's town car, he found himself daydreaming about his room in his parents' home, or better yet, Chanté's small apartment in Cleveland. And that was dangerous. They walked straight from the car into the club, which looked and smelled like a humidor.

"How often do you think they close this place down for a deep cleaning?" Sonja whispered into Asif's ear, making him laugh surprisingly.

"Never," he replied with a smile.

"Sonja," Raphael said. "Come."

Her face fell at his sharp tone and the way he spoke to her — not like a doll now, but a dog.

"I can stay with her while you have your meeting," Asif said.

Raphael feigned a smile. "How considerate," he said, condescension dripping from every syllable. "Unfortunately, I require Sonja's companionship, so we will have to leave you alone for a bit. But please, go to the bar. On me," he added in the kind of tone rich people use when they believe that money solves everything.

Sonja smiled sadly in his direction before turning to follow Raphael.

Asif watched until they disappeared into the crowd before scanning the room. There were too many people to correctly assess the threat level, so he assumed that everyone — literally everyone — was a hostile. Sometimes things were easier that way.

Until he saw her hair.

He thought he was dreaming. Hallucinating, actually, but he moved toward her anyway. The bar was ornate with heavy wood and all types of glass. He'd hate to see this place in a gunfight, but it was pretty to look at, nonetheless. The room was packed and he had to maneuver his way through the crowd toward her, but he'd done that dozens of times and dreamed about doing that thousands of times more.

He hadn't been sure what kind of club this was until a skinny blonde woman in little more than lingerie threw herself in front of him, bringing him to a halt. She said something in Russian, and even though he didn't understand a single word, he imagined it would be attractive to the right man. He didn't know if the complete stranger whose arms he pushed the woman into was the right man, but that wasn't really his concern.

She was.

"Huh? I don't speak—" She sighed. "You don't care."

"I do," Asif said, pushing his hands into his pockets.

Her face lit up, and the man she'd been speaking to thought it was for him for a pathetic second. He opened his mouth to speak to her — still in a language she couldn't understand — but she was already turning toward Asif.

The only good thing about the fact that Asif denied himself time in Chanté's presence was that whenever he saw her again, it was as good as the first time. Maybe even better.

"Well, hello, stranger," she trilled, taking a step toward him.

"Hello, sweetheart," he replied in a soft tone, taking a step toward her.

They were in their own little world. This bar, this building, that man, the blonde, Raphael — all of it fell away.

"What are you doing here?"

"Looking for you," she said, pressing her body against his.

He had to bend forward to keep eye contact, and she pressed the palms of her hands into his chest, rubbing herself against the lower half of his body. Her smile was perfect; not even his imagination could improve upon it.

"Last I checked, you were in Japan."

"And last I checked, you didn't have a death wish."

He frowned, and she lifted her heels from the floor to get closer. "Why would you think that?"

"You're here alone," she said, shrugging.

"Not anymore. I should have known they'd send you," he whispered into her mouth.

Chanté licked his lips and he smiled even wider. God, she was perfect.

He angled his head to the left and bent forward, well on his way to bending himself in half just to kiss her. Just to touch her. Always for her. "Who else is with you?"

"Just me," she sighed.

Asif jerked away a few inches. "What?"

Chanté rolled her eyes and moved her fingers over his chest, circling his nipples through his shirt.

"You're very capable of getting yourself out of anything," she purred, pinching one nipple between two fingers.

This time when he jerked away, he cried out on a soft moan and shut his eyes.

She pinched harder.

Asif's dick was hard and heavy in his pants. Two minutes ago, he'd been a different man, but now, with Chanté's hands on him, her soft curves pressed into his chest, and her cool, minty breath making his lips tingle, he felt like a brand-new person.

With Chanté, Asif felt like himself.

After a few seconds, she released her grip on his flesh. He groaned as his muscles relaxed. That sharp bit of pain radiated from the two hot points on his chest over his body. It took a few seconds more to regain the energy to speak, but he picked up the thread of their conversation easily.

"If I'm so capable, why are you here?"

She took a step back, and he opened his eyes in confusion.

There was a mischievous smile on her face. Her hands moved to her neck dramatically, posing for him — only him — in this room full of people. His heart was racing as he took her in, from the pointed tips of her long, multicolored nails to the obscenely sheer lace of her bodysuit.

"What do you think?" she asked.

"What I always think about you," he rasped.

"Which is?"

"Did you get those done for me?" he asked as her hands moved down her chest and around to cup the sides of her breasts.

"Depends," she said, moving both hands over her soft stomach.

He wondered how far she'd go. If he could get her in a coatroom or restroom fast enough for his hands to follow. But he shouldn't have been thinking about any of that or the dozen other filthy wishes flitting through his brain.

Asif moved fast, pulling his hand from his pocket to cup her waist and yank her forward.

Her hands slapped against his chest as she laughed. He grunted at the lovely sting. "Why are you here, Chanté?" He said those words against her closed mouth.

She spread her lips and sighed against his pout. There are some things more intimate than a kiss. "I'm here to make sure you get out of this without a scratch on that pretty little head."

Chanté

+

Asif

SEVEN

THE BOUNCER CHECKED her driver's license like it was a counterfeit bill. He even pulled out a blue flashlight and inspected it, along with her face, as if she was trying to pull off a bank heist. Now, Chanté wasn't opposed to that, but if she was trying to do all that, she'd be doing it somewhere that wasn't East Cleveland. Respectfully.

After the doing-too-much bouncer had inspected every square inch of her ID, he handed it back and peered at her. "You're the new girl?" he asked.

"Yeah. They didn't tell me if there was an employee entrance or anything."

He nodded. "It's around back. Make sure they show you before you leave tonight. This line gets long, and they'll send you home if you get here late."

"Damn. Okay, thanks. Where do I go inside?"

He motioned with one finger that she should step forward, then walked to the front door of the club and pulled it open. She stepped inside, and a woman at a hostess stand waved at her. "This is Chanté," he called to the hostess.

"New girl?" she smiled.

Chanté nodded.

She pulled open a long black curtain and pointed inside. "Go wait by the bar, I'll call someone to come get you."

"Okay, thanks." She turned to the bouncer. "And thank you, too."

He nodded once. "Welcome to the Brick House. Have a ball."

Chanté's mouth fell open at that corny line. "I hope they pay you enough to say that."

It took a second, but eventually, his face cracked into a half-smile. "They don't. Now get."

Chanté learned early at The Pearl that there were a few people she absolutely needed to be on her side — the bouncer, security, the bartender, and the DJ. She could get by without them, but with those four people in her corner, she could rule any club she danced at. That small smile on the bouncer's face let her know she was well on her way to making him her new friend. He didn't know it yet, but he had two weeks max before Chanté became his favorite dancer at the club, maybe even in the city.

The hostess smiled as she approached. She'd auditioned during a slow night, but tonight, the club was packed, and her mouth fell open at the sight. The last few months at The Petal had been like a ghost town. Even some of the regulars stopped showing up. Chanté only worked a couple of days a week, and sometimes she wasted a whole shift backstage reading for class because there wasn't anyone in the audience to see them dance. But this night at the Brick House was better than The Pearl had ever been.

"Damn," she breathed to herself.

The space was set up with a circular stage in the middle

of the room with low, small round tables and chairs surrounding it almost entirely. Chanté thought it was a bit of a fire hazard, but the gossip around The Petal had been the changing rooms had asbestos, so she decided to call this a hazard of dancing at this club and not complain. So long as the money was good, she'd be fine. Half-naked waitresses shimmied through the thick crowd as best they could, fists stuffed with drinks. The stage was empty for the moment, but Chanté could tell by the mushroom cloud of dollar bills in the air and men jumping up and down that there were at least a few dancers on the floor. She lifted onto the balls of her feet, trying to see one of them— even just a little bit of her — because whoever she was, Chanté wanted to be her friend.

In the middle of all that, the DJ came on the mic to hype up the crowd as the house lights dimmed and the stage lights came on full force. "Make some noise for Pussy Poppin' Petunia!" the DJ yelled, and the crowd popped up.

"What a name," Chanté breathed in awe.

In her Converse, Chanté couldn't see over the crowd no matter how much she stretched her neck or her legs. All she could do was wait until the crowd settled to give her another glimpse of the stage, but when she did, it was worth it. A white woman in a pastel bodysuit was slinking around the stage. She had Chanté at the bodysuit. Chanté loved a dancer who could play with silhouettes and shadows, who knew you could show nothing and everything at the same time and made their time on stage a performance from beginning to end, and Pussy Poppin' Petunia seemed like her kind of people. Chanté's mouth fell open as the woman suddenly ran toward the pole, grabbing it with both hands and swinging her body in a fast arc, and the crowd erupted.

"Holy shit," Chanté cried out and watched the beginning of Petunia's routine.

"Hey! Hey, you!"

Chanté didn't know how long he'd been yelling at her — her attention was otherwise occupied — but she turned toward the bar where a skinny, red-faced man was glaring at her, motioning for her to come to him.

She did so, forcing herself to smile, and even waved.

He didn't seem to like that. "You wanna watch, you gotta buy a drink," he spat at her.

She was confused for a minute until she realized and shook her head quickly. "Oh, no, this is my first day. I'm the new dancer."

He raised his eyebrows and let his gaze move down her body.

Chanté clapped her hands sharply and glared at him. "Don't be rude." Her voice was low and hard, the exact opposite of how she normally sounded. Mentally, she crossed the bartender off her list of allies. She'd get along without him. "My name is Chanté. I just got hired from The Petal."

"And she's with me," a voice called behind her.

Chanté whirled around to find Joi glaring at the bartender over her head.

Joi flicked her butt-length royal blue wig over one shoulder for dramatic effect. "I'll make sure to let Rosé know that this is how you treat new dancers, and probably our customers too."

Chanté didn't bother turning back to the bartender, but when Joi flipped him off, she could only guess it didn't go well. And she didn't care.

"Oh my god, I missed you!" Chanté cried. She hadn't

meant to say that, and as soon as the words left her lips, her face started to warm.

But even in the midst of her overwhelming embarrassment, she couldn't help but admire her friend. She watched as Joi turned her attention to Chanté. Her face and body relaxed as a slow smile spread across her perfect, plump brown lips. There were so many beautiful women in the world, but in Chanté's world, Joi was top five. She had the most gorgeous dark eyes framed by the silkiest strip eyelashes. Her skin was the smoothest shade of dark brown, and the flashing lights from the stage bounced off her in soft splashes of neon. Her gaze moved down Joi's body. She was so fucking sexy, so sexy that normally chatty Chanté was briefly at a loss for words.

Joi pulled Chanté into a hug. "I missed you too." She brushed her mouth low on Chanté's cheek. The corners of their mouths touched, and it took every ounce of self-control Kenny thought she didn't have not to turn her head and do more than just brush her lips against Joi's.

Once Chanté realized it was time to leave The Petal, Joi was the first person she reached out to. Her friend knew all the strip clubs in town and damn near all the dancers. Chanté had hoped she could steer her in the direction of a new club, and she had.

"Are you excited?" Joi pulled back and asked.

"Yeah. Nervous too."

Joi rolled her eyes. "Oh my god, shut up, there's nothing to worry about. You'll be great. I know it."

Chanté turned to look at the stage. Petunia's thighs were wrapped tight around the pole, her torso perpendicular to the ground. She was turning in a slow circle. "I don't know about that."

Joi's cool breath ghosted over the shell of Chanté's ear. "You're gonna make that stage yours," she whispered.

Goosebumps erupted down Chanté's neck.

Chanté turned her head slowly, but Joi didn't move. They were eye to eye, nose to nose, their breath mingling. Some crushes are cute, fleeting things, but some dig down in your bones. And some crushes reminded you of a life that could have been.

It was impossible for Chanté to be this close to Joi, to smell her perfume, to be within half a breath of kissing her without thinking of Asif.

Without missing him.

And Joi, being Joi, smiled sadly at her, smoothing her hand down Chanté's forearm until their palms met and their fingers locked together. "It's okay," she breathed. Her breath tasted like peppermint, and Chanté wondered how the taste would be stronger on her tongue. "Come on, I'll take you back."

She buried that sharp needle of sadness and let Joi lead her across the floor. At the last minute, Chanté glanced over her shoulder at the bartender.

Joi squeezed her hand until Chanté turned back to her. "Don't worry about his narc ass. Josh thinks he owns the place."

Joi led her to a false hallway, toward a door with a security guard concealed in the shadows. He was at least six feet tall and had the look of a college football player whose better days were well behind them. Chanté decided to make him her second new friend.

The man reached for the doorknob as they approached. "Steel, this is Chanté. Chanté, this is Steel," Joi said.

He nodded. "Josh fucking with you?" he asked, his eyes boring seriously into Joi's.

"Nah. He was fucking with Chanté, though, and I had to nip that shit in the bud," she spat back in annoyance.

"You need to stop antagonizing his ass. You know the skinny ones be mean."

Joi stopped at the door and put her free hand on her hip. "I'm not antagonizing his ass, but I'm not about to let him treat me or my people like that. He shouldn't treat anybody like that. And if Rosé won't check his ass and none of the men who work in this place want to, then I will."

Chanté's eyes went wide, and she held her breath. Maybe it was because the man was damn near a foot taller than her, but she wouldn't have talked to Steel like that. Joi had always been more talented than her and definitely more fearless.

Steel was staring a hole into Joi's face. His jaw twitched, and he frowned. "I told you we'll handle it," he said in a low, slow, terrifying grumble of a voice.

Chanté's nipples stood at attention, and so did Joi's.

She stabbed her index finger into Steel's chest. "Then handle it," she said before pulling Chanté through the door.

There was a lot going on in the first few minutes of her first day at her new job, but between Steel's frustrated growl and Joi's ass bouncing as she pulled her toward the dressing room, Chanté was convinced this move was her best decision of the year.

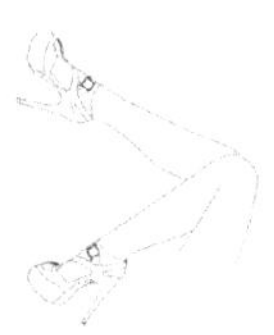

Two years ago, Yuri Malkov was head of the Russian mob's interests in the Midwestern nightlife, a position he'd held for two decades. He'd been preparing to retire and leave his financial interests to his son, which had immediately caused a rift between him and his other children. Two years ago, The Agency sent Asif to Cleveland on a surveillance mission on Malkov's daughter, Mia. Almost as soon as her father announced one of her brothers as his successor — and not her — she'd started using a feminization of her last name, Malkova, and begun setting up her own financial interests, brazenly stepping on her father's toes. Her investment in a strip club in East Cleveland called The Petal had given Asif the opportunity to place a bug in her office, which almost immediately gave The Agency the information they needed to arrest half her family and start dismantling the Midwestern arm of the Russian mob. They'd hoped to flip her as well, but she'd disappeared before they could get to her.

"The subject could be deceased or on the run. We won't know until we know," had been his official conclusion, and he read it again three weeks ago when he got orders to return to Cleveland and check in on the case. He read his final report on the mission closely, not because he'd forgotten the details but because it was the first time he realized how little real information was in it. Beyond a single authorization for increased discretionary spending, Chanté didn't exist in that file. There was no mention of their walks from the club to her bus stop. No mention of the days he spent in her living room watching her dance for him or all the times he'd jacked himself off in peaceful privacy thinking about her. His mission notes were brief, direct, and professional, and even to his own eyes, cold. He could almost forget that he'd met Chanté two years ago except he'd never managed to forget her. And in the end, Chanté was the reason Asif didn't complain about returning to Cleveland. He'd been waiting for permission to get back here since he left. Still, he didn't believe it would actually happen until he stepped off the plane at Hopkins Airport with a fake ID, a carry-on bag, and a determination to see Chanté, even if he had to disobey orders to do so.

"I'll be in the area if you need a ride," Smith said.

"I won't," Asif replied, looking out at the grays and browns of the city — old, abandoned factories dotted alongside half-finished revitalization projects to make the best of a time gone by, dirty snow in the gutters, barren trees against a cool sky.

"You never know," Smith said cheerily as he pulled along the curb, turning to look at him over his shoulder.

"*You* never know. I do. I'll check in tomorrow." He pulled the door open and stepped out onto the curb, slamming it shut behind him with a satisfying push.

Smith, however, refused to let him get the last laugh. He rolled down the passenger window. "I'll be in the area regardless. Have a good night."

Asif rolled his eyes and turned to look at the short, squat building in front of him.

Brick House used to be a refinery or something, but nowadays it was a pleasure palace. A strip club on the main floor, a massage parlor on the second, and storage on the third, allegedly. Asif would have bet real money that whatever was actually happening on the top floor of the building would probably interest the ATF, but that wasn't his business, so he put it out of his mind. He was here to track down a former associate of the Malkov family, not get embroiled in an arms trafficking case.

He started toward the door, but the bouncer stepped in front of him with a wicked glare.

"Back of the line," the man said in a deep grumble.

Asif smiled. "This how you treat your VIPs?" he asked.

The man looked him up and down. "You ain't a VIP until you make it through the door. Before that, you just like everybody else." He motioned toward the line again.

"Unless you play for the Cavs," someone down the line yelled out.

"And the Browns," another person yelled, which elicited a groan from the crowd as everyone started to debate if the *entire* Browns squad deserved to skip the line or only a select few. Asif held up his hands in good-natured defeat and strolled a few feet away to the end of the line. He was standing behind a couple too preoccupied with their own relationship woes to worry about Asif or join the debate about the local football team.

"You said you wanted to do this," he hissed at the woman.

Asif pulled out his phone and pretended to text someone while the couple in front of him had his full attention.

"I-I—" The woman never managed to finish that sentence because the man cut her off, berating her in vicious whispers. Asif guessed that this wasn't the first time they'd been in this predicament. Predictably, when they made it to the bouncer, the man threw his arm over the woman's shoulder and handed over their IDs. Asif slipped his cell phone into his pocket and watched as the bouncer inspected their driver's licenses before ushering them inside.

"ID," the bouncer barked at Asif. The man was intimidating, not too tall, but wide. His arms bulged out of his black, long-sleeved t-shirt and his thighs stretched the fabric of his slacks. There was no need to wonder how this man spent his free time.

Asif reached into his pants pockets with unhurried movements. "You should keep an eye on those two," he said.

"Already on it," Deon replied. "ID."

Asif pulled his fake license from his wallet. He'd already memorized all the information on the card, but he glanced at it just in case — it never hurt to refresh his memory while undercover — before turning it over. "What's the temperature inside?" he asked.

Deon inspected the card with an almost singular focus. Almost. "'Bout the same as always. Chaotic. Not too packed. Good sound cover but a lot of eyes."

Asif nodded.

Deon took out a blacklight flashlight to further inspect Asif's ID. The Agency didn't bother with fakes, especially not domestically, so Deon's blacklight didn't uncover anything, although if it had, the man would have pretended otherwise, which was why he'd been placed here two months ago. Whatever mission he was on was none of Asif's concern; he was simply an asset Asif could leverage to get him where he needed to be. Once he got inside the Brick House, Asif was on his own. Deon wouldn't jeopardize his assignment to save Asif, and vice versa. They might both work for The Agency, but they were just ships passing in the night.

"My shift ends at midnight. Don't fuck up anything before then," Deon muttered.

Asif laughed. "I'd never."

Deon peered at Asif with hard eyes. "You would. You have. Your reputation precedes you."

Asif laughed again. "Good to know."

Deon clicked the button on the back of his flashlight. "If you brought big money, the private rooms are worth your time."

"Do people really bring big money here?" Asif asked flippantly.

"They do if they're 'bout their business."

"And if they're not?"

Deon grinned. "Got a man inside named Steel," he said. "I can count on him to take out the trash if need be." He extended his arm to hand back Asif's ID.

"Good to know that as well."

Deon tipped his head toward the front door. "Welcome to the Brick House. Don't be cheap."

Asif laughed and shook his head, saluting him as he stepped to the side. As he passed, though, Deon dipped his head to whisper low enough for only Asif to hear.

"Got a new dancer starting tonight," he whispered. "Keep an eye out."

Asif's easygoing smile shifted for a moment as he tried to decipher what Deon was trying to tell him. Asif loved mysteries and puzzles, but his least favorite part of the job was trying to decode word puzzles from agents in the field. How the fuck was he supposed to know what "new dancer" was code for when he'd only been in the city for three hours? The only thing he could hope was that he could fit the pieces together before it was too late — whatever 'too late' meant today.

The foyer was surprisingly bright, with light wood floors, white walls, and colorful, abstract paintings hung at eye level. A tall, slim woman with light brown skin and a shockingly bright platinum blonde wig was waiting across the room with a bright smile beaming on her face directed at Asif. "Welcome to the Brick House. Are you meeting a group?" she asked.

"Nope. Just me and my wallet."

"That's what we like to hear," she replied. She looked down at the podium and peeked through a curtain onto the main floor. "We've got one more booth left if you're interested. Right by the stage."

Asif pretended to give this some serious thought before lifting an eyebrow. "What's the spending floor?"

"Five hundred."

Asif had allocated a thousand, so he hoped whoever in Accounting had been policing his expenditures since the last time he was here appreciated these savings. "Let's do it," he said with a smile.

"Follow me."

Asif reached around her and pulled the velvet curtain out of the way. "After you."

There were worse places to work. Every agent had their own preferences, and Asif's leaned toward dim lights, good music, and the ambient vibes of track lighting bouncing off rhinestones while someone shook their ass to the beat.

To each their own.

Before Asif could appreciate the atmosphere, he took stock of the room. He had, of course, seen blueprints and surveillance pictures, but nothing could prepare him for the energy. The stage was empty, but one dancer was topless on a table — clearly an OSHA violation — although he didn't think she would complain based on the piles of bills at her feet. It brought a smile to his face.

The hostess steered him to the right, and he peeked into each booth as they passed.

"Here we are," the hostess said. "I'll send your waitress right away."

"Appreciate it," Asif said, his smile slipping because that waitress wouldn't be Chanté. Of course, he'd looked up The Petal, thinking that should be his first stop when he landed. Finding out Chanté's club had recently closed made his chest hurt. He'd thought about keeping track of her but common sense had stopped him. If he couldn't be with her — and he couldn't — it was unfair to torture himself watching her from afar. It would only be so long before she found someone else; before she forgot about him and moved on. But when he heard about The Petal, he realized he'd been banking on the hope that she'd be easy to find. Chanté was born to dance; he knew that from the moment they met. The way she looked at the dancers, the way she danced, the way she'd danced on him, it was obvious. Sure, it was likely she was just in another club somewhere in the city. Or maybe she'd left the city altogether since she'd probably graduated from college by now. He didn't know, and he shouldn't know, but that didn't mean that he didn't *want* to know.

"Hey, sweetheart," his waitress said, sliding a menu across the table. She had to yell over the DJ on the mic.

Asif started to turn toward her, but he saw something curvy and sparkly in the corner of his eye.

His mouth went slack for a moment before he couldn't stop the smile from spreading on his face.

He breathed her name on a soft sigh.

There was no way she could have heard him, but her head turned in his direction, her mouth falling open for a second.

But then her music started and the lights went out.

At least now Asif knew what Deon was trying to tell him.

Chanté

+

Asif

EIGHT

BACKSTAGE AGAIN, Chanté was almost ready for her performance.

She was trying to go through her routine — a few last-minute stretches, touching up her lip gloss, nothing too strenuous — but she could hardly focus.

Asif wasn't just close, he was in the building. She'd touched him. He'd touched her. He'd made her wet. What else could she ask for? Hell, as far as she was concerned, the mission was over. She'd found Asif, she wanted to fuck Asif, there was no need to go on stage.

"A-are you ready?" Inessa asked. She saw the girl's reflection in her mirror again, except this time she looked excited and much less nervous than half an hour ago. "I am excited to see you."

Chanté smiled and decided to suck it up. She hated to disappoint her fans. At least Asif could see her on stage again. That was always fun. "Yes." Chanté glanced back at her reflection again and took a deep breath. It didn't matter how many times she stepped on stage or how well she knew the routine, those tiny little butterflies in her stomach always came back.

It was the anticipation that got to her. The sound of the crowd, the clink of glasses, the silence when the club went dark before she stepped on stage — Chanté loved all of it. And she loved it when she could feel Asif's eyes on her.

Inessa led her to a heavy black velvet curtain and opened it a crack so Chanté could see the crowd. Chanté nodded and smiled at the younger woman. She said something in Russian Chanté decided to translate as, "Break a leg." She took another deep breath and stepped onto the platform. The house lights were down low, but there was a helpful lighted pathway from the heavy dark curtain to center stage. Even in the dim lighting, Chanté could hardly see the crowd, but just knowing that Asif was out there made her skin warm. She was ready.

She turned her back to the room, placed her hands at her lower back, spread her nails along the top curve of her ass, and held her breath. When the first notes of Miguel's "Do You..." started playing, Chanté felt like a different version of herself. A boneless version that could sway her way around the pole set into the stage. Knowing Asif was here made her feel like that twenty-year-old girl, writhing around that cheap pole she'd installed in her old living room for him. A version of herself that could control every muscle in her body, including keeping the smile on her face even when she needed to concentrate on climbing gracefully into the air.

This routine was an oldie but a goodie, something she choreographed right after she met Asif, actually. She'd been alone in her apartment feeling sad, lonely, and horny — a potent emotional cocktail. She'd also been a little high and pouring herself into movement made her feel good. Every time she told a DJ to play this song, she felt like she was peeling away layers and layers of protective armor to expose her heart on stage, baring herself emotionally as she cheekily untied one side of her skirt and then the other. She imagined Asif in the crowd, Asif on that old couch with a wad of singles making another bulge in his pants, Asif walking into a pub in Ireland, raindrops glistening in his midnight hair. Asif falling to his knees at her feet. Every movement was a testament to her scattered memories of Asif over the years. Loving him held the core of her choreography together. Sometimes she stayed high in the air, other times she happily writhed around on the floor, but either way, she was thinking about Asif.

Chanté lost herself in the song. She moved from the pole to the floor and back again. She put her back to the crowd and untied her corset with elaborate, slow movements; she bent her knees and bounced her ass off her heels. In flat shoes, it wasn't an amazing move, but in six-inch Perspex stilettos it just hit different. Chanté couldn't explain it, but every dancer she knew agreed. An impossibly high heel and a little bit of body glitter could make a muggy day feel like a heatwave. The crowd was silent, focused. In Cleveland, that silence would have spelled the end of her career, but in these upscale European clubs, it was to be expected — she didn't like it, so she cheered each new move in her head. Chanté had long since learned that if no one would cheer for her, she'd have to cheer for herself.

As the song increased in tempo, she let those emotions go and got down to business.

There were stairs set at the far end of the stage, opening up onto the dining area. She crawled her way across the floor and spread her legs lewdly at the top of the steps.

She knew it was Asif by his silhouette. She would know Asif anywhere.

She put her feet on the second chair, hands on her knees, and started grinding toward him as he started up the stairs. By his third step, Asif's hands hit the stairs and he started crawling his way toward her. Crawling his way between her legs.

"I made this dance for you," she whispered.

He sat on the third step from the top, smoothed one hand up her inner thigh, and curled a wad of rubles into her garter. She shivered at his touch. "When they ask you how we know each other, tell them something kinky."

His hand caressed the sensitive skin where her leg met the bottom curve of her ass.

"So tell them the truth. Got it," she said before turning away and walking back onto the stage just in time for the song to end and the house lights to drop out completely.

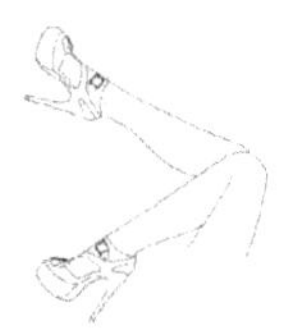

ASIF STOOD IN THE DARK AND WATCHED CHANTÉ'S silhouette disappear through the dark curtain. He used that time to steady his breath and let his dick deflate. When the house lights turned on, Asif smoothed his hand down his stomach, turned, and casually walked back to his table.

Sonja had a look of amused shock on her face and started clapping slowly as Asif arrived. Raphael joined in after a beat. While he didn't seem as shocked as Sonja, he was certainly amused, and far more interested in Asif than he'd been at any other time of their acquaintance. Joseph, however, was glaring a hole into his face. Those were unexpected responses, but Asif could use all of them to his advantage.

At the table, Asif smiled and bowed dramatically in front of Sonja.

"Yusuf, I've never seen you this way," she said and laughed when he did.

"Do you know her?" Joseph barked the question at him, almost as an accusation.

Asif shifted his gaze to the other man for the first time since they sat down. "I do," he replied jovially.

"How?" Somehow, his tone seemed harder, and Asif delighted in that.

"That's personal," Asif said. "Are you alright?"

"You do look unwell," Raphael added.

Hearing the other man's voice seemed to pull Joseph from his rage spiral. Asif took immense pleasure in watching the man splutter through an apology and then gulp down nearly an entire glass of water.

"She's beautiful," Sonja cooed.

"Gorgeous," he said. "And funny too."

"I can't wait to meet her."

"Will she be coming to say hello?" Raphael asked eagerly.

"I hope so," Asif teased, looking around the room. He could feel the heat of Joseph's jealous stare on the side of his face.

The overhead lights started to shift again, but this time into a warm orange light that cast most of the room in shadow. A tall, thin white woman strutted on stage and excitement rippled through the room. This location was a logistical nightmare. Their table was set almost in the center of the audience, exposing Asif on all sides. None of the exits were clearly marked, and the only way to get to any of them quickly was to hop on stage and make a run for it, which he'd only do in a life-or-death situation. He could hear Kenny screaming in his head that *this* was exactly why an agent needed backup, but he ignored the imaginary sound of Kenny's voice just like he ignored the man in reality. That he was right would never sway Asif's opinion.

Besides, technically, he had backup, and she appeared just at the edge of the right side of the stage. One of the track lights caught on the clusters of rhinestones in the center of her bustier, like bejeweled nipples.

She strolled onto the floor, shimmying between the tables with adorable bounces that made her cleavage jiggle invitingly. Asif watched her with a smile on his face. She had his entire attention, which was dangerous, but he didn't care. For a few slow, happy moments, Asif gave himself permission not to worry about anything but Chanté.

And it was lovely.

ASIF HAD SEVENTY-FIVE PERCENT OF HER ATTENTION, but the other twenty-five percent was focused on the mission. She'd meant what she told him and Maryam. Chanté would make sure Asif got out of here safe and sound; she wasn't done with him yet. He was sitting at the edge of a table with a woman to his left, a man to her left, and another man sitting across from Asif. All eyes were on her, but the only ones that mattered were Asif's.

Well, his mattered the most, at least.

"You're beautiful," Chanté said to the woman next to Asif. She seemed surprised at the compliment, which made Chanté mad. She looked at Asif. "Haven't you told her how beautiful she is?"

Asif laughed and stood from his chair. "I've told her. But she can never hear that enough."

"I agree," she beamed.

The rest of the table stood to welcome her, but Chanté focused her attention on the woman.

"I'm Betty," Chanté said, extending her hand.

"Sonja," she replied.

"What?" Asif breathed. "That can't be right."

"It's an homage to Betty Boop," she whispered to him.

"This is Raphael," Sonja said. Chanté reached around Sonja to offer Raphael her hand. He brushed his lips across her knuckles. Chanté didn't like strange lips on her, but his kiss was dry so she didn't complain.

The man on the other side of the table strolled behind their chairs, walking toward her with a singular focus. Chanté offered him her hand and regretted it almost immediately.

"It is my pleasure," he said, bending forward to kiss her knuckles. He didn't have nearly as much tact as Raphael, leaving a wet print on her fingers.

Every time she forgot to bring hand sanitizer with her on the floor, she regretted it. As soon as he started to stand erect again, she smoothly — but quickly — pulled her hand from his grasp and wiped it on the side of Asif's pants.

"It's so lovely to meet you all," Chanté said, taking a step away from him.

She jumped when Asif's hand settled round her waist and pulled her into his side.

"How do you know Yusuf?"

"Wh—" Asif squeezed her waist. "Well, it's a funny story actually. It started in Dubai."

Asif sighed. "Doha," he corrected.

"Really?"

"Really," he echoed. "She was doing an aerial burlesque act."

"You do aerials?" Sonja gasped excitedly.

Chanté glared up at Asif, who had the nerve to smile down at her like the cat who got the cream. "I used to," she ground out and then brushed his arm from her waist. She turned quickly to Sonja and laughed. "Not in ages, though. Yusuf and I go way back," she said, proud of herself for not stumbling over his cover name. "But we don't get to see one another much. We're always traveling in opposite directions."

"Until we're not," Asif said, moving his hand back to Chanté's waist. His fingers curled into her flesh possessively.

She let out a soft sigh at that delicious pinch.

"Betty and I have a knack for running into one another," he said.

Chanté swallowed the tiny lump of emotion in her throat. "It's like fate," she breathed softly, trying to keep her smile in place and her eyes dry.

Joseph grunted unhappily.

EIGHT YEARS AGO...

Chanté always danced like Asif was watching her, and over the years, she'd started to delude herself into thinking that he actually was. That the shadowy figure in the back of the room — the person who was there on one rotation of the pole but gone in the next — was Asif, just popping in to check on her. Just Asif making sure she was okay. She knew it was delusional, just one of those coping mechanisms she learned as a child to make getting through a random day bearable, but it was a coping mechanism for a reason. It comforted her to think that Asif was somewhere, out there in the world, thinking about her, and when he missed her, he dropped by a rundown strip club in Cleveland just to see her. It wouldn't change her life, it didn't bring him back to her, but it did soothe that sometimes-yawning pit inside her that just wanted to be loved.

So when she saw him nestled in a booth all by himself just like the night they met, of course she thought he was a figment of her imagination. But when she flipped her legs over her head to wrap her thighs around the pole, he was still there. And when she lowered to a split on the floor, he'd shifted to the edge of the booth. And when she threw her bra just a little too hard and it landed at his feet, he bent over and picked it up. She got through the rest of her routine with klaxons blaring in her head because after all the years she'd spent thinking about him, dreaming about him, hoping to see him again, there he was.

By the time her music was fading, Chanté was on her knees, back to the crowd, covered in a sheen of sweat and glitter, panting, watching as Asif stood from his booth and walked the short distance to the edge of the stage. He pushed her bra toward her. Chanté couldn't stop blinking, preparing herself for the moment when he would disappear again, but until then, she recorded all the changes she could note.

His hair was longer.

A new scar cut into the left side of his beard, but it was old and healing. She wanted to lick it.

There were bags under his eyes.

He was still beautiful.

She watched as he reached into his jacket pocket and pulled out a stack of bills. She swallowed as he peeled two hundred-dollar bills from the wad and replaced the larger stack in his pocket, like an invitation. She held her breath as he leaned forward and grazed the back of his hand down her side. One finger pulled the strap of her thong away from her skin while the other stuffed the bills around the scrap of polyester.

"Did you miss me, sweetheart?" he had the nerve to ask.

"Yes," she whispered. "And that's not enough money to make it up to me."

It had been two years since she'd heard the delicious timbre of Asif's voice. She felt like her soul was glowing.

Chanté

+

Asif

NINE

CHANTÉ WORKED the floor to keep her cover up and to keep an eye on Asif. She moved from lap to lap under the guise that she needed these men's tips or cared about what anyone in this building thought of her. Anyone besides Asif. Once he and his companions left, her job was done. She hopped right off the lap of the Austrian man trying to convince her to have a threesome with his wife, snatched the wad of bills from his hand, and headed backstage.

The good thing about the other dancers being so cold to her was that once she'd done what she needed to do — and successfully at that — Chanté didn't feel the need to stick around. She changed from her stage outfit, packed her bag, and stuffed her tips into Inessa's bag before pushing out the dancer entrance. Now that she'd found Asif, she wouldn't be coming back here.

She stepped out onto an alley that looked so much like all the other alleys she'd navigated after a night on stage. Sure, sometimes it was hot and humid or freezing cold like tonight, sometimes the alleys were well-lit and guarded, and sometimes she waved at her homeless friend settling down for the night, but they were all about the same to Chanté.

He stepped out of the shadows.

Her instincts should have made her feet stutter to a stop and her heart race, but only one of those physiological responses materialized and not out of fear.

"Shouldn't you be sick of waiting in alleys for me after all these years?" she laughed.

"No," he replied in a low, serious voice. "You shouldn't be here."

"Neither should you," she shot back, walking right up on him. She just wanted to smell his cologne again.

"I told them I wanted to go for a walk, but they probably guessed I wanted to see you again."

"As you should," Chanté shot back. "But I meant here. Alone. Why haven't you been checking in, Asif?"

"This is the first night I've been alone or away from their surveillance. I've been working."

"Alone," Chanté said again.

"I work better that way."

She rolled her eyes. "Bullshit. Kenny always says—"

"Oh, here we go. I don't care what Kenny says. Besides, I *trained* him."

"Then you have no excuse."

"Some missions require a little flexibility."

Chanté smiled and pressed her body against his front. "I'm flexible," she whispered.

"Oh, yeah? Maybe you should remind me," he whispered. His fingers ghosted over her waist, but only for a second.

"Gladly," she said, a soft smile on her face, before she

stepped back and rolled her eyes. "After you get the fuck out of this damn country."

Asif laughed. "I'll do that *as soon as* I get what I came here for. Go home and tell The Agency that."

"I'll do *that* as soon as I get what I came here for."

"I gave you the update. You have proof of life." He stepped back and turned in a circle.

She licked her lips and enjoyed the view. "Sexy, but I ain't come here for proof of life. I came here to take your ass home. Period. I leave when you leave."

When he turned back around, Asif's normally easy smile was gone. "No," he shot back.

She crossed her arms over her chest. "Yes."

He crossed his arms, and Chanté was ready to dig her heels in the sand because they could do this for hours — or a decade. Asif also seemed to be settling in for this fight, but instead of doing so in this cold, dank alley, he rolled his eyes and grabbed the duffel bag from her hand.

"Where are you staying, Chanté?"

She lifted her eyebrows and smiled. "Around the corner, actually."

"Good, let's go," he said, grabbing her by the arm.

"Yes, sir," she purred.

Asif sighed and dropped her bag.

"Hey, that's Gucci!" she whined, but then Asif pushed her against the closest wall. He grabbed her around the back of her thighs and lifted her in the air. Chanté wrapped her legs around his waist like she was coming home. She threw her arms around his shoulders as their mouths pressed together.

Every time she and Asif kissed was like a new chapter to an old book. Sometimes he tasted sweet with a bite like ginger ale and whisky, or tart and smooth like cranberry juice, or the faint, minty remnants of toothpaste, but the overwhelming note of Asif's kiss was that he always tasted like hers. This time, she could taste the desperation, and she deluded herself into thinking that meant he'd missed her — he'd been dreaming about her the way she'd been dreaming about him. He sucked her tongue into his mouth like a man who'd been starving for this one specific dish — her — and she ground her pussy into his hard stomach.

He trapped her against that old, dirty wall and shoved his left hand between her legs. She'd been cursing her thin leggings on the way to the Glass Menagerie, but now she was glad at her inadequate clothing. Glad that he could feel the heat between her legs. Glad the seam gave way so easily to his fingers with a satisfying rip. She moaned into his mouth even before he'd shoved two fingers through her torn leggings, seeking out her hot, wet folds.

"Yes," she groaned against his lips.

"No underwear," he groaned back as the pads of his fingers found her clit.

She scratched at his shoulders as he played with the hard nub until it was engorged with blood and sensitive. She started circling her hips, desperate for more, begging into the gentle cavern of his mouth for him to, "Fuck me with your fingers. Please."

He grunted, hips jutting forward into the empty space underneath her butt, but he didn't give her what she wanted. It was incomprehensible to the people who loved her, but Chanté had always trusted Asif, even though everything in her past said she shouldn't. But she trusted Asif to protect her. She trusted Asif to love her.

The only thing she couldn't trust Asif to do was stay.

Every time he left, it broke her heart, but every time he returned... "Fuck me," she moaned as he finally sank two fingers into her with slow, deliberate, loving care.

Every time Asif returned, it was like he never left.

CHANTÉ WAS HOT AND WET, AND HER PUSSY QUIVERED around his fingers the closer she got to her orgasm. She was shaking in his hold, pressing her mouth to his ear so he could hear her little gasps and moans in surround sound.

All the blood in his body was rushing to his dick. It would have left him lightheaded, but even biology couldn't disrupt his focus. He wanted to get Chanté off. It had been months since the last time he'd touched her in the way he wanted to — the only thing that could stop him from making her come all over his hands was death.

And even then, Asif would put up a damn good fight.

"Oh shit, I'm close. I'm close," Chanté gasped.

Asif turned his head and licked her lips. That was enough to push her over the edge. Her arms and legs locked tight around him and she crushed her mouth against his. He didn't stop moving his fingers inside her. If anything, there was something about Chanté coming in his hand that spurred him on. He dragged the pads of his fingers back and forth around her warm flesh until her voice had gone high and hoarse and she was patting weakly at his shoulder to get him to stop.

But he left his fingers inside her, riding out the last pulses of her orgasm. He also pressed his body against her, sandwiching her even tighter between the wall and his chest. Chanté liked to feel full and secure while she came down from the high of her orgasm. After a decade of fixating on her rather than being with her, Asif always wanted to make their snatches of time together memorable for them both.

He kissed his way across her jaw and down her neck.

"Does that mean you missed me?" she asked in the soft, quiet voice that broke his heart.

"Always," he whispered back.

She moved the hand on her shoulder to caress his cheek. "Then why—"

"Shh," Asif said quickly.

Her hand fell from his face.

"Did you hear that?" Asif asked as he started to pull his fingers from inside her.

She stiffened and held her breath.

When cool air hit his wet digits, Asif shivered and frowned into the crook of Chanté's neck. They stood still and listened. The alley was quiet, but they could hear the faint sounds of a busy street not too far away. He was beginning to think whatever he thought he'd heard was a figment of his imagination when Chanté jumped in his hold.

It was small — just the faint scratching of a shoe sole against rough gravel, like the gravel in the alley. It would have been easy to think it was just someone approaching, but Asif knew what that sounded like. In fact, it was the irregular sound that caught his attention, standing out stark against Chanté's rhythmic breaths.

She let out the air she was holding in her lungs slowly, quietly, perfectly — not wanting to interrupt the mental work she knew Asif was doing. She let him hold onto her as he tried to figure out exactly how much danger they were in.

After a while, he felt ready to talk or interrogate.

"How close is your hotel from here?" he whispered as low as possible.

"Two blocks."

"What's in your bag?"

"Stage gear."

"Heels?"

"Duh," she said with a soft click of her tongue.

"Okay, I'm going to walk you back to your hotel. It could be nothing, but it could be someone following us."

"Wouldn't be the first time," she breathed. "If it is someone following us, what do you want me to do?"

Run. Asif wanted to tell her that she should run, now, immediately, whether someone was following them or not. He wanted her to get as far away from him as fast as possible, but he couldn't tell her that. They didn't have time to get into yet another argument about this.

"Stay safe, and if I tell you to leave, I mean it. Don't fight me."

She brushed her mouth along his beard. The tip of her tongue tasted his skin. "But it's so fun," she moaned.

Asif just barely swallowed his groan. "Chanté," he warned.

Her breath was featherlight in his hair. "Fine. But only because you just made me come."

He kissed her neck. "I'm going to put you down now."

She whined softly, and he kissed her skin two more times. He couldn't help himself.

He lowered her carefully to her feet. She held onto him for as long as possible. He cupped her face, and they stared into one another's eyes. "How do you feel?" he asked.

She shifted on her feet. "My thighs are wet," she laughed.

He bent forward and kissed her, hard and deep. He never knew how much time he'd have with Chanté, and over the years, he'd tried to make sure that every hello and goodbye would be worth it. That when the end came, in hindsight, she'd know he'd never regretted a moment. But chatty as he was, even this was too much for Asif to communicate with only a kiss.

So he made sure to grind his erection against her stomach until she started laughing against his lips.

Chanté

+

Asif

TEN

ASIF'S ATTENTION WAS TORN, which was exactly why he hated working with other people if he didn't have to. And he *didn't* have to. There were other people the agency could have sent. Kenny even though he was on assignment, Lane, Carlisle, Deon — literally anyone who was approved to handle firearms. Anyone but Chanté.

Sure, Chanté had skills, but they were on stage or in code, not in the field. He'd said so on every report he'd filed after a mission with her. In fact, it was the only consistent thing he'd ever written in his after-mission reports.

Keep Chanté out of the field. Please.

Did they listen? Never, and he didn't know why. Well, that wasn't true. Monica and Lane loved her, Kenny was one of her best friends, and those were the only people who could engage Chanté in work she wasn't technically approved to do. Why The Agency head allowed it, he didn't know, but after this mission, he resolved to find out. It wasn't that Asif didn't want to protect her, it was that he didn't want her in the middle of danger in the first place, and he couldn't get anyone to get on the same page as him. Not even her.

"There's my hotel," she said, pointing across the street.

"Great," Asif mumbled. He put his hand on the small of her back and tried to gently push her forward. He realized his mistake as soon as he made it.

Chanté pushed back at his hand and slowed down.

"Come on," he sighed.

"I'm coming," she said, even though she'd technically slowed to a leisurely stroll.

He bent down toward her and she lifted onto the balls of her feet, offering her ear to him. His lips brushed her skin, and she moaned softly. "We're trying to see if someone's following us, remember?"

"I do," she purred, slowing her steps again. "I still don't like to be rushed. You know what that's like, right?" She always managed to accuse him in the lightest tones, as if she didn't care. As if he'd never hurt her.

"Chanté," he whispered, but she shook her head and leaped off the curb, doing a pirouette in the street.

"Be careful," he called out louder than he meant to. The ground was covered in ice and snow and if he let her hurt herself, he would be pissed. More pissed than he already was that someone at The Agency — probably Monica — had put her in the middle of a mission, and in winter at that.

He rushed off the curb and slipped on a patch of ice.

"Ope, careful!" Chanté laughed.

Asif scrambled for a moment until he could steady himself while Chanté took another twirl in the street, unfazed by the weather conditions. He stood slowly. Even though he was the one on shaky ground, his eyes were focused on Chanté's shoes. Her legs. How happy she looked.

For a moment, Asif stood in a snowy street in Saint Petersburg, Russia, watching Chanté have the time of her life. The problem was that it was a dangerous moment. They were exposed, and Asif's attention was divided, and anything could have happened. The fact that nothing did wasn't the point; it never had been. A dog barked somewhere in the distance, jolting Asif out of his reverie and back into the moment. One minute he felt like they were standing under a full sun, the next he came crashing back to reality. His heart was pounding in his chest as he turned in a circle, looking for anything that seemed out of place. It was just that *everything* seemed out of place.

When it came to Chanté, Asif thought everything was a danger. Even himself.

He wrapped his free arm around Chanté's waist and picked her up.

"Ooh," Chanté breathed. She threw her head back. A few of her curls obscured his view, but he kept moving forward.

When he stepped onto the sidewalk and headed straight for the front of Chanté's hotel, the doorman hesitated. Asif glared at the man until he scrambled to pull the door open for them.

"Spasiba," Chanté giggled.

He had to maneuver his way into the hotel lobby, where everyone in the room seemed to stop speaking and turn to look at them. Asif never minded making a scene, but this wasn't really the kind of scene he liked.

Chanté turned her head toward him. "Elevator's over there," she said, jutting her chin to his left.

Asif let out a harsh breath through his nose and moved forward. He didn't even think about putting her down.

"Let me," she said, extending her arm to press the call button. They looked ridiculous. He didn't care. Thankfully, the elevator doors slid open immediately, and Asif carried Chanté inside where he finally put her back on her feet. She pouted adorably while pressing the button to the penthouse.

Asif lifted his eyebrows at her.

She laughed. "I'm not paying for it." But then her eyes shifted to the right, where they had a clear view of the front of the elevator.

"Black dude, all black clothes, about five-ten. He's the one who's been following us."

"What?" Asif asked quickly, confused.

He was about to turn his head when Chanté reached out quickly and grabbed his face. She leaned into him and smiled while his eyes shifted to the left, and he saw the man trying — poorly — to blend into the crowd watching them from the lobby.

"Oh, goddammit," Asif groaned at the same time as Chanté pulled his mouth down to hers.

"How'd you know?" Asif asked as soon as they entered Chanté's hotel room.

She tossed her key onto the table by the door, kicked off her sneakers, and threw her hands into the air to stretch. "Know what?"

"That he was the one following us?"

Asif dropped her bag by the door and bent down, undoing the zipper.

"He was obvious as hell. Do you know him?"

Asif rooted around in her bag until his fingers closed over one of her heels. He pulled it free, along with a pair of her panties hanging off the heel.

"I charge good money for those," Chanté said.

He turned to find her standing in the middle of an ornate living room, just as gaudy and oddly beautiful as he would expect from a Russian luxury suite. "I know," he said. "You recently raised your prices."

Chanté smiled and gasped gently. "Are you keeping tabs on me, Asif?"

Yes. The answer was obviously yes, like it had always been. He knew that, she knew that, but the hitch in their relationship was his refusal to admit it. It was an immature and unproven theory Asif had been using to order their lives and push Chanté away, but it was the only way. It had to be.

"He works for French intelligence," Asif said. "He's a good agent, but wet behind the ears. He'll get better."

Chanté frowned at him. She sucked her bottom lip into her mouth, watching him as if she was thinking. As if she was wondering how to say something she shouldn't. He wanted to hear whatever she was thinking as much as he wished she would keep some piece of her only to herself. But that, too, was the hitch of their relationship: Asif wanted Chanté to lay herself bare for him, even as he refused to do the same.

"I know I'm short and giggly and love rhinestones, but I'm not nearly as helpless as you think I am," she said in a deep, surprisingly serious tone.

Asif stood slowly and tried to smile at her, but he could hardly manage it. "There are a lot of things I know to be true about you, Chanté, and the thought that you were helpless was never a possibility. Never even crossed my mind."

"What did cross your mind about me?" she asked in a small, heartbreaking voice.

He had no way to answer that safely. He could lie, but he hated doing that to her. He could tell her the truth, but that was too dangerous. Neither option was safe. Neither option would keep her safe.

They stood there, staring at one another in a silence so complete the sound of the elevator dinging as it arrived back on their floor saved Asif from this moment.

Maybe he looked relieved, but whatever look flitted across his face only made Chanté's fall. She swallowed and forced a weak smile on her face.

"Don't get any blood on the carpet. I'm gonna take a shower," she said before turning and walking away.

Asif watched Chanté leave the room with a lump in his throat — a lump stuffed with emotions and words he wouldn't burden her with. He wondered if this was how she felt all those times he left. He hoped not, but he knew he was too much of a coward to ask, so he turned his attention back to the matter at hand.

Quietly, Asif toed off his shoes, leaving them next to Chanté's. He took one step on the polished marble and bent down to peel off his socks for better traction before ducking out of the foyer into a living room that was bigger than some houses. "Damn," Asif breathed quietly as he took in the shadowed room that seemed to go on forever. Floor-to-ceiling windows made the already cavernous space seem even bigger, and on a clear day, Chanté must have had a view of half the city. He could see the outline of a baby grand piano tucked in a far corner. Just beyond that, he saw a faint glow of light flick on. Asif didn't know what Chanté's budget was for this extraction mission, but he could bet one of the Agency accountants was going to be pissed when they got her invoice.

The metallic jingle of the doorhandle moving caught Asif's attention, and he managed to duck into the shadows just before the door pushed open. Since he couldn't look around the corner to see what was happening, he closed his eyes to listen instead. Most people relied too heavily on what they could see, pushing aside the rest of their senses. It wasn't always so crucial as to be dangerous, but when it was, there was no way to go back and hone that skill — no way to go back and save your own life. Or Chanté's.

He heard the sound of soft, scraping metal against wood, then metal against metal, then nothing for a few seconds. Behind him, he heard water rushing from a shower and Chanté humming quietly. If he could have told her to be a little quieter so he could focus, she would have started singing at the top of her lungs, so he worked to push those sounds to the back of his mind just in time to hear the door creak open and the person breaking into their room swear softly under his breath. Asif rolled his eyes and continued to wait.

Asif met Marcel once when their paths crossed in Dubai,

where they'd both tracked the same Italian businessman fleeing Europe after a close associate of his was arrested on a string of charges from money laundering to human trafficking. They'd spent only a couple of days unknowingly running parallel missions that ended with Marcel taking his target into custody just an hour before Asif was set to make his own move. He would have been pissed if not for the fact that the goal — getting a corrupt man off the streets — was really all that mattered. All that mattered to Asif, anyway.

He heard when the door snicked closed and still, he waited. He redoubled his grip on Chanté's shoe and prepared. Asif held his breath and flattened his back against the wall. In the bathroom, Chanté hummed louder, and the water and tile amplified the sound, which seemed to put their intruder at ease because Asif heard the first unmuffled sound of his footsteps against the floor. And then another. And another. And another.

Perfect.

Instead of waiting for the intruder to come around the corner and spot him in the shadows, Asif waited until he was closer and threw himself around the corner. The element of surprise was always Asif's best friend.

He swung Chanté's shoe in a tight but vicious arc just about at head height, although he couldn't remember exactly how tall Marcel had been. He was right on target, and if Marcel hadn't managed to jump back, he'd have taken that blow directly on the temple. Still, catching the man off guard worked well enough to give Asif an advantage. He took another swing on the back hand, hitting Marcel in the shoulder, but he didn't take that hit passively.

Marcel bent forward and rushed at Asif, punching him in the gut with his full weight, shoulder first.

Asif grunted all the air from his diaphragm and smashed Chanté's shoe on Marcel's back.

"Ah," the man groaned, so Asif hit him again.

Marcel pushed Asif into a couch and the arm hit him at the back of the knees, giving Marcel an advantage that could prove deadly if Asif didn't pivot. He dropped her shoe and wrapped his arm around the back of Marcel's neck while bunching his free hand into a fist and punching at his kidneys. They fell from the couch with a hard thump, and both cried out when they made contact with the unforgiving marble floor. They scrambled away from one another to regroup. Asif tasted a sharp metal tang as blood filled his mouth before he swallowed it quickly, blinking to adjust his eyes to the darkness. Marcel was panting somewhere in front of him.

Asif tried to regroup, but the first thought that came into his head was that Marcel was now in between him and Chanté. He couldn't have that. He scrambled to his feet right as the overhead light turned on. Marcel was on one knee, just about to stand, but both of their heads turned to her. Chanté was posed next to the piano, a towel wrapped loosely around her body and a frown on her face.

"I thought I'd catch you wrestling. Naked," she said.

"Why would we be naked?" Marcel asked in confusion, his French accent thicker than Asif remembered.

"Why...not?" she challenged in sincere confusion.

Marcel was going to say something else, but Asif rushed at him and punched him in the temple. The man crumpled to a heap.

Chanté squeaked in surprise. "Why'd you do that?"

"Why not?" Asif panted. "I need something to tie him

up with. You wouldn't happen to have any handcuffs, would you?"

Her face brightened. "Of course, I do!" she cried before rushing back into the bedroom.

Asif tried to catch his breath but couldn't help but laugh drily. "Of course, you do."

Chanté

+

Asif

ELEVEN

"YOU'RE BLEEDING," Chanté said.

"I know," Asif huffed. "Do you want to help me?"

"With what?" she asked.

He was holding Marcel under the man's armpits and dragging him into the second bedroom, but he stopped to glare up at Chanté. "With him," he said in exasperation.

She moved her gaze over Marcel's unconscious body. "I don't like 'em passed out."

"What? Not— Help me get him in the room and secured to the bedframe," Asif said, being very specific.

Chanté frowned. "So close, but so far away," she whispered, smiling at him. "No, thanks." She brushed past, smelling like roses. "Protect your lower back. You're getting long in the tooth, old man." She laughed over her shoulder.

Asif stopped to glare at her back — her shoulder blades flexing as she moved — but when she undid her towel and let it drop to the floor, he had to look away and get back to work. It only took a few minutes more to drag the other man into the second bedroom. He seriously thought about leaving the man on the floor, but Marcel didn't deserve that. Besides, the way their job worked, one day it would be Asif unconscious, handcuffed, and at Marcel's mercy, and he hoped the other man would give him the littlest bit of comfort after punching him so hard he fell unconscious. It would only be right. So, he took a few moments to catch his breath before lifting Marcel onto the bed. He quickly undid Chanté's handcuffs — which were, of course, pink and fluffy — and attached the free cuff to the bedpost.

He took another moment for his breathing to go back to normal before he bent forward and patted Marcel on one cheek. "Night-night," Asif whispered before walking out of the room and closing the door behind him.

He found Chanté in her bedroom with one foot on the bed. She was smoothing her palms over her legs, and the rose smell had intensified.

"You should take a shower," Chanté said without looking at him.

He laughed, pulling his sweater over his head. "Are you trying to tell me I stink?"

She giggled lightly. "I'm telling you I want you to smell like my body wash when I fuck you."

Asif's feet were rooted to the floor, but his heart was galloping a hundred miles a minute.

Chanté's back straightened as her hands moved over her knee to moisturize both sides of her thigh. She turned her head and locked eyes with him. She looked so much like the girl he'd met all those years ago, even if her hair was longer, her curls bigger, her ass fatter, and when she looked at him like this, it seemed like more time had passed than the ten years since they met.

But no matter how much history stretched behind them,

he couldn't help but see the cute little waitress he'd met that first night at The Petal.

He took a deep breath and strained the muscles in his neck to make sure he could keep his voice even when he spoke. "Is that what you want, Chanté?"

She rolled her eyes and moved her left hand between her legs. "Is this what you want, Asif?"

He loved the way she said his name. The way she looked at him.

He should tell her no. He'd been breaking Chanté's heart one hairline fracture at a time, trying to push her away by running and never letting her get too close. The distance was all he could give her, but the thing about Chanté — the thing Asif had immediately loved about Chanté — was that she always bounced back with a bigger smile. If someone told her she couldn't do something, she proved them wrong with ease. When someone told her she couldn't have something, she stole it. Chanté was a flower forever in search of the sun. She didn't waste her own time withering in the shade. If he told her he didn't want her, eventually she'd get over him.

He pulled his pants button open and turned to the bathroom.

"Good boy," she whispered.

Asif rushed into the bathroom feeling like a brand-new person, a person he only ever got to be when he was with Chanté. He pulled the rest of his clothes off in breakneck speed and jumped into the shower. He didn't care when the first freezing cold jet of water spluttered out of the shower-head and hit his skin. In fact, he barely felt it. As soon as the spray was steady, Asif dove into the stream. He closed his eyes and let the water baptize him. He couldn't count the number of times he'd imagined that some moment like this would magically free him of Chanté, but over time, he'd realized he could bathe in holy water and it wouldn't matter because he might have said he wanted to get over her, but every cell in his body knew that was a lie. And so did she.

"The pink bottle."

Asif looked over his shoulder and found Chanté leaning into the shower, watching him. She nodded to the right, and he turned his head. The hotel toiletries were in clean white and gold packaging, but on the shelf next to them was a shockingly bright pink bottle that had Chanté's personality written all over it. Asif pressed the bottle open, and the same rose scent he'd smelled on her skin and in the bedroom flooded his nostrils.

"I get it from a cute little shop online. Black-owned. Vegan. Sustainable packaging."

"Are you trying to sell this to me?" he laughed.

"Word of mouth can change the life of a young Black entrepreneur." Chanté laughed. "I'm just trying to be a good consumer."

When Asif glanced at her over his shoulder, she was playing with her nipple, rolling it around between two fingers while her eyes moved over Asif's backside. He looked away and poured some of her body wash into his hand before replacing it on the shelf. He turned slowly, and her eyes lit up as he exposed more of his body to her in a lovely reversal of most of the other moments they'd spent together.

"Do you want me to smell like you?" he asked.

"Yes," she whispered, watching his hand as if it was primetime television.

"Why?"

She smiled softly. "Why not?"

Asif tried to laugh, but he was too focused on keeping

Chanté's attention to do anything else. "You want to mark me."

Her tongue tasted the corner of her smile as she lifted her eyes to meet his. "I did that already," she whispered. "Didn't I?"

Asif took in a sharp, warm breath that smelled like Chanté. "Yeah."

She smiled triumphantly and moved her tongue over her lips.

Asif moved his hand down to his dick. He was painfully hard. He had, in fact, been at least semi-hard since the moment he saw her in the bar. He wrapped his hand around his shaft and started to spread the palm full of Chanté's boutique body wash into his length as he stroked himself for her.

Her laughter bounced around the tile in the room like bells. "That's fifty dollars a bottle," she said, staring at his dick.

"You've stolen enough money from me to afford it."

"True," she chirped before looking at him again. "Don't waste too much time in here."

His face fell as she flounced away. "I thought you were going to come in here with me," he called after her.

"And I thought you'd be mine by now," she teased. Her voice was full of laughter, but his heart throbbed at her words.

He was, but he couldn't tell her that, so he let Chanté leave even though she took all the warm joy with her. He sighed and took a step back under the spray, closing his eyes as the water washed over him again. The rest of his shower was mundane, sad even — the only thing getting him through one moment and the next was knowing that Chanté was just in the other room.

When he stepped from the bathroom into the bedroom with a towel wrapped around his waist, Chanté was lying on her front in the middle of a king-sized bed. Her crossed ankles were raised in the air, a tablet in front of her, with one hand under her chin while she used the index finger of the other to slide up the screen in an endless scroll.

"What are you in the mood for?" she asked.

"You," he said, happy to be honest.

She rolled her eyes. "Obviously. But I meant for ambience."

He laughed, pulling the towel from his waist to wring some of the water from his hair. "What are my options?"

Chanté's eyes shifted to her right as she watched him hungrily. "Mmmm, I've got a little R&B playlist if you want to be romantic." He didn't like the way she said that last word, as if it was an improbability.

"Maybe some other time," he said.

Her eyelashes fluttered before she presented the next option. "I downloaded this erotic indie film. It's supposed to be artsy and horny."

Asif's knees hit the bed. "That sounds like exactly your vibe. Maybe later."

She smiled up at him and turned onto her back.

Asif couldn't have kept his gaze on her face if he tried, and he did think about trying. It was just that while the thought was flitting through his head, Chanté had started to spread her legs. She bent one arm behind her head while the other drifted over her chest. One finger circled her areola teasingly. "Are those—" He had to clear his throat to continue. "Are those my only options?"

Her fingers were dancing down her chest to ghost around her belly button. "Have you been watching Kenny and Maya's videos?" she asked.

Asif smiled. "A bit."

"Did you see the cowgirl one?"

"Like riding him or wearing a costume?"

"Both," Chanté giggled. Her hand moved between her legs. "She set up a camera so you can see him disappearing inside of her over and over and over—"

Asif dropped his towel and reached for her closest leg, dragging her across the bed. She laughed, batting her tablet out of the way. Her chest was rising and falling slowly, but he did his best to focus on her face.

She pressed her feet to the edge of the bed to readjust herself so she could spread her knees, making room for his body between them.

"He gets her so wet," Chanté teased. "And she rides him so hard."

He nodded, reaching down to scrape his short nails up her shins. Chanté's back arched as she tried not to burst into laughter. "Still ticklish?"

"Sometimes," she gasped, and then her back arched clear off the bed and she moaned loudly.

Her pussy was a furnace against the palm of his hand. He had to reach down to squeeze his dick at the base just to keep his lust in order. Just to keep himself in check. It had been months, nearly a year since he'd let himself indulge. Since he'd gotten this close to a naked Chanté.

"What if I told you you're all the ambience I need?" he said, bending over to lick at her nipple. Well, it was supposed to be a lick, but one taste of her skin and the reins of his control slipped. He opened his mouth wide and engulfed as much of her breast as he could.

Chanté's groan was desperate as all the months of their separation finally found an outlet for release.

He smoothed the palm of his free hand down her arm while the hand between her legs started to move. He pressed the heel of his hand into her clit and her back bowed. His fingers teased her opening without the pressure. Best case scenario, Marcel would be out for a few hours, and Asif planned to use every minute of their time alone making Chanté come. Worst case scenario, the man would wake up to the sound of Chanté and Asif fucking; hopefully, he would enjoy the soundtrack.

His hand moved behind her neck. He cupped the back of her head and lifted his own until the tips of their noses touched.

"The only soundtrack I want is my skin slapping against yours while you scream," Asif said in an even voice.

Chanté opened her mouth to reply, but all that came out was a high-pitched groan as he worked two fingers inside her. Their gazes were locked as he touched her deep. Her panting breaths were warm and sweet on his lips.

"Can I record it?" Chanté whined, forever a bubbly pit of horniness.

Asif brushed his mouth against her lips. "Next time," he said.

Her moan tasted like honey on his tongue.

Chanté sucked Asif's tongue into her mouth like she was starving. His fingers sawed in and out of her with frustrating and enticing precision. She moaned on nearly every breath — when the pads of his fingers brushed her g-spot, when his thumb caressed her clit, as their tongues tangled together — and Asif licked every one up.

It had been just under ten months since she'd fucked Asif. Chanté had been doing a residency in Miami and Asif had a long scheduled layover while he waited to catch up with an asset on a flight to Boston. They had fourteen hours together. Chanté couldn't remember much about the month she'd spent in Miami, but she could describe every minute of that night with Asif. Her old mentor, Dr. Charbonneau, used to say that Chanté's brain was exceptional. He would probably be frustrated to hear how much of her exceptional brain was dedicated to remembering moments like this.

Asif's wet hair hung over his shoulders in long, dripping curls. She felt every drop of water as it fell on her skin. She grabbed him, trying desperately to pull him onto her, desperate to feel the weight of him on top of her. But Asif being Asif, he smiled and pulled away.

She scrambled to keep him close, her fingernails raking at his sides.

His hand was firm behind her head as his dark eyes bored into hers. "Do you think about me when you're with other people?" he asked.

She rolled her eyes. "Duh. I think about lots of things when I'm fucking other people." Her eyes went wide. "Remember Joi?"

Asif groaned, and Chanté craned her neck to lick the last remnants of that sound from his bottom lip. She moved her hand between his legs and caught his next groan on her tongue. She stroked him slow and lazy because they both knew there was more to come.

Finally, Asif gave her what she wanted, pulling his fingers from her pussy but lying heavy and hard on top of her.

Chanté didn't waste any time wrapping her arms and legs around him, holding him close. From experience, she knew this was futile, but she'd never managed to break the habit of hoping that maybe this time — maybe next time — he would stay.

His hand dug through her curls and massaged her scalp as he looked deep into her eyes and slipped one of his wet fingers into her mouth.

He leaned forward and took another of his digits between his own lips. They stared at one another while sharing the taste of her pussy on his skin.

She shifted her hips to press her sex against his coarse pubic hair and his length. She shifted back and forth, rubbing her pussy against the underside of his dick. But then it wasn't just her arching her back and grinding her hips. With Asif's help, she wet every inch of his shaft as he worked her lips open.

"Fuck," Asif said, pulling all the way back. He had to force her ankles apart and then push her knees back to the bed. "Hold your legs open for me."

Chanté nodded frantically as she shoved her hands under her knees and then spread her legs as far as they would go, which was pretty damn far, pushing her thighs flat on the bed.

"Fuck," he whispered reverently before bending over and placing one strong kiss on her clit.

"Yes," Chanté hissed.

Asif gripped the base of his dick with one hand and her right inner thigh with the other.

"Put it in me, baby," Chanté whispered.

Asif smiled briefly but shook his head. "Not yet." Instead of moving inside her, he laid the length of him on top of her pussy and started to move his hips again. The fat tip of his dick poked her opening and then moved up to glide through her wet lips.

She and Asif whimpered together.

They both jumped when it touched her clit, retreating quickly down and back again. They started grinding their genitals together frantically, panting and moaning in harmony.

"Asif," she moaned. "Please."

Chanté screamed when he pushed inside her in one long, liquid stroke. His shaft had been nudging her toward release for so long that one stroke was all she needed, but Asif didn't retreat. He knew what Chanté liked and he gave it to her, fucking her through that first orgasm, galloping toward another. He climbed onto his knees, punching his hands into the mattress next to her head, and started humping into her with sharp thrusts.

Soon the room filled with the sound of their skin slapping together, just like he'd wanted.

These were always such precarious moments for Chanté. When Asif was inside her, looking into her eyes like he loved her, she wanted to tell him that she loved him back, but she couldn't.

Her love was a thing they agreed not to acknowledge — the big, glittery elephant in the room of their relationship — for now. Chanté'd had a choice all those years ago to move on from him, to let those feelings she'd felt for him in Cleveland fade as she moved further and further away from that city and the girl she'd been when they met. But she chose to let those feelings consume her because the alternative — giving up on Asif — wasn't an option.

She pulled him down onto her and he gave her his full weight. Their hips moved together and apart and back again. Chanté slipped her fingers into Asif's hair and pulled his face to hers. She felt like her entire body was on fire, like every nerve ending Asif touched was on high alert. It was the scarcity mindset, she'd realized years ago; every part of her body knew she wouldn't have Asif for long, so she hoarded every touch, every grunt, every stroke, every panting breath, everything.

Chanté's thighs were trembling as another orgasm neared, and she pressed her lips shut in case she said something she couldn't, something Asif knew but wasn't ready to hear.

He moved his mouth over hers. "It's okay," he whispered against her lips. "Just come, baby. Just come for me. I've missed you so much."

The admission broke something inside her, something Asif had shattered years ago. Her muscles locked in place and she clung to him with everything she had. She closed her eyes and swallowed her moans, shuddering around his shaft from her core through her hips and thighs. Asif never stopped moving, but he did slow down, thrusting harder inside her until he was close.

He tried to pull away, but she dug her nails into his back and that was all it took. Asif lost control of himself and came inside Chanté in a wet, messy gush. Her muscles unlocked and she cried out, but Asif covered her mouth with his. They kept grinding into one another desperately, as if their bodies refused to let go. As if this was where they belonged — because as far as Chanté was concerned, they did. She was just waiting for Asif to accept their truth.

When they finally stopped moving, they were covered in sweat and gasping.

He rested his forehead on hers, and they breathed life into each other as they caught their breath. "You shouldn't have come after me," he sighed.

It didn't hurt anymore, or not as much as it used to. She raised her hands to cup his face, scratching lightly at his beard. "I shouldn't have done a lot of things when it comes to you, Asif, but I chose you. Every time, I've chosen you. Even when you weren't ready to choose me back."

Chanté

+

Asif

TWELVE

MARCEL KNEW what a concussion felt like. He blinked awake in a bright room that might have been impressive if it wasn't so gaudy.

"He's awake," a female voice trilled.

He lifted his head from the pillow and started seeing dark spots in his vision, so he closed his eyes again.

"I think he might have a concussion," she whispered.

"Nah, he's alright," a voice he recognized said. He heard footsteps, then a few seconds later, the bed depressed to his right. "You probably want this medicine, though."

Marcel cracked open his right eye and looked at him. Asif looked enough like the man he'd first seen in Dubai, but there were subtle differences. His hair was a little bit longer, his beard was a little bit thicker, and now that he wasn't pretending to be a novice day trader out of his depths, he looked more relaxed with a charming smile on his face. He was also shirtless, hair down and loose falling over his shoulders.

He lifted a glass of water in one hand and showed him two pills in another.

"I wouldn't accept directions from you, I'm surely not going to take unknown medication from you."

"It's just aspirin, and I'm actually great with directions."

The bed depressed on the other side, and Marcel closed both eyes. He took a deep breath before opening both eyelids slowly to look at the other side of the bed.

He recognized the dancer from the stage and the alley as he'd followed them to this hotel. She leaned on the bed, one palm pressed into the mattress, the other arm lying over the curve of her side, showing off her curves under the pink satin nightgown that was barely long enough to hide anything that should be hidden. He forced himself to look away from her body to focus on her face. "Do you know how dangerous this man is?" he asked.

She nodded excitedly.

"And you're okay with that? With this?" he said, jiggling the arm above his head and the handcuffs attaching him to the bedpost.

"Those are mine," she replied happily. "And this isn't the first time they've been used like this. I mean, not *exactly* like this, but not so far off."

"Are you an agent too?"

Her face crumpled. "Eww. No. I'm not fucking up my manicure fighting anyone." She held up her right hand to show off her long, sharp nails, each with its own unique pattern of bright pinks, yellows, and cream polish. She shrugged. "But I'm a bit partial to their cause. Sometimes. And it really is just aspirin."

"Why should I believe you?"

She lifted onto her knees and pressed herself against his

side. Her gaze moved over his face as her smile faded to a serious line. And then she brushed her hand softly over his temple. "You shouldn't," she said, "but at this point, what do you really have to lose?"

"She's got a point," Asif said, stealing the words from Marcel's brain.

"Fine."

Asif helped him sit back against the headboard, dropped the pills into his hand, and offered over the glass.

Marcel took a quick gulp of the drink, then, realizing he was thirstier than he thought, he downed the rest of the water.

"Feel better?" Asif asked.

"No. I could smash this over your head," Marcel mused.

Asif laughed. "You sure could. But then what?"

Marcel's eyes moved to the pink handcuffs over his wrists.

Smiling at him, Asif nodded his head to the woman. She was sitting on both knees, looking at him, bright and eager. Toying with a chain around her neck, she slowly pulled a key from her cleavage.

Marcel breathed slowly before trying to lunge at her, but Asif grabbed his right shoulder, pinching at the already-sore muscles there in a tight grip.

"Ah, shit! Shit, okay."

Asif let go quickly and Marcel punched at the mattress, clenching his jaw as the pain subsided.

"I know she's beautiful, but if you try to touch her again without her permission, I'll break every bone in both your hands."

The woman gasped prettily. "I think he means it," she whispered.

"I think he means it as well," Marcel said, grinding his teeth at the ache in his shoulder. He turned to Asif. "What's your plan? You just going to keep me locked up in this room?"

"Ooh," she sighed.

Asif glanced at her and moved a hand to his mouth to hide his smile. "As fun as that sounds, I don't actually have the space in my brain to handle a hostage. All I need you to do is stay out of my way and let me gather the information I need about Verinac's operation."

"Are you just on reconnaissance or do you plan to take him in?"

Asif's eyes lifted. "Just recon. You?"

"I am as well."

Asif squinted. "I don't know that I believe you."

"What does it matter? Verinac is a French citizen under investigation by French intelligence, what we do with him is none of your concern."

"You're right, it's not," Asif conceded, and his face became pensive. "It's just that the information I'm trying to gather becomes next to useless if the man disappears or is arrested before we're ready. His contacts will burn their paper trail before we can even discover it."

The woman scoffed, and Asif's mouth almost lifted into a smile. Even though he didn't look in her direction, Marcel could tell she had his full attention.

"Why don't you compromise?" she asked.

"I'm open to that," Asif said.

Marcel sucked his teeth. "This is a lovely little performance, but—"

"You should have seen the one we put on while you were asleep," she purred.

No one moved, but chicken skin erupted all over Marcel's skin as the tension in the air thickened. It took all the strength in his body not to join Asif in his attentions. He swallowed hard and loud. His lips stuck together when he opened his mouth to speak, and he ran his tongue along them. She made a sound that was the filthiest thing Marcel had ever heard.

"What do you want?" he rasped.

"Help me get the information I need, and then give us three months to set some chess pieces on the board, and I'll share everything I recover." Asif smoothed his hand over his beard.

"And if I say no?" Marcel asked because no one can head in a wise direction without counting all the paths.

The other man sighed. "Then I'll leave you here, attached to the bed" — his eyes flitted to Marcel's wrist — "and hope for the best."

"I can promise you one month, but I will ask for three. Unlike your bosses, mine don't enjoy me making deals in the field."

Asif smiled. "The job offer still stands."

"And my answer is still no."

"Pity," she said.

Marcel relented and shifted his gaze in her direction, still trying not to let his eyes stray below her neck.

"Do we have a deal?" Asif asked after a while.

She winked at Marcel, and he turned away.

"We have a deal as soon as you unlock these handcuffs."

"Another pity," she said, although this time there was a playful note in her voice.

Asif stared at him for a long, silent moment before lifting his right hand and beckoning her forward with two fingers.

That small movement made Marcel's stomach clench, but then she lifted onto her hands and knees. She crawled over Marcel's outstretched legs, her eyes on him as she leaned toward Asif until the other man's fingers brushed her chin. Her eyelashes fluttered as she turned and let Asif lift her mouth to his.

He couldn't stop his eyes from wandering over the thin straps of her pink satin nightgown. Her clothes barely covered a fraction of her body, and what it did succeed at covering, it did so poorly. At this angle, she was practically spilling out of her nightgown at the top and bottom.

Marcel had heard...things about The Agency, about the way they moved through the world, the tactics they used to close their cases. They were legendary and infamous all at the same time, but Marcel had thought those were just rumors. Just things other agents said to soothe their egos when The Agency turned their assets and swiped their targets. But as he watched the woman suck Asif's tongue into her mouth as his fingers caressed the chain around her neck, he had to consider that maybe there'd been a kernel of truth to those stories.

But that was an investigation for another time. Right now, all he could concentrate on was forcing his dick not to harden in his pants. He could have looked away, though; he just didn't want to.

Asif pulled the chain over her head, and she settled back onto her knees, watching Marcel while he watched her. Even while Asif unlocked the handcuff on his wrist and Marcel massaged his numb arm to bring the feeling back, he and the woman watched one another.

"What's your name?" he asked.

"Betty," she chirped. Marcel frowned.

Asif shifted on the bed. "Can we talk about this cover name?"

"No," she said flatly, still watching Marcel.

Asif sighed and turned back to him as well. "Her name is Chanté. Where are you staying?"

Marcel laughed drily and looked toward Asif. "I'd never even think of telling you that."

"Fine. Raphael likes to have a salon of some sort every Friday."

"Tomorrow," Chanté added helpfully.

"I can't get you in—"

"I'll handle my own invitation," Marcel said, swinging his legs toward Asif until the man stood out of his way.

He stood slowly and took a deep breath in through his nose, until the room stopped spinning.

"Do you need me to take you home?" Asif asked.

"I'd rather let you cuff me again."

"I'd rather that too," she added.

Asif's face lit up. "She doesn't make that offer to just anybody, and rarely more than once."

Marcel felt woozy again, but probably not from his head injury. "We don't operate like your Agency in French intelligence."

"Another reason to consider switching teams."

"No," he said again, and the man shrugged. "Do I need to sneak out of here?"

Asif frowned. "What do you mean?"

"You two made a scene in the lobby and everyone saw me follow you. Now I'm leaving, and I look like I've been through a lot," he said. His clothes were rumpled, and he had a split lip.

Chanté slid from the bed, crowding against him. Her

nightgown pushed up to the crease of her thighs, and he held his breath.

She leaned close, tilting her face toward his. He moved his hands behind his back, not trusting himself when she was so close and smelled like candied roses. Asif chuckled softly behind him.

"If anyone asks," she whispered with a hungry smile, "tell them I like it rough."

Marcel jumped when Asif's hand squeezed his shoulder. The man's mouth brushed against his right ear. "It's easiest when you don't have to lie."

Marcel nodded slowly before slipping away, rushing from the room.

There was much he didn't know about The Agency, but that tense encounter had taught him that apparently, some of those stories he'd heard were, indeed, true.

"So, he's a spy too?" Chanté asked.

"Mmmhmm," Asif said absentmindedly.

"But he doesn't work with you?"

"Different agency."

"Do they have a better name than just '*The Agency*,'" she said, twirling in a circle. The hem of her nightgown lifted into the air, showing off the bottom curve of her butt and the shadows of her sex.

Asif swallowed. "Bureau d'Espionnnage Française."

Chanté came to a stop and frowned at him. "So...no," she said definitively.

He didn't stop. Asif walked up to her and easily lifted her in his arms. She wrapped her limbs around his waist. He missed touching her when they were apart. Holding her. Kissing her. Smelling her. It had never been only about the sex; if it had, he wouldn't have spent so many years running from her. In Asif's business, sex was easy; it was the inevitability of breaking her heart that he couldn't bear, but he did it anyway. The only solace he could offer was knowing that he was breaking his own heart as well.

He kissed a path across her collarbone and down across whatever exposed skin he could touch, then moved his mouth over her breasts, sucking her nipple through the soft material of her lingerie.

She kissed his hairline softly, gentle butterfly kisses that broke his heart. "You have to leave, don't you?"

Instead of answering, Asif bit her nipple and smiled when she pressed her pussy against his stomach.

She kissed her way to his ear. "You can tell me. I won't break."

He held her against him with one hand so he could move the other between her legs. She was so soft. And wet. Everywhere he touched her, she felt like the most expensive velvet, and he couldn't get enough. She moaned into his ear while he massaged her lips, bumping against her clit just to drive her wild. It wasn't about breaking her; it was about breaking himself.

He took his mouth from her chest so they could look at one another. "There's nowhere in the world I want to be more than here."

"No?" she asked in a voice as delicate as porcelain.

He shook his head. "Have you seen the video where Kenny gives Maya the massage?"

Her face lit up. "Oh my god, put me down."

Asif did as she asked with a smile.

"It's gonna be so good, come on." Chanté grabbed his arm and pulled him back into the bedroom. He slipped his fingers into his mouth and tasted the beginnings of her desire.

They had all night.

Chanté

+

Asif

THIRTEEN

EIGHT YEARS AGO...

"WHAT'S YOUR LAST NAME?" Chanté asked while lowering her ass directly onto his lap.

He grunted and licked his lips before he could collect himself enough to speak. "Is that a requirement for a private dance?" Asif asked. He tilted his head back to look into her eyes.

"Social security number?" She pressed her palms against his chest before sliding her hands up to his shoulders for stability.

"Seems a bit steep," he said, clenching his fists at his side to stop from touching her.

She leaned forward. Their smiles almost touched. "Last known address?"

"That's a lot of very personal information," he said. "This dance better be worth it." His words were a choked whisper that seemed to please her.

Chanté rolled her hips, moving her pussy along the length of the hard protrusion she could feel trapped down his right pantleg. "You know it will be." She gripped his shoulders and pulled her cleft slowly back up along that length.

Asif's eyes fluttered closed, just for a second. He licked his lips, but the tip of his tongue brushed her top lip. She licked his taste from her mouth. She was close enough to accidentally kiss him, and at The Petal, she might have; no one would have been there to know or care. But this was her first shift at The Brick and she didn't want to give any of the other customers the wrong idea.

Chanté leaned back and bounced heavily on Asif's lap. He laughed and huffed out a hard, pained, amused breath. "But if you're not interested—"

Asif didn't even think. He moved both hands to her ass and squeezed.

Chanté rolled her hips forward into his waist. She shook her head slowly and moved even slower to push his hands away. "This isn't The Petal," she teased, circling her hips on top of him, dipping her head to almost kiss him again. "They won't let you touch me here."

Asif strained his neck to get closer to her mouth as she retreated. "Where will they let me touch you?" he asked.

She slid from his lap and sat next to him in the booth, slouching back against the seat.

He readjusted his erection while looking at all of her, the curves of her breasts and stomach and hips and the way her small panties disappeared between her thick thighs. "I can't tell you my name, Chanté," he admitted in a choked whisper.

She moved her legs into his lap. "Can't or won't?" she asked, toying with the knot at the center of her chest, the flimsy material the only thing hiding her hard nipples from his gaze.

He lifted his eyes to her face. "Can't," he said.

Her body stilled, and she gave him all her focus. Most dancers believed that the best way to make a living was to be always in motion —— always moving around the stage, customer to customer, and, if necessary, club to club. Chanté tended to buy into that belief, but sometimes it didn't apply. She pored over everything she knew and didn't know about Asif.

Taken separately, there was very little to note. Cleveland was a big city, and in her line of work, it wasn't unheard of for men with money to appear and disappear out of nowhere. Even before she started dancing, Asif hadn't been the first man to tell her a name she'd come to suspect was anything but real. And at the end of the day, who was really hard up enough to give a stripper their personal identifying information, in the middle of a club, no less? None of this was strange, but Asif appearing out of nowhere again made her brain itch.

Obviously, Asif wasn't who he said he was, which was fine, but who was he? And should Chanté leave well enough alone? One of those questions was easy to answer.

She sat up in the booth and removed her legs from his lap.

"Did you come here to find me?" she asked.

He frowned and shook his head slowly. "This is just a happy coincidence."

She smiled. "I don't believe in coincidences." She slid out of the booth. "Whatever you came here looking for is your business. If you don't want to make it mine, leave me be." She turned to walk away, but his voice stopped her.

"Is that what you want? For me to leave you alone?"

She smiled at him over her shoulder. "If you want to

know what I want, I'll be in a private room in the back of the house."

She wished she could trust that he was following behind her — the last time she'd looked away from Asif, he'd disappeared for two years — but she couldn't look back. She kept her back straight and her chin high as she navigated her way through the round tables littering the space in front of the stage. It wasn't easy to keep her composure while squeezing through two dancers on each side of the aisle shaking ass like rent was due — hell, it might have been — or a rain of bills making a cloud in the air before cascading over a woman on her back with her ankles behind her head.

There was just so much to see.

But she could see this display anytime; this might be the only time she saw Asif for another two years.

Still, she didn't verify he was following her until she parted the velvet curtains that led to the VIP area. She turned slowly to look out on the floor.

But all she could see was Asif, gliding toward her with his hands shoved inside his pockets and an amused smile on his face.

He came up behind her to whisper in her ear. "You didn't think I'd say no to you, did you?"

Up close and with her hair providing cover, Asif's lips brushed Chanté's skin, and she shivered at his touch.

"I did, actually," she whispered and felt him frown.

He moved his mouth to her shoulder and kissed her, soft as a feather. "Let me make it up to you."

She swallowed a lump in her throat. She could have said what she was feeling — that he already had — but that was letting him off too easily.

Joi had only pointed in the direction of the private rooms

during her quick tour, so she aimed herself toward a hallway she could barely remember and tried not to betray the fact that she really had no idea where she was going. She was doing okay right up until she came to a literal fork in the hallway.

"What the fuck?" she spat under her breath.

"Everything alright, Chanté?" Asif asked.

She turned to glare at him but felt herself coming up short. She'd missed his smile. "This is my first night," she hissed.

"This really is a happy coincidence."

She turned around quickly, fighting her own smile. "I told you, I don't believe in coincidences."

She jumped when his left hand cupped her left hip. He squeezed her flesh and gently pushed her to the right hallway.

It took a little bit of work, but eventually, Chanté gave in and started to stomp down the hall. He chuckled softly. "How many times have you been here?" she hissed, realizing her anger wasn't about her confusion but about the thought that he'd been in the city but hadn't come to see her. It stung.

"This is my first time too," he said. "When'd you leave The Petal?"

She looked over her shoulder at him. "Two months ago, just before they closed."

"Why'd they close?"

She shrugged and turned away. "Saraiya said the building needed more work than she could afford, especially after her co-owner skipped town."

"Damn," Asif said. "I liked that place."

"Not enough to come back," she said before she could stop herself. He squeezed her waist but didn't reply. Chanté didn't believe in crying at work, but in that moment, it took everything she had not to break her own rule.

The hallway curved to the left, reminding Chanté of a funhouse. Maybe it would have been nice on another night, but she felt like every step she took was sucking all the previous joy that had buoyed her steps here.

She stopped at the first door and knocked.

"Occupied!" someone yelled.

"Sorry," Chanté called back, her face heating in embarrassment.

Every club had a different etiquette system and she knew she'd learn The Brick's soon enough. It was just something about feeling so out of sorts in front of Asif that made her feel exposed and anxious when she so rarely was.

She walked to the next door and knocked. They waited in silence, and when no one called out, she slowly opened the door, careful just in case. Thankfully, the room was empty when she opened it, but she couldn't bring herself to walk inside.

Asif leaned against the wall next to the door. He watched her in silence for a few minutes, and she tried to think of something to say that wouldn't expose her emotionally more than she already had.

"Are you still in school?" he asked after a while.

She nodded slowly. "I'm getting my master's in information technology and cybersecurity."

He smiled. "Of course, you are. I always knew you were brilliant."

"Did you?" She turned to look at him finally and was immediately devastated by how beautiful and sad he looked. "Why'd you disappear? Can you tell me that?"

He shook his head. "I *can* tell you that if I were here, I

would have been at The Petal every night. As soon as I got into town, that was the first place I looked. For you."

She blinked quickly, still trying not to cry. "There are phones. Emails."

He inched closer. "You don't need me," he said. "I knew that the moment I saw you. The first time I saw you on stage. You don't need me."

She rolled her eyes. "I don't," she agreed. "But that doesn't mean I didn't want you. What did you want?"

Somehow, the sadness on his face only seemed to sharpen, and it made her heart throb in pain. He reached up to grab one of her curls. He let it smooth through his fingers and watched it as if he couldn't bear to look at her, but she couldn't look away from him.

It felt like half an hour passed before he finally spoke again. "My wants and my responsibilities never meet. It would be unfair to lie to you about that."

"But it's fair for you to just drop into my life?" she asked.

He shook his head. "Absolutely not. If you were to ask me, I'd tell you to send me away." His thumb moved through her curls to brush her cheek. "You should ask me."

She shook her head. "I'm not going to let you put this on me. We're adults. I've spent the last two years thinking about you. Fucking myself with every sex toy I have thinking about you. Fucking other people thinking about you. I feel exactly the same way about you as I did the last time we met. If you don't feel the same, tell me, and I'll get another girl in here to dance for you."

His fingers caressed her face as he inched closer. "When I left you last time, I swear I could taste you on my tongue for months after that. Every time I thought about you, I could taste you. Every time I ate something good, I was tasting you.

Every time I missed you, my mouth filled with the taste of your pussy."

Chanté's body was on fire, every inch of her.

He leaned forward and brushed his mouth over hers. "It's been so long," he whispered against her parting lips. "This is exactly where I want to be. I can't stay, but you can give me something to remember when I'm gone."

"And what about me?" she moaned into his mouth.

He grabbed her hand and moved it to a lump in his pants. "This is all for you, and I didn't bring singles."

Her heart and pussy fluttered.

ASIF HAD BEEN DREAMING ABOUT A MOMENT LIKE THIS. For the last two years, no matter where he was in the world and no matter what identity he was assuming, damn near every time he closed his eyes, he imagined sitting on a couch while Chanté stood above him.

"What kind of music do you want?"

"What—" Asif stopped to clear his throat. "Whatever you want. The music doesn't matter."

She cut her eyes at him. "The music always matters."

She was scrolling through her phone, stealing glances at him, while all his attention was on her. "You still have a roommate?"

She looked at him and bunched her eyebrows together. "Did I tell you about him?"

"You extorted me for his dinner on our first date, but I didn't know you lived with a man."

She snorted in laughter. "Was that a date?"

He laughed. "I bought you dinner, you scandalized that poor waitress—"

"That poor waitress stabbed a customer like two months later," Chanté interjected.

Asif lifted an eyebrow. "Did they deserve it?"

Chanté looked back to her phone with a small smile on her face. "I plead the fifth," she mumbled.

"You scandalized that poor waitress, and then I walked you to the bus."

Chanté pressed something on the phone and soft music started to play through the Bluetooth speaker. "Um, you're absolutely skipping the part where you became my short-term sugar daddy and guinea pig."

"Guinea pig?" Asif cried. He was ready to keep protesting, but Chanté had started to walk around the pole in the middle of the room. Her fingers caressed the metal, making Asif shift uncomfortably in his seat as his dick slowly swelled in his pants.

"You mean you remember me mentioning my roommate one time but forgot our business arrangement?" She shook her head as she turned away.

"I haven't forgotten anything," he replied, his gaze focused on the curve of her lower back, right above the place where her thong disappeared between her cheeks.

Chanté abruptly grabbed the pole with both hands and hoisted herself up into the air.

"I thought The Petal had just gotten a new owner," he said, his pulse racing.

She wound one leg around the pole and swung the other out for momentum. She moved in a slow rotation, arching her back for the best view of all her curves.

"You remember that?" she asked.

"I remember you thinking I was your new boss when we met."

She smiled serenely and slid down the pole. When her feet hit the floor, she started those slow circles again. "Yeah, she showed up at the end of that shift, I think. I don't remember seeing her much. She didn't do anything that changed my life one way or another. Saraiya was still the boss as far as I was concerned. She made sure I had good shifts as a waitress and gave me my start as a dancer. The Petal was her baby."

"What's she doing now that it's closed?" he asked.

"I was thinking about crawling to you," she said, out of the blue.

Asif sat up straight, preparing himself.

"I thought about it, but I don't know how often they clean these floors."

His gaze moved to the floor with a frown. "I didn't think about that."

"It's best not to think about it," she said, walking toward him with slow steps, one foot in front of the other, in a way that made her hips look rounder, sexier.

Asif reached down to grab the head of his dick. His mouth fell open in a soft gasp, which seemed to please Chanté at least. "Maybe next time," she sighed.

"Definitely."

"She's doing some feature gigs at clubs in Chicago."

"What?"

"Saraiya," Chanté said. "She moved to Chicago to get her money up. She said she'll be back to open up another club, but I doubt it."

Asif was having a hard time concentrating, the parts of

his personality fighting for supremacy in this moment. The mission needed him to keep her talking, but lust wanted her to talk about getting on her knees in more detail.

She stopped just out of arm's reach and spread her legs, swaying her hips side to side to the slow beat as the singer crooned over the song. Her hands went to her back, and Asif held his breath as she slowly untied her top, first behind her back and then behind her neck. She let it fall to the floor dramatically.

"Her girlfriend left her."

"Who?" Asif said. He was listening, he just found himself caring about anything that wasn't her less and less.

Chanté reached for her the ties at her waist. "Saraiya was dating one of the other dancers, Kay. They were kinda messy, but I think they loved each other. Or Saraiya loved Kay, but then one day, she just...*poof!*" — Chanté pulled the strings on her bikini bottoms — "disappeared."

"Come here," Asif groaned. Chanté took a step back.

Asif scooted to the edge of the couch. "Chanté."

"Asif." She had the nerve to moan his name.

He felt like he was going out of his mind. "Chanté," he hissed.

She turned back to the pole but he was up from his seat in a flash, wrapping his arms around her body from behind.

"You're not supposed to touch me," she laughed.

"And you're supposed to do as I say," he said, knowing that would go over poorly.

She threw her head back and laughed loudly.

There was a lot to see — the swell of her breasts, the hard, pointed tips of her nipples, the gentle curve of her lower stomach, all of it jiggling as she giggled — but all he could see was her face and how beautiful she looked when she was happy.

When he got to make her happy.

It hurt to know how rare this moment would be. He couldn't change that, but he could make their time together something they would remember.

Her laughter died on a sultry moan when his touch ghosted over her nipples and back again. She whimpered when he pinched one and then the other before rolling them between his fingers. Her hands moved to her stomach, pressing against her body.

"Don't touch yourself," he said.

"But—"

He had to move her hair out of the way with his chin. She jumped when his lips touched the outer shell of her ear. "Have you been waiting two years to touch yourself or do you want me to do it?"

"What a ridiculous question," she whispered, arching her back as he pulled her nipples away from her body, not enough to hurt, just enough to make her wet.

And when he finally moved a hand between her legs, she was dripping down her thighs.

"Oh my god," she cried out as one slow, moody song bled into another.

Her head fell back onto his shoulder. She closed her eyes and sighed happily as he used his fingers on her. She whispered plaintive curses and started to circle her hips like she was riding him. Fuck, he wanted her to ride him.

"More," she begged, jutting her hips forward.

He thought about it. Hell, he started grinding his erection into her ass, he was thinking so hard about it. Asif had been dreaming about pushing his fingers inside her damn near since the night they met, but there were more pressing matters at hand. He hadn't been lying to her outside. Asif wanted to taste Chanté, not like a man starving but like someone who could remember a specific dish from a small restaurant halfway across the world and needed to try it again.

He wet his fingers in her slick folds, circling her clit lightly, but refused to even get near her opening. He moved his hand on her chest, played with her other nipple, and touched her everywhere he could reach because he wanted to drive her wild. He wanted to frustrate her until—

"Enough, oh my god," she cried out, breaking out of his loose hold.

It ate at him, but Asif let her create some space between them for the moment.

"Fuck," she whispered, grabbing her own breasts and squeezing. "Why do you want to know about The Petal so much?"

Asif's brain felt like it had been pickled in lust, so it took a few seconds longer to register her words than normal. "What do you mean?"

It was an odd sight. Chanté was rolling her nipples between her fingers, but instead of being as lost as he was, her eyes were serious and laser-focused on his face. "You keep asking me about The Petal. Why? In fact," she said, tilting her head to the side, "I still don't know why you were there when we met."

There should've been alarms blaring in Asif's brain because that look on Chanté's face was dangerous. The last thing any spy wanted was someone thinking too hard about the circumstances of their acquaintance.

"Chanté," he said carefully, but she shook her head.

"You said you were there on business when we met."

"I was," he lied.

She smirked at him. "Unless the business was flirting with me, you weren't."

He smiled while running his fingers through his hair. "Business comes in many forms."

She laughed and squeezed her breasts again, using her own touch to focus her thoughts. "Tell me about it."

He licked his lips, but she crossed her arms over her chest, depriving them both.

"I'm serious. Tell me why you were at The Petal. Tell me why you're here."

This was the exact opposite of how he'd wanted this to go, but he was trained for this possibility. A cover could fall apart at any time; the trick was to do everything possible not to die and not to let the mission crumble with it. Not necessarily in that order. He didn't think this was a life-or-death situation, so all he had to do was come up with a believable enough story to redirect Chanté's focus. Easy. Except it wasn't because in that moment, Asif realized the last thing he wanted to do was lie to her.

"I was looking for Mia Malkova."

"Who?"

"The boss you were worried about."

"That wasn't her name," she said, rolling her eyes in irritation.

Asif rolled his eyes back. "Yes, it was."

She thought about that for a few seconds. "Seriously?"

"Yes," he said in exasperation.

"Hmm. Why were you looking for her?"

Asif chose his words carefully. "Because she was a criminal."

Her eyes went wide. "Oh shit, she was! I remember that now. When she disappeared, there was all that shit in the news about her family. But I mean, like…it was a strip club, what do we expect? Jesus, you aren't a cop, are you? You're sexy, but I have standards."

"I'm not a cop."

She exhaled in relief. "Okay, good. So, like…where'd she go?"

He shrugged. "That's why I'm here. It's been two years and she hasn't resurfaced. I came to Cleveland looking for any sign of her, but The Petal was closed, so here I am."

Chanté nodded. "I guess that makes sense. So, is there a reward for finding her?" she asked.

And even though Asif's heart was racing, he couldn't help but laugh. "Do you know something you want to share?"

"Nah, I wasn't joking. I really didn't know anything about her, but what if I can find her?"

"How would you do that?"

She rolled her eyes again. "Getting a master's in information technology and cybersecurity. I can help."

"We've got a lot of people working that angle."

"But none of those people are me. Who is 'we'?"

"I can't tell you. What are you proposing?"

"I'm proposing you pay me money to find my old boss."

"Obviously. How?"

"I take wire transfers."

"Chanté…" He groaned and ran his hand over his beard. The scent of her pussy immediately filled his nostrils and his mouth started watering.

She shrugged. "I don't know, I literally just found this out. But I'm off tomorrow and my roommate has a team building day at his job. You can come over, and I'll have a plan by then."

"Okay."

"And if you have a figure I agree with, I'll share that plan with you."

"This feels *very* familiar."

"I bet it does. Do we have a deal?" she asked, sticking out her hand.

He thought about it, like *really* thought about it. The answer should have been 'no' for a list of reasons so long he could hardly comprehend them. But he also had to consider the reasons to say yes, didn't he? There weren't as many as the other column, but they weren't inconsequential. For instance, even though The Agency had some of the best IT experts, maybe Chanté could give him a fresh perspective on the case. So, that was one thing.

Her breasts were two more points to consider.

And then there was her pussy, which was top of the list.

He sucked his index finger into his mouth.

Chanté whimpered softly and rubbed her thighs together.

He grabbed her hand and pulled her against his body. She stumbled into his arms with a yelp.

"Can we talk business after I eat you out?" he muttered against her lips.

"God, I missed you," she groaned into his mouth.

Chanté

+

Asif

FOURTEEN

ASIF THOUGHT the ceiling in Chanté's hotel room was what entering heaven probably looked like. The crown molding was intricately carved around the border of the room and the mural painted dead center over the bed was a beautiful landscape of rolling hills and blue skies. It was peaceful and serene, and Asif felt like he'd ascended to whatever the next phase of life was while Chanté's throat opened for nearly half the length of his dick.

"Fuck," Asif groaned.

Chanté groaned back and Asif discovered another plane of existence.

He closed his eyes and tried to hold the fibers of his being together, but he was losing the war.

Chanté's left fist had an iron grip on Asif's dick, which in and of itself would have been amazing, but she was using it in tandem with her lips and tongue and throat along his shaft. Sometimes she stroked him as if her hand and mouth were locked together. But other times — like right now — when her mouth lifted toward the head, her fist moved down toward the base before they came back together, and it was making Asif weak. The muscles in his abs and back were spasming as Chanté rushed him toward an orgasm he was mildly worried he wouldn't survive.

But if this was how he died, he wouldn't complain. What was there to complain about? Nothing. Not a thing. This was heaven.

"Fuck!" he yelled as she practically ripped the orgasm from him.

Asif was panting, gasping, and blinking up at the ceiling while the obscenely wet sound of Chanté sucking him dry filled the room. The acoustics in here were amazing, but they'd figured that out last night as the sound of their moans and skin slapping together had boomed like surround sound. Chanté's hungry slurping crackled over Asif's skin like light-ning, threatening to make him hard again.

Although he was still hard, so maybe it wasn't that much of a threat.

Abruptly, Chanté's mouth and hand disappeared from around his dick. He groaned as the cool air of the room hit his wet, spent dick.

She crawled up the bed to straddle his stomach, putting her wet pussy against his already overheated skin. Chanté appeared above him with bright eyes and a close-lipped smile on her mouth as she lowered her face to his.

He opened his mouth for her soft lips and then the warm gift of his own release. His tongue tangled with hers as he tasted his own salty come. He managed to lift a hand to the back of her head so he could keep her close, not that he thought Chanté was going anywhere.

Well, except to scoot herself down his body so the wet tip of his dick could nudge at her opening.

He had to get going. There were things to do today before Raphael's salon, but if Chanté wanted him inside her one more time before he left, he wouldn't be the one to reject her.

In all the years they'd known each other, he'd told her no far more than he liked. This yes was far too easy.

ONE MORE TIME INSIDE CHANTÉ TURNED INTO A FEW more times, but at least one of those times was in the shower, so it all worked out in the end.

It was mid-morning by the time he stepped onto the street in front of Chanté's hotel. He walked a few blocks in a random direction. He could never know for sure if someone was following him, but if they were, he hoped to confuse them without a plan and, crucially, lead them away from Chanté.

He turned onto a busy street. In the distance, he spotted a line of taxis and made his way toward them in unhurried steps. Twenty-four hours ago, Sonja had been his only ally. Much had changed in the last ten hours, but he'd had no time to process it. Chanté had kept him busy.

But in the frigid light of day, there was much to consider, more moving pieces for Asif to account for and keep safe. By the time he slid into the first taxi at the front of the queue, he'd started to pull together the threads of a plan. He wished he had more time, but he also wished he was on a tropical beach with Chanté, so he would just have to make it work and get the hell out of this country as fast as humanly possible.

He had the taxi let him off around the corner from his hotel, just in case.

The doorman recognized him immediately and rushed to open the door. Asif nodded in his direction.

"Mr. Mahmoud," Artyom said as soon as Asif stepped inside the lobby.

"Good morning."

"We were worried about you."

Asif laughed, shaking his head. "No need. I was simply enjoying the gems in this wonderful city." He turned to smile at the man and a sharp sting erupted along his back where Chanté had scratched him with her long nails. He was exhausted, but the memory of her hands clutching at him made his dick throb.

Artyom rushed from his stand toward Asif, but he kept moving toward the elevator.

"Sir," Artyom whispered as he got close. Asif lifted an eyebrow and pressed the button to call the elevator. "You have a visitor."

Asif's dick deflated and he turned to look around the lobby.

"Not here, sir. In your room."

"You let someone in my room?"

"No. No, of course not. She said you gave her a key, and as she's been here before, we assumed," he licked his lips nervously. "I assumed she was telling the truth."

"Ah, okay. Thank you," Asif said, patting the man on the shoulder.

"You're welcome," he sighed in relief, but didn't move.

"Thank you," Asif said again.

"You're welcome."

The two men stared at one another before Asif realized the truth of this moment. He reached into his pants pocket just as the elevator door opened. He didn't count the bills in the stack before stretching out his arm. They shook hands briefly to exchange the money and Asif stepped onto the elevator.

"If there's anything else you need," Artyom offered.

"You'll be the first to know," Asif said, smiling until the elevator doors slid closed.

He took a deep breath and shut his eyes, trying to center himself before he had to deal with Sonja. It took a handful of seconds before the elevator came to a halting stop on his floor. By the time they slid open, Asif had the easy smile on his face that Sonja had come to know. He pushed into his hotel room with the same force as he let the memories of his night with Chanté scatter to the corners of his brain.

At least momentarily.

"Are you going to tell me how you keep breaking into my hotel room?" he asked Sonja.

She jumped at the crash of the door and his loud, booming voice. Asif was expending far more energy than he had to spare, but bravado could be lifesaving.

"That sounds so...criminal." Her voice was strong, but he could see the slight tremor in her hands. She was sitting at the desk across from his bed, in an all-black skintight body-suit, heeled black boots, and a long, thin gold necklace hanging down her front. She looked elegant and out of place, but she always looked that way.

"Are you not a criminal?" he asked, tossing his room key onto the dresser.

"Are *you* not a criminal?" she threw back.

"Touché. How long have you been here?"

"Not long. In fact, I was just about to leave you a note."

"About what?"

"Tonight."

"The salon?" Asif asked.

She nodded quickly. "I believe they're going to close their deal tonight."

Asif rolled his eyes. "What happened at the club?"

She pursed her lips. Another agent might have pushed her, reminded her that her escape was dependent on this deal, but she knew that. Sonja was anything but unintelligent. All Asif had to do was wait.

"They agreed that Raphael would sell Joseph all his stock of drone missiles."

"Can he get more?"

She shook his head. "There's a supply chain issue." Asif opened his mouth but she answered his question first. "He didn't say what or from whom, just that he might have to go into hiding for a bit after this deal."

"Fuck!" Asif yelled, loud enough for Sonja to jump in her seat. "Sorry."

She forced herself to smile, but he noticed she'd also grasped the pen on the desk in her left hand in an iron grip.

"Is there anything I can do to stop it?" he asked.

Sonja shook her head. "The deal is as good as done," she said. "All they'll do tonight is exchange money for the coordinates where Joseph can retrieve his drones."

"How?" Asif asked, his head tilting to the side.

"What do you mean?"

"How is Raphael giving him the coordinates?"

"Oh, he keeps sensitive information like that on a computer."

"A computer?" Asif asked, already imagining Chanté finishing this in an afternoon.

Sonja, once again, seemed to guess the paths his brain had traveled. "It's not connected to a network and it's locked in a room that only Raphael can access."

"What kind of lock?"

"Pin tumbler."

Asif crossed his arms as his brain started racing. "I can work with that."

"It's right next to his office," she said.

"There are cameras all around the penthouse."

"You noticed?" she asked.

He stared at her for a brief second and she smiled. "Of course, I noticed. Is there security on the premises? Someone watching the cameras?"

"Yes. No," she said, her smile widening as she caught on.

"If I can get access to whatever's on that computer, theoretically I won't need a deal."

"Theoretically," she agreed.

Asif nodded. "Okay. That's fine."

Her eyebrows lifted in surprise. "Just like that."

"Of course not, but I have" — he looked at the watch on his wrist — "almost eight hours to figure it out."

"And me?" she asked.

"I'll let you know when we arrive tonight."

"We?" she asked, a smile on her lips. "Will your lovely little dancer be on your arm?"

"Yes," Asif said, feeling a mixture of fear and excitement at that.

"Good." She stood from the chair and shrugged into her black fur coat. He expected her to strut from the room without another word, but she hesitated.

"Is there something else?"

She swallowed. "I would not let your dancer get too close to Joseph, if I were you."

Asif's jaw clenched at that. "Thank you."

She nodded once and then walked from the room.

Again, Asif waited until he was sure she was gone to check the room. He made sure she hadn't found any of his hidden tech or left any behind. But rather than leave it all in place, he threw it on the bed, pulled out his duffel bag, and began to pack.

This small hotel room had been fine while he'd been on his own, but Chanté was across the city alone, and he couldn't have that.

Besides, if Chanté was going to be his backup, he might as well use her. And let her use him.

He snatched his emergency phone from its hiding place under the dresser drawer. Chanté had a phone number; Asif knew it by heart but had never used it. Whenever he wanted to get in contact with her, usually to ask where the hell a large chunk of money in his bank account had gone, he sent her a message to an email address he suspected was only for him but was too scared to confirm.

Packing. Will return in one hour. Will need your help tonight.

Do you think mainframes get lonely?

Chanté

+

Asif

FIFTEEN

MARCEL'S ARM was still sore when he woke up.

Sometimes, he wished for the kind of work that allowed him to take a sick day, but the adrenaline rush of his actual job was usually enough to push away those small aches and pains.

He'd just stepped from his hotel room when he saw her glide through a door down the hall. He'd read Sonja Bershov's file, but seeing her in person last night at the Glass Menagerie had been almost as distracting as waking up on that bed with Asif and Chanté. He'd expected to see her again tonight, but now that she was in front of him and apparently alone, he resolved not to waste this unexpected opportunity. He stilled as she walked in the opposite direction of his door to the elevator. He held his breath until she stepped onto the lift and the door closed, then took off in the same direction on a run. But instead of calling the elevator back, he took the stairs, two at a time, down to the lobby. He made it down to the first floor just as the doorman pushed the door open for her.

It was easy to fall into step behind her after that. Easier still when she walked slowly in a clear path. Easy to follow her into an old building that had been repurposed into a large department store, and even easier to keep an eye on her in the sparse morning crowd.

He didn't know what he hoped to find or if following her would uncover anything of note, but this job was as much about patience as anything else. He had time before the salon tonight and Sonja was beautiful. Marcel had taken detours for far less worthy reasons.

"Excuse me, do you speak English?" Marcel just touched the point of Sonja's elbow.

She was standing at a makeup counter, staring at a display of a cosmetics brand he'd never heard of. The model was almost shockingly pale and the colors on the display underneath the graphic seemed to just be variations on the same ivory shade. He'd been watching her for the last half-hour, and this was the first time she'd stayed in one spot for longer than twenty or so seconds. After a full minute, he started to believe something was wrong; after two minutes, he acted.

She blinked at his touch, but the rest of her was still frozen.

"Miss?" Marcel said softly, holding onto the edges of his English accent. He wasn't worried it would slip, he was worried the flat language wasn't strong enough to capture his emotional intentions. So much of this work required a careful — if not intimate — connection, and of all the languages he felt comfortable working in, English sounded worst to his ears.

Marcel's gaze was focused on her eyelashes as they fluttered closed and open again. He stepped forward. He didn't want to crowd her, but he felt suddenly protective and hoped to shield her from the view of other people.

"Are you alright?"

"I have to special-order my makeup?" she said.

"Excuse me?"

Her eyelashes fluttered again. "They don't carry my shade in this country," she said and then turned her head slowly in his direction. "Whenever I run out of foundation, I have to get it shipped from a different country, or make sure to buy some while I'm traveling. Isn't that absurd?"

Her eyes were mesmerizing — endless dark brown pools. Sad pools. They shimmered over with tears.

"My sister is a ballerina," he said. She blinked again. "She's always wanted to be a principal and she will be one day, but when she first started dancing as a little girl, she used to weep because her shoes never matched her skin."

Sonja's lips opened on a gasp. "Bednyy rebenok," she whispered.

He grinned. "She's never been weak and used to steal our mother's makeup as her tint."

Sonja sucked in a sharp breath and her eyes lit up in amusement.

Marcel shouldn't have been telling her this story, not just because it was real. His little sister Aïssa was currently in the corps de ballet at a ballet company in Grand Est, with firm plans to be a soloist within the year. No, the real reason

Marcel shouldn't have shared this story with Sonja was because he liked making her feel better.

"Did she get caught?" Sonja asked slowly. Her Russian accent was stronger than he expected. He liked it. He liked her lips.

"Of course, she did, but after her punishment, our mother bought her a bottle of her own." He let himself show her a genuine smile — something else he found hard to do while in the field. When he realized he was still holding her elbow, he squeezed. Yes, offering Sonja comfort felt very good.

They stared at one another for a second before she turned fully toward him. Reluctantly, he let go of her arm.

"Did you need some help?" she asked.

It was his turn to blink for a few seconds before he remembered why he was here. "Ah, yes, sorry. I was actually wondering if you can point me in the direction of the men's shoe department?"

The right side of her mouth lifted briefly into a smirk, definitely not a smile. "Is that *all* you want?"

She didn't mean to sound so suggestive; he knew that. Nothing he'd glimpsed of her since he'd been tailing her had indicated that. Still, his brain was captivated by the emphasis she put on that one word. Once again, it took him a few seconds to get back on track, but now he had another dilemma.

It didn't matter how many times he practiced the language of this offer, it would always stumble from his mouth. "I can offer you a way out," he said in a flat tone that didn't dislodge his smile.

She squinted. "I'm sorry?"

He wanted to touch her again, but he moved his hands behind his back. "Every time I've seen you with your husband, you look like his pet bird." She flinched and her soft mouth hardened. "A bird whose wings he's cut. You deserve much more than that. An actual wounded bird deserves more than that. I would like to offer you a pathway far from his reach."

She laughed derisively. "Do you know how many men have given me this same offer?"

"Hundreds. Thousands," Marcel replied seriously.

The earnestness of his tone stunned her for a second. He watched her prepare to strike at him and then mentally take a step back to reevaluate.

Her eyelashes fluttered again before she licked her lips. "It's never real," she said. "Men, especially, will offer you the world only to get what they want. And once they get it, they behave as if the lint in their pockets is too expensive for you."

"What do you have to lose?" Marcel asked.

"Everything."

He flinched. "You've smiled more in the last two minutes than the last two weeks. If you think this is everything, I am devastated for you."

She pressed her lips together as her brow furrowed in confusion. She was considering this, but he didn't get his hopes up.

"What if I say yes and then tell Raphael you're investigating him?"

He shrugged. "What if you let nature take its course and set yourself free?"

"You are good with words," she said.

He smiled and stepped forward. "I am."

"You smell good," she purred.

"You're beautiful." The words slipped from his lips.

"He's not my husband," she said with a smile.

"That is *very* good to hear."

Chanté

+

Asif

SIXTEEN

CHANTÉ ALWAYS TRAVELED with one of Kenny's old threadbare sweatshirts at the bottom of her suitcase. It was in a terrible state and had been since she plucked it out of a donation pile. There wasn't much special about it besides the fact that it had once been Kenny's, and sometimes when she was feeling homesick, she liked to throw it on, pull the hood down low over her big forehead, and feel at ease. She would have done the same with one of Caleb's sweatshirts, but he didn't believe in casual clothing, and on her best day, one of his shirts would be an ill-fitting crop top on her. And Asif never stuck around long enough for Chanté to develop an attachment to any of his clothing — although she'd always been partial to how good she felt when taking off her own clothes for him. But she couldn't think about that now, and for once, she didn't pull Kenny's sweatshirt on to stave off a mid-morning depressive episode; this was about business.

"Good morning," Maryam said as soon as the video call connected.

Chanté recognized the wallpaper behind Maryam's head

from her office. "Good morning," she said, trying to sound a normal kind of chipper and not 'Asif had railed her most of the night and her thighs were sore' kind of chipper.

"Do you have an update?"

"I do!" Chanté didn't mean to say that as loud and eagerly as she had, but Asif had railed her most of the night and she was in an excellent mood.

Maryam rested her right elbow on the arm of her desk chair before resting her jaw onto her knuckles. Chanté found it difficult to read Maryam generally, but when the woman's eyebrows lifted, she thought she detected at least a sprinkle of amusement, but maybe a little judgment too. "I'm listening," Maryam said.

Definitely a little judgment. "Okay, so...uh... I found him?" she shrugged. "I thought I had more than that."

Maryam nodded. "Wonderful. Do you have a plan for making contact?"

Chanté frowned and squinted at the screen. "I did that. Like I said, I found him."

Maryam squinted back in silence before laughing drily and shifting in her seat. "Do you mean to tell me that..." She laughed while steepling her fingers in front of her.

Chanté shifted uncomfortably in her seat. Under the table, she pulled the sleeves of her sweatshirt down to cover her hands, fidgeting under Maryam's shocked gaze. The woman might have been almost two thousand miles away, but Chanté knew enough about her to be terrified.

"Let me get this straight," Maryam said. "It took my agents a week to confirm that our agent had disappeared without a trace and forty-one hours for you to locate him *and* make contact?"

Chanté looked around and nodded. "I don't know about

your other agents, but yes on my part. It would have been thirty-five hours, but Russian counterintelligence tech is kind of a bitch and I had a harder time than expected working through the probability data for where he might be, blah, blah, blah," she said, rolling her eyes as she eased into her comfort zone of topics. "In the end, I just had to make a decent guess, and it paid off!"

"That it did. I can understand why Monica has recommended you for fieldwork."

"Ew," Chanté said. "No. I only show up when it's fun. I don't want to learn how to shoot a gun."

Maryam laughed. "With the right partner—" She cut herself off before nodding her head. "One foot in front of the other. What is your plan? His plan?"

Chanté sat up straight, nodding studiously. "Okay, so tonight, the target is having an event at his penthouse. I'll go as Asif's companion." Chanté couldn't help but stop to smile here. "I don't know the details yet, but I think Asif needs me to hack into an encrypted computer. Maybe? He's on his way back."

Maryam nodded for her to continue.

"Anyway, if all goes well, we should be out of here late tonight and back to headquarters... Or wherever."

"It's not the most..." Maryam took a deep breath, and Chanté watched her search for the most diplomatic word in this situation. "It's not the most detailed plan, but Asif has proven himself quite adept at getting himself out of tight situations."

There was a vulgar joke on Chanté's tongue, and she bit the inside of her cheek to keep it to herself.

"Should you need assistance with extraction, please tell the agent that there are assets in the vicinity."

"I'll try, but—"

"But he doesn't like asking for help," Maryam finished with a shake of her head, but a fond grin on her face. "Still," she continued, "remind him that he is not alone and does not need to shoulder the burden of protecting you on his own."

Chanté frowned. "Protecting me? I'm fine. I don't need protection. And he doesn't—" She stopped speaking abruptly. Maryam didn't need to know what she was thinking. It wasn't part of the mission debrief that Asif was amazing at so many things but protecting her wasn't one because he wasn't around long enough to do so.

"I'll relay the message," Chanté replied with a nod.

"Good. I look forward to your and Asif's return."

Chanté smiled even though she thought the likelihood that Asif wouldn't just disappear before they made it back to London was incredibly slim. But then she remembered that paper file on Maryam's desk and her heart started racing. "And you'll answer my questions?" she asked in a small voice. "About...him?"

Maryam smiled. "I am a woman of my word," she said before disconnecting the call without even a hint of a goodbye.

"Rude," Chanté sighed with a loud, long exhale before ripping the sweatshirt over her head. She wasn't naked under the sweatshirt, but when she looked at her own image in the webcam, she did look a little topless. Thankfully, the person she was calling wouldn't care.

"Hi! Oooh," Kierra cooed. Kierra had answered the call while lying on her stomach on what looked to be a bed. If given the time, Chanté could have figured out exactly where Kierra was — and by extension, Monica and Lane — but she tried to only do that when she was being paid or was extraordinarily bored. But what little Chanté could see of the room behind her was obscured as Kierra hopped to her knees, bouncing on the bed. "Monica," she yelled, reaching for the hem of her t-shirt. "It's Chanté. It's happening!"

"What's happening?" Chanté asked, eyes widening as Kierra lifted her shirt to expose the bare undersides of her breasts. She wasn't wearing a bra.

Kierra froze at her question, and Chanté fought some of her own best demons not to take a screenshot in that moment, but Lord knew she wanted to fail.

She flopped back onto her stomach, licking her lips, eyes darting side to side. "Um...what's up?"

"I need some help," Chanté said.

"Please be more specific?"

Chanté bit her lip. "I don't know how much I'm allowed to tell."

"*Please* be more specific," she ground out.

"Okay, so I'm somewhere with someone and we have plans tonight, right? But I don't know what to wear."

Kierra frowned. "Oh. Okay," she said sadly before turning to her left. She listened to someone Chanté couldn't quite hear before shaking her head, definitely sad. "False alarm. I got overexcited. Nothing to report. Chanté." She listened for a few more seconds before smiling and licking her lips. "I'll tell her."

"That Monica?" Chanté asked.

"Yeah. She said you shouldn't freeze your ass off for Asif."

Chanté's eyes went wide. "Don't say that. Anyone could be listening?"

"You're the hacker," Kierra said.

Chanté nodded and looked to the side. "Yeah, that's how I know."

Kierra shrugged. "Don't worry about it. Anyone who knows enough to be listening in on us definitely knows who Asif is."

Chanté nodded because that made a lot of sense, actually.

"So, what's the event? What are our options? And do you have a credit card, just in case?"

Chanté nodded excitedly, pulling her tube top higher up her chest. Kierra's mouth formed into a knowing 'O.' "Okay, so salon, that I'm hoping is code for orgy. Lots of stage gear and a couple gowns. Duh," Chanté answered each question in turn.

"Oh my god, yes. I can see why you called me. Take me to the suitcase. Let's have a fashion show." Kierra stretched out of view of the camera for a second. When she came back, she had a bag of pick and mix candy in front of her. "I'm ready."

Chanté laughed while she grabbed her laptop and walked into the bedroom.

"Ooh, that place looks expensive."

"Naturally," she replied.

She tried to be tidy when she traveled, not because she was the neatest person in the world but because fucking around with The Agency meant that sometimes she had to make a hasty exit. She still got misty-eyed about the pair of strappy heels she left in a safe house in Argentina. She'd never quite forgiven herself for that mistake. Although, a month later, Asif had sent the shoes to her with a note to be more careful, stoking the fragile flame of her infatuation with him. She didn't know how Asif had tracked those heels down; all that mattered was that he had, and she'd never left her belongings behind again.

But she and Asif had wrecked the bedroom last night. Some of the sheets were bunched at the foot of the bed, but they'd thrown most of them onto the floor, with half the pillows and the clothes Chanté hadn't even been wearing. She smiled looking at the mess they'd made.

"Ooh, I know what that smile means," Kierra said.

Chanté looked down at her laptop screen. Kierra took a bite from a piece of candy without dislodging her own smile. She chewed and lifted her eyebrows suggestively.

"It doesn't mean anything," Chanté said, lying terribly.

"Of course," Kierra said. "And Lane and Monica let me tag along to *all* their missions because they can't live without my tactical support." Kierra winked, but Chanté's response was very serious.

"There are so many kinds of *tactical* support."

Kierra and Chanté stared at one another for a few seconds before bursting into laughter.

"Okay, if I set you here, can you see?" Chanté asked, putting her laptop on the bedside table. It was the only place in the room she and Asif hadn't compromised.

"Turn around," Kierra said.

Chanté did as she suggested and looked over her shoulder. "Look good?" she purred.

"Is that a bite mark?" Kierra asked.

Chanté covered her butt with her hands. She wasn't naked! But her shorts didn't leave much to the imagination, and based on the way Kierra was smiling while chewing on her candy, the other woman was definitely letting her imagination run wild.

"Can you behave?" Chanté cried, her face almost as hot as her pussy.

"First of all," Kierra said, holding up her index finger, "that's rich coming from you. Second of all, no." Kierra lifted her middle finger in the air but then twisted her arm around and slowly bent her two fingers toward her, as if beckoning Chanté forward or simulating something far more interesting.

"I prefer three," Chanté teased.

"I'll remember that. Now, strip. Let's see what we're working with?"

Chanté's mouth fell open and she bent forward, hands on her knees, cleavage teasing Kierra. "You wish. Hold, please."

Kierra sighed. "I do wish."

Chanté ducked to her left toward the closet. She hadn't hung up much of her clothing since she'd mostly brought gear for the stage. She hadn't expected to run into Asif so soon and she'd needed to be prepared for weekly shows like any other residency. But if she'd known an orgy might be on the table, she would have packed differently!

She started with a floor-length long-sleeved scooped neck velvet gown she loved. She wasn't entirely sure why she'd brought it on this trip except it seemed like something dramatic enough to entice whatever Eastern European criminals she might encounter. She looked at her reflection in the mirror on the back of one closet drawer. She looked lovely, of course, but did it scream orgy?

"Nope," Kierra said as soon as Chanté moved back into view of her webcam.

"It's gonna be too much work to fuck around all that fabric, and there's nothing worse than having to drag your clothes from room to room like you're staying in a hostel looking for a free shower stall. Also, getting come out of velvet is just annoying. Trust me. Next!"

That was sound enough reasoning for Chanté, so she ducked out of view again, pulling her dress carefully off. "Maybe next time," she said, putting it back on the hanger. She'd only hung up a few things, and with Kierra's voice in her head, she tried to figure out what might work best. "I don't know," she mumbled to herself.

"This is an orgy but also work," Kierra's voice called from the laptop. "Think tight, some coverage but not too much, and I say short, but that's just 'cause I love your thighs. Also, just in case you need to run," she added that last tidbit helpfully.

"Good points," Chanté said.

"That's what I'm here for. Help and hand jobs," Kierra said with a laugh. "Oh my god, where did you come from?"

Chanté's heart raced at that. She turned toward the bedroom door, clasping a breast in each hand, wondering how she'd fight an intruder in just a thong. She could do it, but how? Thankfully, the room was clear, and Kierra's laughter was blaring from the laptop. Chanté grabbed a dress from the closest hanger she could reach and pulled it up her body. It was tight, short, and thanks to the low dip in the back, gave her both easy access and enough places to hold some SD cards if Asif needed. Or if she needed.

She moved back in front of the camera to an interesting view. Instead of Kierra's face, she saw her bare stomach and Lane's tongue circling her belly button.

"Ahem," Chanté said.

Lane's eyes moved to the webcam. He smiled and dipped the tip of his tongue into Kierra's navel. "Well, hey there,

Chanté. I didn't know we had company." He moved his hand over Kierra's stomach while he spoke, his fingers moving down out of sight.

"Kierra's helping me pick out something to wear to a possible orgy," Chanté said.

Lane's eyebrows lifted before he turned to look up Kierra's body. "Is it happening?" he asked in a slow, deep drawl.

Kierra sighed sadly. "No. False alarm. But...she's with Asif."

"Oh, ho, ho," Lane laughed, turning back to Chanté. "Are you now?"

"I'm his tactical support," Chanté said defensively.

Lane's arm moved. Chanté couldn't see what he was doing, but she thought she heard a moan. "Kierra's great at that."

"Is this what you're gonna wear?" he asked.

"It's an option," she replied.

He tilted his head from side to side with a grimace on his face.

"Wait, you gotta see the whole thing," she said, turning around to show off the back.

Lane whistled slowly and Kierra laughed softly. "That's a showstopper," he said.

Chanté looked over her shoulder again, beaming at the laptop. "Kierra, what do you think?"

Lane helpfully moved the laptop so Chanté could see Kierra's face. She was lying back on the bed, blinking up at the ceiling. Lane said something before Kierra turned toward it. She licked her lips and squinted at the screen before lifting onto her right elbow. Her nipples were hard.

"Yeah. Yes," Kierra said. Panted. "Love it. But a bra would have been nice for holding—" She broke off for a second on a high-pitched note. She closed her eyes and breathed through whatever Lane was doing off-screen.

Chanté crossed one foot in front of another, pressing her thighs closed while her pussy clenched. God, those three were a lot. In the best way.

It took a moment for Kierra to get back on track, but she was definitely struggling to speak when she did. "A bra would have been good for small tactical gear."

"I agree, but I'll figure it out. I'm gonna let you go, okay, hon?"

The laptop moved again on a loud moan. When he came back into view, Lane was licking his lips. "Don't run off just yet, sweetheart. We're here to help." He was breathless.

"Um, no, I think I got it. I'm okay," she said, and by okay, she meant ready to hop back in bed with a vibrator as soon as she closed her laptop.

"Well, if you need us, you know where we are." He smiled while Kierra's left leg moved behind him to frame his head. "Virtually, I mean. We're only a video call away."

"Okay," Chanté sighed.

The video call shut off right as Kierra started pulling Lane's head down toward her body, and he went with a smile.

Chanté

+

Asif

SEVENTEEN

EIGHT YEARS AGO...

"WHAT ARE YOU DOING TODAY?" Kenny asked.

"None of your business," Chanté replied before throwing her arms in the air and bending backward for a full-body stretch.

Kenny was sitting at their small dining room table, eating a dry slice of the high-protein bread he swore by — which tasted like cardboard — and drinking a cup of plain black coffee. She'd watched him eat this sad breakfast damn near every morning for years, but to each his own.

"What are you doing today?" she asked, walking into the kitchen to make her own breakfast.

"None of your business," he mumbled around a bite of toast. "What are you cooking?"

"Nothing," she said, pulling out a carton of eggs. "Is there any coffee left?"

"You're closer to the coffee machine than I am," he sighed in aggravation.

"You're always in such a bad mood in the morning. Is it 'cause you're hungry?"

"I'm eating."

"My question stands."

"Do we have to do this *every* morning?"

"If you're going to starve yourself every morning, I guess so. It's your move, though."

He sighed. Chanté smiled before turning back to the coffee machine. "Oh, there's coffee!"

Kenny stubbornly waited until Chanté had taken her first sip of coffee before responding. "I have an all-day team building exercise with my ROTC group. I need to leave in half an hour. I'll be back by six. Yes, there's more coffee. Can you please make me some egg whites?"

Chanté smiled at him. "See how easy it is to be nice to me?"

He rolled his eyes and stuffed the last sad, dry bite of his toast into his mouth.

"I have a friend coming over to help me with some routines. I was going to kick you out, so I'm glad I don't have to."

"You can't kick me out of *our* apartment," Kenny said.

"Yeah, I can. The same way you kicked me out last month when that stacked cashier from the grocery store stopped by."

"I didn't kick you out, you were heading to work."

"I was willing to stay behind," Chanté said, waggling her eyebrows at him.

"No," he laughed. "We did that once. No more."

She sighed. "I'll never understand why you hate fun so much."

Kenny sighed and stood from the table. He put his plate in the sink and took his mug of coffee with him back toward his bedroom. "Forget the eggs, I don't have time anyway."

"Your loss," Chanté said, then yelled louder to make sure he heard her. "In so many ways!"

"Shut up!" he yelled back.

Asif slipped into Chanté's building behind a delivery man and took the stairs.

He wasn't overeager or anything, he was just trying to get his steps in.

Asif pulled the heavy metal door from the stairwell open and stepped into the hallway. He hadn't been here in years, but as soon as the old Formica flooring crinkled under his step, he felt like no time had passed. The thought of seeing Chanté in a few minutes — seconds — had his heart pounding in his chest and his dick swinging low and heavy in his sweatpants.

But when he strolled around the corner, he came face-to-face with Kenny and felt like someone had dumped a bucket of ice water on his head.

Asif rolled his eyes and let out a hard breath.

Kenny's eyes went wide. "What's wrong?"

Asif put a finger to his lips and moved his eyes to his front door. "Lower your voice," he said.

Kenny nodded quickly. "I have a field exercise in fifteen minutes," he said. "They told me to be ready in four minutes." He checked his watch. "Three minutes."

"Then you better get going." Asif stepped to the side.

"Um..." Kenny turned to look at the front door. "My roommate's still in there."

"Okay," Asif said.

"Is there something you need?" Kenny asked.

"How much time do you have left?" Asif replied.

He hadn't exactly forgotten that Chanté's roommate had been recruited into The Agency, he'd just pushed it to the far corners of his brain. Thinking about Kenny meant thinking about Chanté, and he couldn't invite that kind of longing into his brain any more than he already had. He'd spoken to the recruit a few times, and each conversation had gone about as awkwardly as this. If he'd been on top of his game, he would have checked Kenny's schedule and just come a few moments later. If the taste of Chanté's pussy hadn't been fresh on his tongue, maybe he could have spared a moment to come up with an excuse on the off chance he ran into the other man — but he'd woken up so fucking horny.

It was a good thing Asif had a reputation for being a dick.

Kenny looked at his watch again, and when he lifted his eyes to Asif's, the panic was starting to show.

"She's not—"

"In any danger," Asif finished his sentence. "This is routine. Just a quick check to make sure your space hasn't been compromised. She won't even know I'm there."

"I—"

"Two minutes goes faster than you think, and refresh my memory, what's the penalty for holding up—" Asif didn't even get to finish his sentence.

Kenny tore off down the hall, his sneakers squeaking against the floor. Asif turned to watch him disappear, listening to the sound of his retreat. But he didn't move. He imagined Kenny rushing down the same stairs Asif had just ascended, darting through the lobby, maybe running into someone bringing their dog in from a walk. Asif checked his own watch. He imagined Kenny catching his breath on the curb and the nondescript van pulling up in front of him. He waited until he could imagine Kenny on his way to his field exercise, too far away to turn back.

Asif wondered what Kenny told Chanté he was doing today, but that was none of his business. So long as Kenny was out of his hair, he was a happy man. He turned and knocked on the door. He pressed his ear to the wood and listened. Nothing.

No matter.

Asif looked left and right, confirming the hallways were clear, before squatting down and pulling his lock pick set from his jacket pocket.

Chanté planned to just take a quick shower, but she made the mistake of putting her Certified Hits playlist on before she hopped in the tub and her quick cleanse turned into nearly half an hour of her singing and dancing, almost slipping and falling while she soaped up her body. By the time she hopped out of the shower, she wasn't just clean; she was in a great mood and absolutely ready for Asif to show up today. She didn't know when, but she hoped it would be sooner rather than later. If Kenny said he'd be back by six, he'd be back by six, and she wanted to spend as much time with Asif as possible.

She brushed her teeth, washed her face, and looked at her reflection in the steamy mirror. "You got this," she told herself. "You're gonna get that dick." She'd been waiting years for this, and she was more than ready.

She blew a kiss at her reflection, opened the bathroom door, and was about to turn toward her bedroom but decided she wanted another cup of coffee.

"Holy shit!" she screamed as soon as she turned the corner into the living room.

Asif was standing in her kitchen, sipping something from a mug, his eyes bright as he looked at her. He lowered his cup to the counter and smiled, big and wide. "Good morning," he said.

"The fuck are you doing in my apartment?"

"Waiting."

"How the fuck did you get in here?"

"Your roommate let me in," he replied.

"Abso-fucking-lutely not. Kenny barely wants to let the maintenance man in. No way he let you in and then left while I was in the shower."

"Is it 'cause you walk around naked?" Asif asked, his gaze moving slowly down her body.

"Obviously. Did you break into my damn house?"

He had the nerve to shrug as if that wasn't a crime. "You gonna call the police if I say yes?"

"I don't believe in cops," Chanté said.

"Then I might have."

Chanté put her hands on her hips. Asif licked his mouth and bit his bottom lip to tame the full force of his smile.

"Can you teach me how to pick a lock?" she asked.

A laugh burst from Asif's throat. "Of course, that's your response. What if I was someone really dangerous? What if I am someone who's really dangerous, Chanté?" He'd started out lightheartedly, but Chanté watched as his voice and face became serious, if not pained.

"I can take care of myself, Asif."

"I broke into your house while you were in the shower. I've been here for nearly twenty minutes."

Chanté frowned. "Then why didn't you join me?"

He took a deep breath. "I— Chanté, you—"

"Asif," Chanté said. "Calm down."

"I'm calm," he said, smoothing his hand over the top of his head. Looking stressed as hell.

"Sure."

"You're so damn vulnerable, Chanté," he whispered. "But you don't even know it."

Chanté thought Asif was spiraling, and a large part of her wanted to rush across the room and wrap him up in her arms — and legs — to make him feel better, but it had been years since they'd seen one another. Years since he'd walked into her life and made her think she could have something she wanted desperately and then ripped it away. Years since she stopped getting sad every time the shadowy figure in the crowd turned out to not be him. Years since she learned to live with the aching hole he left in her heart.

"You don't know me nearly as well as you think you do, Asif. You've never stuck around long enough. I'm gonna throw some clothes on," she said, turning down the hallway to her bedroom. "Don't drink all my damn coffee," she yelled over her shoulder.

Chanté

+

Asif

EIGHTEEN

THEY WERE DRESSED and ready to go, but Asif was hesitating, and Chanté was wasting time debating about whether to paste a lip stain on her pillowy lips or something glossy.

He was pacing in the living room while she stared at her reflection in the bathroom mirror. "We don't have all night, sweetheart."

"Of course, we do," she called back flippantly. But then he heard her feet on the tile as she reappeared in the hallway.

She made his mouth water.

"Happy?" she asked sarcastically, and his gaze moved down her short, thick body.

"Very."

"Come on, let me give you some goodies."

"We don't have time," Asif sighed, even as he started walking toward her.

She laughed. "I'm saving those for later, but if you're

going to try and copy an entire hard drive, you need something to clone it with."

"I have—" Asif said, but she cut him off, lifting a silver chain with a black diamond-shaped pendant hanging from it.

"What's that?"

She dropped the charm into her hand and pulled a piece of the gem off. "USB-C that I might have customized a bit. You can wear it inside Raphael's home and no one will think twice about it. When you get to the computer, plug it in. Depending on how much data we're talking, you should only need a few minutes."

"That's surprisingly low-tech of you." Asif laughed as she capped the connector again.

"I know, and I'm devastated about that. Don't tell anyone."

Asif laughed and plucked the chain from her hand. "Your secret is safe with me."

She looked up at him with a vulnerable smile. "Promise to be careful?" she whispered.

He threw the chain over his head and moved his hands to her face.

"Don't mess up my makeup," she whispered.

He nodded. "I know you don't have any reason to believe me, but I hate lying to you. Don't make me."

She nodded softly. "Okay."

"If we get separated—"

She cut him off, moving her hands to the gem on his chain, tucking it carefully inside his shirt. "Don't make me tell you the truth," she said.

"Okay. Kiss me."

Her face lit up, and she lifted onto the balls of her feet. It wasn't a compromise, but this thing he had with Chanté was how Asif reminded himself that there was still something beautiful to live for.

THEIR CAB PULLED ALONG A CURB IN A PART OF SAINT Petersburg Chanté would have loved to explore. The money was oozing as far as the eye could see. Even in the gray-white of winter, she could only imagine the kind of wealth that lived behind these doors.

"We don't have time for that," Asif whispered against her ear.

"You don't even know what I was thinking," she said.

He laughed, handing over a wad of cash to the driver. "Of course, I do. Wait here, I'll get your door."

She watched him stand from the car and then round the back of the cab, pulling the door open. Frigid air hit her bare legs, and she shivered excitedly. He stuck his hand into the car, and she slipped her fingers into his hold.

He pulled her carefully onto the sidewalk and then into his body, slamming the door in one fluid motion.

"We don't have all night," she whispered.

"We surely do not."

Asif rolled his eyes, and they turned to find Marcel standing on the sidewalk, watching them.

"So, you came?" Asif said.

Chanté covered her mouth, giggling into her palm.

Marcel rolled his eyes. "I am trustworthy."

"You say that as if I am not."

"I wouldn't trust any of you," Chanté said.

"I agree." They turned to find Sonja walking toward them in a long deep red silk kimono dress.

"Damn," Chanté whispered because she was the only one who could speak, apparently.

"Uh, um… Sonja, this is my friend, Marcel."

Her eyes flickered to the other man, assessing him coolly, gaze looking him up and down. "Yusuf, you have such beautiful acquaintances."

Asif enjoyed watching the man squirm and take a breath before he could reach for her hand. Chanté let out a little purr as the other man brushed his mouth over Sonja's skin.

"Please tell me this is an orgy," she whispered.

Sonja turned her attention on Chanté. "What has Yusuf been telling you, Betty?" she laughed.

"He told me it's a salon, but I am always full of hope."

"Is that it?" Sonja asked.

He could feel the excitement radiating from her. Chanté loved when people met her horniness with their own. Asif hated to dampen her excitement, but things were about to get tense and they didn't have time to waste.

He threw his left arm over her shoulders. "Let's get back on track," he said.

Chanté sighed. "If we must."

"What's the plan?" Sonja asked, and Marcel whipped his head back and forth.

Asif nodded at him and got to work. "I need to know where the computer room is."

"Third floor, door next to Raphael's office," Sonja answered quickly. "But the camera—"

"I'll handle that," Chanté said.

"What about me?" Marcel asked.

"And me?" Sonja echoed.

He looked at Sonja. "I need you to stay with Betty and keep her safe." He looked her deep in the eyes, and she nodded seriously. He shifted his attention to Marcel and rolled his eyes. "And I need you to watch my back."

"Can I watch him watch your back?" Chanté whispered.

He bent forward to kiss her forehead. "Maybe later."

"You two are quite sweet," Sonja whispered sadly.

INSIDE THE BUILDING, SONJA AND MARCEL WERE standing on the threshold of the open elevator. He was a few inches shorter than Sonja in her heels and he was looking up at her like she was a goddess — which was understandable — or as if he was waiting for her to tell him to get on his knees — which was relatable.

Chanté slowed her steps so she could experience whatever was about to unfold, but Asif's hand was at the small of her back, pushing her forward. She glared up at him, and he shook his head. "We're working," he mouthed as silently as possible.

She rolled her eyes and turned back to the elevator just in time to see Sonja running the tip of her nail down the length of Marcel's tie. Marcel made a choked sound that was very pleasing to Chanté's ears.

Asif cleared his throat and Marcel jumped, stepping into the elevator, just out of reach of Sonja's searching hand. Sonja glanced back at Chanté and winked before they followed the man inside the small box. In the penthouse, the elevator opened onto a short hallway. The large metal front door to Raphael's house was a carved, imposing monstrosity.

"Rich people waste good money on the most annoying things," Chanté whispered. Marcel stifled a laugh.

They watched as Sonja pulled a long chain from deep in her dress to unlock the door. She beckoned them to follow her inside with a graceful sweep of her hand.

They stepped into a tame sitting area with men in suits standing around, chit-chatting with glasses of champagne in their hands, and a waitress circumnavigating the room with a tray of canapes leading her way.

"Has it started yet?" Chanté asked in confusion.

"Yes," Sonja replied, leading them forward.

They walked down a narrow hallway. Chanté heard the party before she saw it. "Oh, my," she breathed with a smile on her face.

This sitting room was a bit larger than the other and no one was speaking. Instead, a thicker cluster of people were standing against the walls, watching two sweaty men fuck one another in the center of the room. One man was pressing the other's face into the carpet, one foot on the floor, slamming his hips into the other man's ass. The only sound in the room was hard grunts and slapping skin, music to Chanté's ears.

"Chanté." She shivered at Asif's warm breath on her ear. "The cameras."

"Yes, you can re— Oh, sorry," she laughed softly, coming to her senses. "Got it."

Her left hand moved to the earring dangling from her lobe. She had a friend in Arizona who was obsessed with developing functional but beautiful tech accessories. Chanté had hooked him up with The Agency, and he'd been subsidizing his starving artist lifestyle with defense money for the past couple of years. His other friends might have judged him, but Chanté knew what it was like to worry about making rent. Besides, when she bought earrings with the capabilities to disrupt cloud syncing, she hadn't known she'd ever need them, but tonight, she did!

"It'll take a few minutes to fully disrupt the networks, so don't rush," she whispered.

He pressed his lips to her temple. "I never do."

"Yusuf, you should go," Sonja whispered.

Asif nodded at her words, but he was looking down at Chanté.

"I'll take care of her," Sonja said.

"I'll be okay," Chanté added. "And so will you."

He kissed her lips lightly, quickly, before moving behind her toward a door just ahead of them that led to the dining room. Asif stopped at the door to glance back at her, but only for a second before he turned and rushed away.

Chanté watched that empty doorway, her heart pounding a fast and terrified beat against her rib cage.

"Would you like to keep looking?" Sonja asked.

Chanté plastered a smile on her face. "Always," she said, which was true enough.

Chanté

+

Asif

NINETEEN

"SO, IS SONJA ONE OF YOURS?" Marcel asked once they'd cleared the kitchen.

"One of mine?" Asif asked, turning on the man with raised eyebrows.

"Not... Not— That's not what I meant?"

Asif couldn't stop walking because time didn't matter until it did, and this moment was the latter. "Then what'd you mean?"

Asif was trying to strike a balance of getting where he needed to be quickly without attracting any unnecessary or unwanted attention. He led Marcel down a narrow hallway that opened up onto the dining room, where a small, mostly male crowd was gathered, smoking. The air was thick in here and Asif wanted to open a window, but this haze could be helpful in a pinch, so he covered his mouth and rushed through the room as fast as he could.

Once they were in a hallway full of fresh air, Marcel spoke again. "I mean is she, you know—"

"I don't," Asif said, moving around the library. No one

even noticed them; this crowd was engrossed with two women playing a high-stakes game of strip chess. That wasn't how Asif would have started the evening, but if he had his way, he would have been balls-deep in any part of Chanté rather than leading Marcel up a flight of stairs fully clothed. A waste.

Marcel grabbed Asif's hand and pulled, jogging up the stairs so he could look Asif in the eye. "I mean, is she one of us? Can we trust her?" Marcel asked, tipping his head close.

Asif could only wonder how they looked to an outsider, but since at least one of his cover stories would be that he was taking Marcel somewhere to fuck, he let the man stay where he was. Besides, Marcel smelled like a warm, husky cologne and bitter cold, and it was surprisingly attractive.

"Why? Are you looking to mix business and pleasure?" Asif asked.

Marcel's head reared back and his eyes went wide, but he didn't object.

Asif let out a low, guttural laugh. "I trust Sonja about as much as I trust you and maybe more than you can trust me."

The man rolled his eyes.

"We don't have the luxury of perfect allies in this moment, but she wants to get out of here as much as we do," he said, not sure exactly what answer Marcel wanted, one way or another. "Just be careful with her."

Asif jogged up the next few steps. This wasn't the only staircase in the house and Asif had only been up here a couple of times — just enough to log its location in the floor-plan he'd built in his head but not enough to arouse suspicion. The staircase curved onto the third floor, and while it was much quieter than the main floor, it was by no means without action. He eased his way onto the landing which led directly to a long hallway. Asif could see the darkening sky through a window far on the other side of the building. He knew that on either side of that hallway were two small bedrooms and a full bath. But the stairs opened up onto a rotunda that had an office, a large sitting room where the man often entertained, and a locked door he now knew was very important.

"What's up here?" Marcel asked.

"Lots, actually."

Marcel sighed, and Asif led him to the right. The most interesting thing about this penthouse was that the floorplan didn't make any fucking sense. There were likely dozens of reasons for that just based on the age of the building and the hysteria that comes over rich people when they have the opportunity to design anything. Thankfully, Asif didn't have to figure out the why of this structure; all he needed was to make it work for his needs. The part of the floorplan that made the least sense but was the most useful was the small alcove just outside an even smaller powder room.

Like every other wall in the house, dark wainscoting was topped by moody, floral-patterned wallpaper that wasn't to Asif's taste but made it very easy to hide when the lights were low, and so he made sure they were. He stopped next to the powder room door and reached behind a wall hanging, feeling against the wall until his hand moved over the light switch.

Marcel looked up as the chandeliers dimmed the smallest fraction. Barely enough to be noticeable, but just enough to hide.

Asif tipped his head to the alcove and led Marcel in that direction. He'd just ducked inside the alcove and started to turn around when the sound of raucous male laughter started to fill the hallway.

On the other side of the rotunda, the door to Raphael's office was slowly opening.

Marcel's eyes widened, but Asif was already reacting. He reached out to grab the man's shoulder and pull him forward. Their mouths touched and Asif cupped the back of the other man's head, feigning an intimacy, but his eyes were trained on that door.

Asif watched with a hungry clarity as the door opened and Raphael stopped to speak to someone in the room, his back to the rotunda. He was speaking quickly in French, nodding his head. Asif couldn't catch every word, so he focused on the other voice and felt very sure that it was Joseph Herman.

"Is it them?" Marcel asked, his breath mercifully minty and slightly cool.

"Yeah."

Raphael laughed, nodded, and finally turned from the room. Asif lowered his eyelids and started to move as if he and Marcel were making out. Thankfully, the other man didn't need to be told to keep up. His hands moved to Asif's back and they shifted.

Raphael smiled, watching them for a few seconds before reaching down to adjust himself in his pants and turning to Asif's left, to the only other door Asif cared about. He pulled a key from his breast pocket and turned it. Raphael was amazingly reckless. He left the key in the lock and the door open while he moved inside. Asif kept up the ruse with Marcel but used their proximity to give him the fastest, quietest brief he could.

"There's a computer up here. I need to copy the hard drive."

"Do you need me to pick a lock?"

"No, I need cover. He's in there now. Once it's clear, I'll slip in and get to work."

"If he comes out?"

"There's only going to be one way in, one way out."

Marcel grunted.

"There's a gun in the potted plant behind me. If you have to, take the shot."

Marcel nodded.

And that was that. Considering that this team was forced on him, he appreciated working with someone who didn't need to have his hand held. Asif pulled Marcel's body against his as Raphael came from the small room. He glanced toward the alcove, locked the door, and walked quickly back to his office. Glancing in their direction once again, Raphael squeezed his dick one more time and pushed the door open. Asif saw Herman's profile, confirming his identity. Raphael walked inside and pushed the door closed behind him. Before it clicked shut, Asif spotted a hand that belonged to an unknown person.

"Fuck," he breathed.

"What?"

"There's someone else in the room, but I don't know who it is." He pushed away from Marcel.

The other man stumbled back a couple of steps. "What do you want to do?"

Asif considered the closed door, his brain running through this unexpected problem. Finally, he made the best decision he could under the circumstances. "Stick to the plan. Take the shot."

Marcel nodded and stepped aside so Asif could get to work.

THE THING ABOUT RICH PEOPLE AND THEIR SECURITY was that it was never as good as it seemed. So many of them wasted money on a small team of guards, but Asif thought if someone needed that level of protection, more times than not, they also needed a one-way ticket to The Hague. If they were less annoying and actually rich, they probably spent a small fortune on a state-of-the-art home security system, which was better but not great because how effective can the tired person watching your security cameras be when you have the dumb ass nerve to email yourself all the passwords and codes to your doors? Hypothetically speaking. So in some respects, Raphael's retro use of an old pin tumbler lock was more secure than most setups — it was just that Asif could pick damn near any lock in his sleep. The few seconds it took until the last tumbler turned felt like a year, but Asif didn't rush it.

Once the lock opened, Asif pressed down on the handle carefully and pulled the door open slowly. He wanted to leave it open to make leaving easier, but there was nothing worse than getting caught because a door that should have been shut tight wasn't. Although getting caught coming out of a room was a close second, but that was a worry for five minutes from now. He glanced in Marcel's direction, nodded, and then plunged inside the glorified closet, pulling the door silently closed behind him.

The room was unremarkable. There was a safe set into the wall on his right. Asif was desperate to crack it, and if he hadn't been in such a tight spot, he might have. But tonight, the only thing he needed was sitting on a plain desk pushed against the far wall.

He moved to the computer and nudged the mouse with his knuckle, turning the screen on. He pulled the chain over his head. He had to search the computer tower for the right port — staying focused to make sure he didn't freak out if he couldn't find the right one — and then pushed the USB drive into place.

For a quick second, nothing happened, and Asif worried he'd underestimated the difficulty of this plan. But then, the computer screen glitched in a familiar way, and Asif watched as whatever code Chanté had put on this drive went to work. After a few seconds, a progress bar appeared on the screen. Asif's heart froze at the estimated time of five hours.

He fought the urge to scream at the top of his lungs, managing to get to work on a Plan B. He wondered if he could pry the hard drive out with his bare hands. It wasn't the best plan, and to be honest, it would make him feel like he'd wasted the last two weeks of his life, but if it got the job done, it got the job done.

Thankfully, the progress bar started to move, and five hours became three and then two in a matter of minutes. He exhaled in relief. Soon enough, there were only ten minutes left. He pressed himself against the wall next to the door, slowed his breathing, closed his eyes, and listened to the atrium on the other side of the door.

Asif should have spent the next five minutes planning his exit, but he didn't. Instead, he lied to himself. In his brain, he got Chanté out of this house and preferably the country in the next few hours. He imagined taking her to Italy and hiding away on the top floor of a sinking hotel in Venice, fucking her while the sea ate away at the inlet city. He'd spent the last two weeks in the field and he would be forced to take a mandatory holiday anyway, so why not take it with Chanté?

If she'd let him.

A soft ding pulled him out of his fantasy and he let it go, just like he always did with his dreams of Chanté. There was nowhere he could take her in the world where he wouldn't worry about putting her in danger. So, he'd get her out of here and say goodbye. She should be used to that by now.

Leaving was surprisingly easy. He pulled the USB stick out of the computer and quickly put it back to sleep. He made sure to attach it to his necklace and tuck it back into his shirt before he went back to the door. He gave a last longing look at the safe, took a deep breath, and pushed the door open with a flourish before stumbling out of the room.

Chanté

+

Asif

TWENTY

MARCEL WAS STILL CONSIDERED wet behind the ears in French intelligence.

No matter that he was one of the youngest recruits into the agency, or that in his first year, he'd been an integral part of a mission that had stopped a bioterror attack on a major holiday weekend. Never mind that he'd far outpaced his peers to the point that, as far as he was concerned, he had no peers. He wouldn't say that aloud, but he knew it was true all the same.

So far, the only significant mar on his career was Asif and that mission in Dubai.

Since then, he'd been waiting to cross paths with Asif and The Agency again, but playing lookout from the shadows while Asif did the hard work of copying a computer that could close his case was not what he'd been expecting. Still, he couldn't imagine how else this mission could have gone or what he could have done differently.

And then there was Sonja, but Marcel was trying desperately not to think about her.

Asif had only just disappeared behind the door, but every second felt like an hour. Unfortunately, waiting was the worst part of the job, and Marcel still struggled with it.

He stood just back from the alcove opening, enough in shadow that someone would have to squint to see him. Asif's gun was heavy in Marcel's right hand. Even though he wanted to lean against the wall out of sheer boredom, he knew that would be a mistake.

"Shhh, my darling, be quiet."

Marcel's brain snapped to attention at those whispered words. He took half a step back, hoping the shadows would consume him whole while his eyes moved wildly around the rotunda, looking and listening for whoever was coming.

Nothing moved for long seconds until finally, two people appeared at the mouth of the long hallway across the room. Marcel's eyes moved to the computer room door and then back. He thought he was seeing a short, round man and a tall, slender woman, the former hanging off the latter. With the dimmed lights, Marcel couldn't be sure of much, but he watched them intently, making sure at least some of his attention was on the other doors around the rotunda.

The tall figure pressed the short figure against a wall. They didn't move for a few moments while Marcel readjusted his grip on his firearm and his eyes bounced around the room. The seconds ticked by even more slowly than before somehow. Marcel could barely hear the sounds of the orgy picking up down below, but the silence up here was almost deafening.

Until a loud moan filled the space.

This had never happened to him before, but from what he'd heard about The Agency, their representatives had a knack for getting themselves into situations like this. Situations like the tall figure spitting into their hand and then the loud, wet slapping of skin on skin.

Marcel shifted his gaze away to give them some privacy, but no matter where he let his eyes settle, all he could hear was the sound of a man being jerked off while his moans echoed around the rotunda. He was finding it hard to concentrate, or to ignore his body's response to what he was hearing.

He prayed silently for Asif or the short, round man to finish quickly. He didn't care which one, he just wanted to get the fuck out of this alcove.

"Schneller," the man groaned loudly, pulling Marcel's gaze back to them. It was very obvious now what the tall person was doing, and he looked quickly away.

Marcel's heart was pounding against his chest. He was starting to sweat. He wondered how the hell he was supposed to write this up in his post-mission report.

And then three things happened all at once.

First, and most excruciatingly, the man came in one long guttural moan.

Next, the door to the computer room burst open and Asif ran out into the rotunda, zipping up his pants as if he'd been in the bathroom and maybe not alone. The couple against the wall jumped and turned toward Asif.

"Oh, what's going on here?" Asif laughed.

The man against the wall started blustering in German, but the tall one's attention was focused on Asif. Marcel watched as they wiped their hand on the German's coat and started to turn their body fully in Asif's direction. They looked deadly in a way that made very little sense under the circumstances but presented Marcel with two options and not enough seconds to weigh them. First, he could aim his gun and clip them in the shoulder. Easy, but loud.

He went with the second option as soon as it entered his mind.

"Didn't mean to interrupt," Asif said, putting both hands in the air.

Marcel shoved the gun in the back of his pants under his coat, unzipped his pants, and plunged out of the alcove's shadows, stumbling as if he was drunk.

"There you are," he slurred, reaching down to tuck his shirttails back into his pants. "That is not the toilet, and there might be a dead plant in there."

As he moved toward the head of the stairs, his gaze was focused primarily on Asif, but his peripheral vision was entirely on the German and the tall figure hovering over him. From the corner of his eye, he saw their demeanor change. In seconds, their back bowed the tiniest bit as they turned back to the German man, wrapping their lean body around his side.

"Don't go in there for a few minutes." Asif laughed at him.

They made eye contact and began to chatter at one another across the rotunda. Marcel hardly knew what he was saying because none of it mattered. The only thing that mattered was getting the fuck out of here with Sonja and Chanté in tow and intact.

They were rounding toward the top of the stairs when the couple moved back toward the hallway. The tall figure pushed the German down the hall as Marcel and Asif finally met at the stairs.

Marcel turned toward the hallway just in time to see the German disappearing through a door while the tall figure glanced in their direction, their dark face as impossible to read as stone.

"Did you get it?" Marcel asked as the door closed and he turned his attention back to Asif.

"Of course, I did. Let's go."

They turned together toward the mouth of the stairs but only made it two steps down.

The office door opened as Raphael came laughing into the hallway.

"Yusuf!" he called. "I thought I heard your voice. Join us!"

"Fuck," Asif said, the word echoing around the rotunda.

"We're going to fuck," Asif continued before Raphael could fully process his outburst.

"That can wait," Raphael said breezily. "Come."

They were so close. In fifteen minutes, he could be out of here with the least amount of hassle possible, but not with Raphael looking at him.

The other man's eyes narrowed and his smile tightened. "Come," he said again, with far less ease than before.

"Can I come?" Marcel asked in a voice that managed to sound drunk and sexually suggestive. The voice was so good Asif turned toward him with a smile. He didn't know if Marcel could see the appreciation on his face or if he cared, but if he did, he didn't let it deter him. Marcel shrugged. "I'm not going to let you get away that easy," he said in a surprisingly good American accent.

Asif's mouth fell open.

"Yes, come," Raphael called cheerily. "Before you come." He laughed at his own joke.

Back on the landing, Raphael beckoned them forward excitedly. Asif prayed he didn't get stabbed; he didn't have time to recover from a knife wound.

"You have a remarkable knack for finding the loveliest people wherever I take you," Raphael said, clapping Asif on the back. "I will remember that."

Asif tensed as he walked into the room, preparing himself for the unknown. "Joseph, hello," he said brightly, offering his hand to the other man.

Even though Asif had just seen the man twenty-four hours ago, Joseph looked at him with a bored ignorance before offering a limp hand. Asif could let many things fall off his back, but a lackluster handshake irritated him to no end, so he let the man's hand go and shifted his attention away.

He locked eyes with a tall, thin white woman with an icy blonde pixie cut framing her angular face.

Asif hadn't seen Mia Malkova in the flesh in a decade. Once upon a time, Asif had made the periodic return to Cleveland part of his annual schedule. It had been his job to return to the town where he'd met Chanté and stop by Malkova's former haunts, trying to drum up any news of her whereabouts. He'd handed off that task to another agent as soon as Chanté moved away, but here she was, standing in front of him.

His brain and pulse started running a hundred miles a minute.

"Ah, Yusuf, let me introduce you to another of my business associates. Mia Malkova, this is Yusuf Mahmoud."

"Yusuf, I have the unfortunate task of telling you that I cannot move forward with our deal."

Asif tore his eyes from Mia's face, glaring at Raphael.

"But," the man said in a squirrely whine, "I believe Mia can."

"I don't know Mia." Asif ground out this lie, focusing on the danger in this room rather than disbelief that he'd finally found the woman who'd brought Chanté into his life.

"And I do not know you," Mia said. "But Raphael tells me that we have one thing in common."

"Oh?"

"Money," she said.

Asif huffed out a laugh. "A wonderful foundation for a new acquaintance."

Mia reached into her jacket pocket and pulled out a card, extending her arm but not stepping forward. Asif let her win this subtle power play and took the two steps forward to pluck the card from her hand.

He looked down to find Russian embossed neatly on the thick cardstock. "I'm sorry, I don't read Cyrillic script."

"My address is on the back. When you're ready to do business, you can find me there," she said. "Now, if you'll excuse me." She walked from the room in a slow gait.

"If you will excuse us," Raphael said.

"Sorry?" Asif asked as a man and woman appeared in the doorway, naked as the day they were born. The woman moved into the room, around Marcel, and pressed herself against Joseph's front, while the man started to undress Raphael.

"Yes. Please, excuse us."

Marcel rushed from the room back into the hallway.

They were still within earshot when a loud groan sounded through the upper floor.

Chanté

+

Asif

TWENTY-ONE
EIGHT YEARS AGO...

CHANTÉ HAD PLANNED to dress up for Asif, but he'd pissed her off so bad she didn't even want to. There was a hamper of clean clothes she'd been meaning to put away tucked into a corner. Reaching inside, she threw on the first t-shirt and shorts she saw, not even bothering to put on a bra or do her hair. She caught a glimpse of herself in the standing mirror by the window and smiled because she was still cute. She was always cute, she just didn't look like the version of herself she'd wanted Asif to see. She didn't look like the version of herself on stage or even the waitress he'd met all those years ago; she looked pretty and regular in her wrinkled, oversized black t-shirt and running shorts — even though Chanté didn't believe in running. She seriously considered throwing on a light wash of makeup — maybe some mascara and a little tinted lip gloss — but he didn't deserve it, she decided, and pulled open her bedroom door.

"Oh, fuck!" she screamed because Asif's tall body was filling her doorway.

She backed away — Kenny would kill her — heart

pounding against her chest. She opened her mouth, panting, eyes wild. "What the fuck are you doing?"

"Waiting. For you."

"In the living room. You should wait in the living room."

"You sure?" he asked and had the nerve to grin.

"Don't smile at me," she said, crossing her arms and leaning on her right hip.

"Oh, sorry," he said and leaned against the doorjamb. He crossed his arms to mirror her stance, a smug grin on his face.

"I can kick you out of here," she said, not entirely sure how she'd do it but knowing she would.

"You can," he said breezily, "but do you want to?"

"I want you to stop getting on my nerves."

He laughed, and Chanté pretended not to feel her pussy tingle. That was none of her business and none of Asif's, either. He reached into his pocket and pulled out a slip of paper.

"Do you know what this is?"

She rolled her eyes. "I barely know you. Of course, I don't."

He tried not to laugh and offered it to her. She stared at his hand, he stared back at her, and they entered a stalemate.

Chanté was stubborn and settled in for the long haul.

"How much time do we have before your roommate gets back?" he asked.

She held out for a few more seconds before caving and stomping toward him to snatch the paper from his fingers.

"Careful," he sang.

"Oh. Shit," she said, staring at all the zeroes on the check.

"That's all yours," he said, but then snatched it back. "After you get me the information I need."

"Bitch," she hissed back.

"No need for name calling," he teased. "I want to give you this check. But I need you to give me something in return."

Chanté had had more than a few wet dreams about Asif over the years, but the stark difference between this very real moment and her dreams was that his cute little speech would have ended with 'I need you,' and minutes later, he'd have her face down and ass up on her queen-sized bed. Also, the check he gave her would have maybe had one more zero.

Also, his hair would have been down by now.

"Fine," she said, rolling her eyes and turning toward her desk.

When Chanté moved to Cleveland from Detroit, she had sixty-four dollars in her wallet and three hundred dollars in her checking account from the state of Michigan. In the last six years, Chanté had turned that three hundred and sixty-four dollars into cushy accounts to make sure she'd never be a ward of the state again. She liked pretty things, shiny things, and skimpy things, but she didn't open her wallet to spend money without serious consideration unless she was buying computer equipment.

She and Kenny had gotten new desks when an office store went out of business, and a friend who worked in the university's campus works department gave her the desk chair for thirty dollars and a lap dance, but everything on top of the desk was state-of-the-art and modded out by Chanté herself.

She pulled her chair out and plopped into her seat.

"Mia Malkova," she whispered to herself.

"Malkov," Asif corrected.

"What?" she asked, glaring at him over her shoulder.

"Malkov was the family name, but they started using a

feminized version to confuse some of their international contacts, especially the ones they were ripping off and Mia ran with it."

"Feminized it," Chanté said, nodding in approval.

"So, if you're looking for her in official documents, Malkov is another option."

"Huh. And how do you know this?" she asked. "Which agency do you work for?"

His smile was big and bright in that moment. He walked into the room and leaned against her dresser. "When did you realize I wasn't who I seemed?"

She glared up at him while she thought. "Nothing about you made sense," she said. "Not from the beginning. You were way too smooth for a place like that."

"The Petal was charming," he said. "Not the kind of place a man can forget easily." His eyes wandered as he spoke, settling appropriately on her mouth.

"I know that, but a man that looks like you isn't supposed to know that. You were supposed to be..." She motioned with her hands as if she was bouncing a few words back and forth between her palms, jostling her breasts side-to-side. "You were supposed to be an asshole and a bad tipper."

"I'd never."

"And you weren't supposed to walk me to my bus stop," she said quietly.

"That was my favorite part," he whispered before lifting his eyes to hers and plastering a bigger, faker smile on his face. "Is that when you knew?"

She shook her head. "I think I knew when you came back," she said, her skin warming at the memory of Asif on his knees, one of her legs thrown over his shoulder, his tongue lapping at her soft folds. She shivered quietly in her chair.

"Why then?"

She licked her lips and his gaze focused there, so she did it again. "If you'd walked in that club, seen me, and ignored me to chase after a new dancer, I would have assumed you used me two years ago and got what you wanted. No big deal. Happens every day. But you came back like leaving was out of your control. You ate me out like that taste would have to last you a while. Maybe even the rest of your life."

Now his smile was sad. "What agency do you think I work for?"

She shrugged and turned to her computer, booting it on while she spoke. "Definitely not local pigs," she said, making Asif laugh. "The only thing they're good for is corruption and laziness. I thought maybe something federal," she said, "but ain't no way they'd let you seduce an innocent college student." She laughed to herself as she pulled up her dark browser and got to work.

"Maybe they don't know," Asif whispered.

Her fingers were flying over her laptop one second and frozen the next.

She turned to him with a fake smile on her face now. She dropped her voice to something husky and oozing. Something mocking. "Am I your dirty little secret, Asif?"

His tongue peeked out of the left corner of his mouth. "I have a lot of secrets, Chanté. Most of them aren't even my own. Any man would be lucky to be able to brag about you."

It had been two years, but those words and the stabbing pain in her chest were just as devastating as when they met. She didn't know how he did it, or why, but Asif had this unique ability to make her feel as if she was flying up into the atmosphere and then freefalling with only his words. And most importantly, she couldn't figure out why he would.

She turned back to her computer. "I have a program that'll run her name through most of the state databases. I can jump from there to regional or federal, it's up to you. Although I imagine you could do that on your own," she said, turning to see how he reacted.

"Let's stick to local and state for now," he said.

"Mmmhmm, thought so." She turned back to her screen.

"You haven't heard anything about her?" Asif asked, inching closer.

"I haven't even thought about her since before you left. She wasn't important to me. She was important to Saraiya, though."

"The woman who owned The Petal?" Asif asked. Chanté nodded. "The one who's in Chicago now?"

"That's her."

"Do you have her number?" Asif asked, sounding impatient.

"Of course, I do, and no, I won't be giving it to you."

"Chanté," Asif said.

"No, and there's no amount of money you can offer me to change my mind. I don't give my friends' numbers to strange men."

"Am I really—"

She sucked her teeth and rolled her eyes, refusing to let him finish.

"Fine, can you call her for me?"

She thought about that for a few seconds, weighing her options against her ethical code. "Alright," she said, reaching for her phone. She turned the chair so Asif couldn't get even a glimpse of the screen while she called. Once Saraiya's line started ringing, she put it on speaker.

Asif was surprisingly unmasked, looking at the phone with hungry anticipation. But as the phone rang and rang, his face fell.

From experience, Chanté knew Saraiya didn't have a voicemail box set up on her line, but she let the phone ring long enough for him to get the hint.

"Sorry," she said.

"It's fine. Is there anyone else who might know anything about Saraiya or Mia?"

She started to shake her head, but then a face and titties appeared in her head. "Maybe Joi?"

"Who's Joi?" he asked.

She frowned up at him, offended on her friend's behalf. "Do you remember that private dance with—"

"Oh, Joi," he said.

"Yeah." She licked her lips, remembering Joi's thighs spread around Asif's hips.

"Can you call her?" he asked.

"I can," she sighed. "Or we can go see her."

She didn't know why she said it except that she knew Joi usually kept her phone on silent on her days off. Also, years ago, Joi had sat on Asif's lap with hard nipples and body glitter smearing on his suit, and that memory had gotten Chanté off hundreds of times while he'd been away.

Chanté had never forgotten her offer, and by the way Asif was looking at her, she guessed he hadn't either.

Chanté

+

Asif

"WHO IS IT?" Joi sighed into the intercom, irritation dripping from each syllable.

Chanté pressed the button to speak. "Chanté. I need a favor." She let go of the button and smiled at Asif. He was leaning against the building and watching her like a hawk.

"You in the wrong place for favors, Chanté."

"You say that, but I know you love me," she chirped back, beaming up at Asif.

In true Joi fashion, she pressed the intercom button so Chanté could hear her aggrieved sigh. "Is this life or death?"

"Nope."

"Girl," Joi whined.

Chanté pressed down on the button. "You remember that guy from The Petal I was obsessed with?"

"A man?" Joi cried incredulously. "Absolutely not. I know more than a few dancers you were obsessed with, though."

Chanté started to press the button again, but Asif

covered her hand. "Which dancers?" he asked while grinning sexily at her.

She rolled her eyes and shucked his hand off. "Duh," Chanté said to Joi and Asif. "I love pussy, but that's why you should remember him. He was coming around before I started dancing and you gave us that couple show."

"Oh, him!" Joi said. "Oh, he was fine and sprung as fuck off you."

Chanté blushed and looked away. "No, he wasn't."

He moved closer. "Yes, I was."

"Shit," Joi said, although only half the word made it through the speaker before the front door to her building buzzed to let them in.

"Seriously?" she sighed as Asif rushed around her to pull the door open.

"So, I was the only man, huh?"

"At The Petal," she corrected. "I've had lots of men since you left."

He bent forward to whisper into her ear. "I want to hear about them too." Chanté's body froze, but Asif pushed her forward with a gentle hand in the middle of her back. She led him to the stairwell and up to the second floor.

Chanté had been to Joi's apartment only twice before this. Joi was one of the few dancers Chanté knew who had nearly impenetrable boundaries between work, life, and play. There was never gossip about Joi fucking with other dancers or customers. She didn't stop by the club on her day off. And she didn't party with her coworkers. Even though she liked Chanté and had never failed to help and guide her, Joi didn't let anyone at the club get comfortable in her life outside of work. It meant a lot for her to entrust Chanté with her real address, and she hoped bringing Asif here wouldn't fuck that up.

Chanté knocked on Joi's front door as Asif moved behind her, putting himself in full view of Joi's peephole. She heard footsteps on the other side of the door as they waited. When Joi pulled the door open, there was a bright smile on her face and a matching one on Chanté's lips.

Joi was wearing a skimpy pair of red silk boxers and a matching lace camisole. But the real change in her appearance was that instead of the long blue wig she was wearing at the club, her thick, curly hair was plaited into two cornrows down either side of her head, hanging just over the front of her shoulders. She couldn't explain it, but thinking about twirling her fingers around that braid made Chanté's mouth water.

"Well, well, well, if it ain't Mr. Sad and Freaky," she said, looking at Asif.

He moved forward, his chest bumping into Chanté's back. He put both hands on her waist. "Not too sad right now," he said as a greeting.

"This the dude you took to the private suite yesterday?" she asked Chanté.

"How'd you hear about that?"

Joi smirked. "I asked Steel to look after you."

"Look after or keep tabs on?" Chanté asked, crossing her arms over her chest.

"Whatever you wanna call it. And I'll take that as a yes. So, you're back in town and came to find your girl?"

Chanté's shoulders tightened at that question. Every word felt like it was full of landmines, and she was terrified at how Asif might respond.

He squeezed her waist. "First thing," he said.

It wasn't true, but it made Chanté's skin tingle.

"And now you two are here on my doorstep," she said. No question. Hard nipples.

"Like I said, we have a favor to ask."

Joi licked her lips. "That right?"

"No— not that," Chanté said. "We just had a question about someone we worked with at The Petal."

Her grin fell into a frown. "Only person I talk to from there is you."

Chanté tried not to smile, but Asif's hands moved to cover her lower belly and he pulled her back into him.

Joi huffed out a soft breath and she was grinning again. She stepped back and opened her door for them. "Y'all get in here. My neighbors are nosy as fuck."

The two times Chanté had visited Joi, she'd never made it over the threshold, only dropping by to pick up a bag of shoes Joi wanted to give her and to get a donation for a fellow dancer out on maternity leave. They kicked off their shoes at the threshold and Chanté followed Joi into her apartment with wide eyes. "Joi, oh my god."

"This is beautiful," Asif echoed.

There were plants everywhere — crowded on floating shelves along the walls, draped over the tv stand, vines hanging over the screen, low pots in corners, all over the place. Everywhere Chanté looked, there was a different shade of green. It had to be at least ten degrees warmer once they were fully inside her apartment.

"Alright, what y'all want to know?" Joi asked, walking into the living room and sitting on her couch. Reaching for an ashtray on the table, she lifted a neatly rolled joint to her lips and inhaled. Chanté licked her lips as Asif moved to stand next to her.

"I asked Chanté about Mia Malkova," Asif said, taking the lead now that there were a few walls between them and Joi's neighbors.

"Who?" Joi asked, letting out a thick white puff of smoke on that word.

Chanté moved her hand to her stomach as it grumbled in lust. "The white girl who was supposed to help Saraiya get the club in shape."

When she remembered, Joi's face shifted into a sneer, and she sucked her teeth. "Oh, her predator ass."

Chanté's eyebrows shot up. "Predator?"

"As far as I'm concerned, yeah. She only got with Saraiya because she knew she needed the money. She fed that girl all kinda pipe dreams about building a future together when it was clear as day she only wanted to be there to fuck dancers."

Chanté's mouth fell open. "What? Wait, did you...?"

"Fuck no," Joi said.

Asif nodded. "Don't want to mix money and sex."

Joi screwed her face up. "I get butt naked four days a week. Mixing money and sex is how I afford all the fertilizer I need." Her eyes moved back to Chanté. "I don't fuck mean people, rude people, racists, bigots, people who don't tip well, men who don't wash their ass, women who don't clean their nails, and comics of any gender."

"Uh," Asif said.

Chanté nodded vigorously. "Good list. All I remember about Mia is that she up and disappeared one day, but I didn't pay too much attention to her."

Joi shrugged. "That's basically what happened. Saraiya was crushed, but that was probably a good thing 'cause she was too sad to notice when Kay bounced up out of there."

"Kay?" Asif asked.

"Another dancer. Terrible, if you ask me, but those broke men loved her."

"But she didn't leave until a few months later," Chanté said, trying to remember something about that time in her life her own sadness at Asif's disappearance had eclipsed. "Why is her leaving connected to Mia?"

Joi pursed her lips at Chanté. The look of disappointment was palpable.

"Oh shit!" Chanté cried out. "Kay was fucking Mia behind Saraiya's back."

Joi nodded in slow motion. "Among others, but apparently, she was the favorite side piece."

"Are you sure?" Asif asked.

"Wouldn't say it if I wasn't." She smiled.

"But how do you know she left 'cause of Mia?" Chanté asked.

"I got a homegirl who used to work at this bar Mia's family owned on the other side of town. She was the one who told me Kay used to slink her ass over there when she wasn't working. She overheard them talking about moving to San Diego or some shit."

"Damn," Chanté sighed.

"You sure about that?" Asif asked, and then corrected himself. "About the San Diego part, I mean."

"Oh, I mean, I guess. I know it was somewhere in California for sure."

"Okay. Thank you. I need to make a quick phone call. I'll be right back." He aimed the last at Chanté.

She nodded at him, and they watched as he rushed to the entryway and out the door.

"You brought a cop to my apartment, Chanté?"

"Not a cop, maybe a fed," she said in her defense. "But he's cool."

She laughed. "That's your pussy talking, but I get it. You wanna hit?" She offered Chanté the joint.

"Ooh, thanks." Chanté walked across the room and sat on the couch next to Joi.

She grasped the joint just under the bit of paper damp from Joi's mouth. She had an essay to write tonight and didn't want to be too tired to bullshit for three to four double-spaced pages, but she decided she could get a little high.

She and Joi were sitting side by side, bare arms and legs touching. It wasn't the first time it had happened. In fact, a year ago, Chanté and Joi had been grinding on each other in just string bikinis for a bachelorette party. That one night paid for a full semester of Chanté's half of the rent. But when Joi wound a finger around one of Chanté's delicate curls, this moment felt different — more intimate — than the full three hours of that party.

"You fucked him yet?" Joi asked.

She shook her head, pulling the smoke into her mouth.

Joi reached out and gently grasped Chanté's chin, turning her head so the two were face-to-face. "You could have called me for that shit on Mia."

Chanté nodded, holding the smoke in her lungs.

"So why'd you bring him all the way over here, Chanté?"

She'd always loved the way Joi said her name. The way she could challenge her with her warm eyes and lopsided grin.

Chanté's eyes went wide. Joi licked her lips and dipped her head.

Chanté watched her face come closer, and when their lips touched, she opened her mouth. Their lips sealed together, and Joi sucked the smoke from Chanté's mouth before moving her tongue to lick along the seam of her lips.

"Just send me a report. I'll look at it tonight. Or tomorrow," Asif said, glancing toward Joi's door.

He listened to the junior agent ramble on the other end of the line, going over the names, approximate dates, and locations Asif gave him. This should have been a quick phone call, but the baby spies always needed so much hand-holding. This was exactly why Asif did everything he could to shirk training them. Let Monica and Lane do that since they loved putting his life in danger so much.

But sometimes, he had to do something so basic like call in a report and interact with them, and it was torture. Someone like Monica would say that was a prime reason to become over-involved in their training. Asif disagreed. He closed his eyes and leaned his head back on the wall next to Joi's front door and listened to the other voice tremble while repeating everything Asif just said, nearly verbatim.

"Great," he said when they were finally done. "Now, get to work." He hung up before they could speak again, shaking his head in frustration.

He didn't know if what Chanté and Joi had told him would amount to anything, but he did know chances were high that his time in Cleveland was limited. His time with Chanté was once again coming to an end. He sighed and pushed the front door open, already trying to figure out how to say goodbye.

Wondering if there was a collection of words he could string together that would get her to forget about him this time.

His brain went completely blank, however, as soon as he stepped back into Joi's living room and found them making out. His time with Chanté was coming to an end, but it wasn't over yet.

He watched them for a few moments with a smile on his face. He'd had some of the most vivid dreams of his life thinking about those two together. But just like that night, Asif found it nearly impossible to look away from Chanté. Her fingernails grazing Joi's skin, her tongue sliding against Joi's, and her cute thick thighs spreading as she contorted her body to lean into the kiss.

Asif didn't get jealous normally, but watching her kiss Joi made him sad only because he hadn't gotten the chance to kiss her yet.

He cleared his throat. They didn't stop. He gave it another try. This time, Joi's eyes opened. She looked up at him through her eyelashes. He couldn't see it, but Asif could feel Joi's smile, and it made his pulse race.

He cleared his throat again.

Chanté pulled away from Joi's mouth with a sigh. She turned to him, wiping at her chin with a frown. "Asif, why are you just standing there? Most men dream about a moment like this?"

He didn't like that and frowned at her. "If I just wanted to get my rocks off to two women fucking, I could have done that anywhere else in the world."

"And you probably have," she said.

"A time or two," he replied with a smile. He didn't want to lie to her — at least not any more than necessary.

She pursed her lips shut while Joi tucked Chanté's hair behind one ear.

Asif wanted to walk to her, but he was torn about making promises with his mouth they both knew he couldn't keep with his actions. But he wanted to make promises.

"I came back for you," he said, which wasn't a lie. He could say no to any mission, especially one that would put him back in the middle of an old cover. But when they put Mia Malkova's file in front of him, he'd never even thought to say no. Because of Chanté. "You know I can't stay, though," he said, as gently as possible.

"I didn't ask you to stay," she said.

That was true, but even Asif knew it was only by technicality. The last time he'd been here, he'd left before Chanté could ask him for anything of consequence, like his heart.

He gave it to her anyway.

Asif walked across Joi's living room and wrapped his hands around the sides of Chanté's neck. He could feel her pulse racing against his palms. Her body seemed to soften in his hold, as if she'd been craving his touch and felt secure here. It made his dick hard.

He brushed his thumbs under her jaw. "Ask me for something," Asif whispered, even though he knew it was dangerous to even open this door.

Her eyes fluttered open and she licked her lips. "Give me something to remember you by when you're gone."

He bent forwarded and licked across her bottom lip. "I can do that," he whispered into her mouth.

"We all can," Joi said. "In the bedroom, though. I don't want to corrupt my plants."

Chanté

+

Asif

TWENTY-THREE

EIGHT YEARS AGO...

EVERY TIME MONICA was assigned to debrief him after a mission, she always asked if there was anything he wished he could have done better. His blustery first answer was always that he had no regrets, but when she asked about Cleveland, he had many. He'd wondered if he should have picked up Mia when he had the chance. He'd second-guessed his decision not to put her under surveillance. He'd quadruple-guessed his decision to use Chanté as an entrée into the club. But his biggest regret was about something he couldn't record in his personnel file.

Every day since the night he left Cleveland the first time, he regretted not fucking Chanté when he had the chance.

Joi led them down a short hallway to her bedroom. She had Chanté's right hand in her left, while Asif held Chanté's left. Just before Joi pushed the door open, Chanté turned and looked over her left shoulder at him and licked her lips. He smiled at her, trying to seem calmer than he felt, because what Asif felt was a tidal wave of lust. Everywhere he looked — her bouncy curls, her soft arms, her long eyelashes — made him feel like something molten was slowly racing through his veins, burning him up from the inside out.

Joi's room was small and sparsely decorated. He could imagine this space as a sanctuary for her — a place to relax and rest and fuck, and as much space to do it as possible.

There were blackout curtains covering the window to their right and a vase with a single rose on her bedside table. Her bed was covered in pillows and a soft, emerald velvet throw. Besides his bedroom in his parents' house, Asif didn't actually have a home of his own — he spent too much time in the field. If he had an apartment, he thought he might decorate it like this. He started to think something he shouldn't and shut it down internally at the same time as Chanté squeezed his hand.

Joi welcomed them inside her room with a bright smile as she let go of Chanté's hand and turned to face them. "Where do we start?"

Chanté jumped onto the balls of her feet excitedly and even threw her hand in the air. "I know," she squealed, and Joi smiled down at her. She was bouncing up and down, her breasts jiggling invitingly, as she looked between Asif and Joi like a puppet master.

Asif tugged at her hand and pulled her back into him. He wrapped their joined arms around her stomach, but Joi's eyes were focused on Asif's other hand as it circled Chanté's neck.

Her mouth opened on a soft sigh that shifted into a smile.

Chanté was predictably responsive to Asif's touch, and it made him smile against her temple. She pressed her ass against the bulge in his pants and mewled lightly from deep in her chest.

"I only have one request," Asif said, whispering against her hairline.

She tilted her head back and looked up at him, squirming against his body. "Tell me," she said in a greedy moan.

"Anything you want me to do with her, I get to do with you first."

She giggled excitedly. "Deal," she cried out and stuck her tongue out at him.

He swooped down and sucked her tongue into his mouth. She tasted like happiness and his wildest dreams.

Asif tried to devour her, licking deep, pressing and retreating and coming back for more. She laughed and moaned into his mouth while they pressed against one another below the waist.

When Joi spoke, it was as if she'd plucked the words from his brain. "I want this but naked," she sighed.

The next moan Chanté breathed into Asif's mouth could have doubled as a laugh. He wanted every moan of hers to taste just like that.

Joi's forehead brushed against his as she kissed the tip of Chanté's chin, making her groan loudly.

Asif opened his eyes to watch Joi kiss her way down Chanté's neck. She leaned back and cupped her breasts in both hands. Even through her t-shirt, her nipples were hard points. Asif's hips jumped forward and Chanté laughed — or at least tried to. With his and Joi's hands on her, Chanté was quietly falling apart between them.

He pulled back and lifted his eyes to Joi, who was toying with Chanté's nipples through her shirt, grinning excitedly at which touches made her jump.

Asif hated to interrupt her fun but... "I bet she's wet."

With her lips momentarily free, Chanté groaned so

loudly it made the hair on his arms stand up. Asif nodded once, and Joi reluctantly let go of Chanté's left breast, pressed her palm against Chanté's stomach, and let it move down. He watched with bated breath. Even when Joi's hand disappeared from view, Asif stared at the spot where he'd last seen it, excited and desperate for what he knew was coming.

Chanté extended her tongue until just the tip grazed the bottom of his beard. Needy was beautiful on her.

"She's warm," Joi sighed.

Chanté sucked in a sharp breath and spread her legs.

"Put your hand in her shorts." Asif wanted this to sound like a command, but he was also too excited to keep the edge of desperation from his voice.

"Are you giving orders?" Joi asked.

Asif didn't know what Joi was doing with her fingers, but based on Chanté's light panting, she loved it.

"I believe in democracy," Asif said. "And I'm a switch. I don't give a fuck who says what, so long as we're all covered in come at the end."

Chanté lifted onto the balls of her feet and cried out into Asif's beard.

"I can see why she likes you," Joi said.

"I've already seen why she likes you, but I'm ready to see it again."

Joi moved back so Asif could watch her hand slip inside Chanté's running shorts.

"Oh god," she cried out, and Asif couldn't blame her. Nor could he stop himself from grinding his dick against her ass.

"She flooded her panties," Joi said. "She's hot and slick and—"

"Yeah," Chanté moaned.

"Tight," Joi finished. "I can't wait to watch her stretch open for your dick."

Asif grunted and moved his head to kiss Chanté again, licking her moans greedily from her tastebuds.

He could have stayed like this forever, to be honest, or at least for the next few days until The Agency sent him a new name and a plane ticket to some other part of the world. Hell, if Joi managed to keep Chanté groaning on his tongue like this, he'd be willing to go AWOL for a couple days. They'd send Monica and Lane to retrieve him, and if anyone could understand his position, it would be them. But just in case that next mission was coming, he didn't want to waste a single moment.

"Get on the bed," he whispered against Chanté's lips, but he was talking to Joi.

He pulled Chanté back against his chest. She was panting and shivering, her hips circling against Joi's hand still buried in her shorts.

"Get on the bed," he said again.

She grinned at him and pulled her hand free. She was slow and deliberate just like she was on stage, and it was just as sexy here as every time he'd seen her dance. Asif and Chanté watched as she brought her hand to her mouth, flattening her tongue against her wet digits and licking the taste of Chanté's pussy from her skin.

Chanté shivered wildly and Asif tightened his hold on her.

After she'd licked her fingers clean, Joi pulled her camisole over her head and pushed her shorts to the floor, exposing miles of milk chocolate skin. She turned from them and crawled onto her bed.

Asif sucked in a harsh breath.

"She has the prettiest pussy," Chanté said wistfully.

"You want to taste it?" Asif asked, even though the answer was obvious as hell.

Chanté answered by pushing her shorts down her body.

"And what do you want me to do to you?"

Joi turned to face them, bent her legs, and planted her feet as far apart as she could manage. She moved her right hand between her legs and started lightly playing with her clit.

Chanté turned to look at him. "Did you miss me while you were gone?"

"Every day," he said, happy for the chance to tell her the entire truth.

"Then I want you to do all the things you dreamed about."

Asif laughed. "Say no more." He unwound his arms from her body and grazed his knuckles over her round belly. He pulled her t-shirt up and over her head. His hands skimmed down her sides and pushed her shorts down her legs. He playfully sank his teeth into her soft hip before smacking her hard on her right ass cheek and stepping back.

Asif enjoyed watching Chanté walk away from him to climb onto the bed, right between Joi's legs. Her mouth went immediately to Joi's small breasts, her bright pink tongue slithering around Joi's brown areola before she sucked the hard nub into her mouth.

"My god," he groaned at the best view in the world — hands down — and started undressing himself.

Chanté was half a dozen shades of the creamiest brown skin he'd ever seen or touched. Joi was her own different shade of deep browns and Asif couldn't manage to get his clothes off fast enough. He couldn't join them fast enough.

He couldn't get inside Chanté fast enough or push deep enough.

He was just about to climb on the bed when Joi pried her tongue from Chanté's mouth to look at him. "Grab that basket on the dresser first," she said.

"What?" he gasped in frustration.

Chanté moved her greedy mouth back to Joi's breast.

"We play safe here," she said, every word a soft moan.

Asif turned around frantically, missing the medium-sized wicker basket on the top of her tall dresser from excitement alone. He rushed across the room, his semi-soft dick slapping against his thighs.

"Oh," Asif said when he looked down into the basket. "Smart."

"I know," Joi moaned.

Asif turned around to find Chanté pushing Joi onto her back, one of her nipples between Chanté's lips while she rolled the other between her fingers. She also spread her knees wider, giving Asif the best view yet of her round ass cheeks, the slightly darker brown of her thighs, her dark brown lips glistening with her excitement, and the beautiful light brown as her pussy unfolded.

Asif grabbed the basket and rushed back to the bed. He climbed onto his knees, his dick hardening and pointing the way straight between Chanté's legs.

Chanté was kissing and licking her way down Joi's stomach, and Asif started rifling through the basket, plucking out one condom for himself but looking for something else.

Chanté shifted as she moved down Joi's body, and her ass bumped into his dick.

"Shit," he hissed, reaching down just to rub the head of his dick over one ass cheek. He just wanted to spread his precome into her skin, just for a second, before he got back on track.

"Red," Joi moaned.

"Huh?" Asif and Chanté asked at the same time, both sounding drunk on their own lust.

"Dental dams are in the red packaging," she groaned.

Chanté grunted against Joi's belly button, and Asif plucked a red foil package from the basket before setting it aside. He ripped the package open and Chanté popped up, pressing her ass against his balls.

"Thanks," she breathed before diving back between Joi's legs.

Asif watched her unfold and smooth the dental dam in place. She ran her thumb down Joi's pussy, just feeling her. Asif couldn't help smiling proudly as she lowered her head to cover Joi's pussy with her entire mouth.

Joi's back arched off the bed and she grabbed at the sheets over her head. Her nipples were hard, dark points.

Asif wished he could leave his body in that moment and see it all from a great height. He couldn't bear to miss a single second of all that was to come. He felt paralyzed by his own desire.

Abruptly, Chanté lifted her head and turned to frown at him. She shifted her hips, rubbing her ass against his groin and pulling a loud moan deep from Asif's throat.

"I need you," she moaned. "Inside me. Just so we're clear."

And just like that, Asif was back in this moment with Chanté. She was the only person who'd ever been able to grab him — keep him — so easily and firmly. Only her.

He reached down and smacked her hip, a deliciously

gratifying crack filling the room. "Heard," he said. "Now get back to work."

Joi clearly agreed, putting her fingers into Chanté's curls and moving her mouth back into place.

Asif reached for the condom, using all his training to keep his fingers from shaking as he ripped it open, rolled it into place, and finally, *finally* got to sink his hard length into Chanté's wet depths.

He couldn't stay, but he'd never be in a hurry to leave.

Chanté

+

Asif

TWENTY-FOUR

CHANTÉ LET Sonja lead her through the seemingly never-ending loop of one room opening into another, each with its own unique sexual environment. Under other circumstances, Chanté would have delighted in exploring each room as a voyeur — or more — but sometimes in the field, she struggled to let herself go and keep her brain on track. She could fake it if she was playing against someone she knew — and was interested in otherwise — but really, she let herself go only because she felt safe with Asif, Kenny, Monica, and Lane. Nothing about this party made her feel safe. She'd had such high hopes about this experience, and disappointment only seemed to increase her anxiety about Asif's safety.

"Interesting," Chanté said in a high-pitched voice. She didn't want to sound excited, just not judgmental, but watching a man crawl on all fours in a Dalmatian onesie, following behind a couple holding his leash just didn't do it for her.

"Not this either?"

"Not for me. Personally. Nope."

Sonja smiled calmly at her, tugging at their joined hands toward the doorway. "What are you into?" Chanté asked. She didn't want to monopolize and waste Sonja's prime orgy time.

"None of this," Sonja said in a sad voice.

They walked into the library, the biggest room Chanté had seen thus far, and the other guests were taking advantage of it. She was too busy looking at Sonja. The woman was a complete unknown to her. She didn't know why Asif trusted her, just that he did, but now she wanted to know how she'd become attached to a man Asif and Marcel were trying to take down. It wouldn't be the first time she'd known a woman tied to a man far beneath her.

"The light must be beautiful in here just before dawn," Chanté said, settling her eyes above the pile of flesh writhing together in the middle of the room.

A soft smile spread across Sonja's mouth. "It is," she said wistfully.

They made eye contact and Chanté licked her lips. She was trying to figure out the best way to broach the subject of getting Sonja away from these people.

"Chanté?"

She froze.

Monica had been suggesting Chanté go through field training, and in that moment, Chanté realized there might have been some merit to that recommendation because when she heard her real name, her nervous system went into shock, and there was no hiding it. Sonja was too close for her to play it off. This was the exact kind of response Kenny said could get her killed, and it pained her to prove him right.

But she wasn't ever without resources.

"Play along," she whispered to Sonja. The other woman's eyebrows shot up, but once again, she didn't miss a beat, nodding down at her.

Chanté put a smile on her face and turned quickly. "Hi," she said but then choked on that word.

Her eyes darted left to right at the two women standing in front of her. The tall white woman to her left was notable, but her eyes kept sliding to the right.

"Kay?" Chanté breathed.

The woman grinned, just one side of her mouth lifting. "I knew that was you."

"And you were right," Mia Malkova said. "Vezeniye."

Chanté hadn't seen Mia Malkova in a decade. She likely never would have recognized her if not for the fact that it was Mia who brought Asif into her life, not just once but repeatedly. For years, Chanté had hoped never to find her again, worried that if she did, Asif would cease to exist. But outside of that, Mia had stopped being a real person to Chanté, if she ever was, years ago.

But Kay she remembered vividly.

When Chanté was a waitress only dreaming of twirling around a pole, Kay had been like a goddess to her — all the dancers at The Petal were.

"You have grown into such a beautiful woman. I knew you would."

Chanté huffed out a laugh, anything to stop herself from shivering as Mia Malkova teased one of her curls and gently smoothed it between her fingers. "I don't think I've changed all that much, actually." She tried to make her voice sound light, vapid, young — the voice she used when she wanted bigger tips. "Um, thanks," Chanté said, glancing at Kay. "What are you doing here? How wild."

Kay shrugged but turned to look at Mia.

Chanté made the mistake of following Kay's line of sight to find Mia staring back at her, a lascivious smile on her face.

Detroit was technically home, but it was Cleveland that felt real to her. She became her own person in Cleveland. She added one more safe pillar to her found family in Cleveland. And she fell in love with Asif in Cleveland. Her six years there were some of the best of her young life and her time at The Petal was a highlight.

By all rights, her time at that club was a blip, but because The Petal was where she met Asif, Chanté remembered everything. She remembered the smell of the bus she took to work, the feeling of the music traveling from the slightly sticky floor through the soles of her heels, how her feet ached at the end of her shift, how good Asif looked the first time she'd spotted him in that booth all those years ago.

"Kay," Chanté breathed in awe. "You look amazing. It's like no time has passed at all."

Kay's eyes shifted toward the floor, but only for a second before she met Chanté's eyes again. She forced a smile on her face, but it didn't touch her flat, dead eyes. A sinking feeling settled low in Chanté's gut.

"What a surprise to find you here," Mia said, injecting herself into the conversation again.

"I know, right?" Chanté laughed. "It's crazy where life can take you. Um, this is my friend, Sonja," she said, putting her arm around Sonja's waist.

All three women's eyes lifted to Sonja, who seemed to blossom under the attention. "Hello," she said.

"You're lovely as well," Mia said.

Sonja pressed her fingertips against her chest, and out of the corner of her eye, Chanté saw Kay's smile fall into a frown.

Sonja started speaking to Mia, thankfully.

"What have you been up to since you left The Petal?" Chanté asked Kay in a soft whisper.

"She's been traveling with me," Mia said, pulling Kay closer into her side. "And what about you?"

"Dancing," Chanté replied. "I have a few clubs around the world where I like to be, which is nice. I never liked staying in one place for too long."

Mia nodded slowly. "We agree."

It was such a small thing, but Chanté hated when one person in a couple responded with 'we' in this way. She managed to suppress the frown she felt at Mia's response, but just barely.

"Are you dancing here in Saint Petersburg?" Kay asked.

"I am," Chanté chirped.

"Where?"

"I debuted at The Glass Menagerie yesterday."

Mia scoffed.

Chanté's face froze at her rude response. She really couldn't remember much about Mia from a decade ago, but she could immediately see why Joi still had nothing nice to say about the woman.

"You should dance at my club."

"Oh, you own a club here?" Chanté pretended to care.

Mia reached into her pocket and pulled out a card. "We open at sundown. I would love to see you on our stage."

Chanté forced another smile on her face as she carefully grabbed the card from Mia's hands. She didn't want to even accidentally touch the other woman's skin.

Mia turned to Sonja. "You would, of course, be welcome as well." The woman's gaze moved down Sonja's chest. Chanté didn't like that and squeezed Sonja's hand.

"She doesn't dance," Chanté said.

Sonja squeezed her hand back and turned to her. "But I love to watch."

They smiled at one another and Mia interrupted once again. "As do I."

Chanté didn't like the tone of Mia's voice and glared briefly in her direction before turning to Kay. She saw now what she'd missed in the disorientation of seeing these two after so many years. Her eyes dipped instinctively to Kay's waist, where she saw the deep indentations of Mia's fingers in the skintight fabric covering her skin. Chanté knew that touch would bruise, and as soon as the word formed in her brain, her eyes darted to Kay's arms — there was a dark scar on her forearm, one more slightly lighter up near her shoulder. The woman was practically naked, and Chanté's eyes skipped around her form, finding the remnants of nearly a dozen marks on her brown skin. They could be from anything, sure, but working in strip clubs for so many years had inadvertently given her a PhD in signs of domestic violence. She didn't know for sure, but she had a gut feeling she refused to ignore.

She lifted her eyes to Kay's face again. "What about you, Kay?" she asked.

"What about me?" the woman asked.

"Do you still dance?"

Mia pulled at Kay again. "Three nights a week," the other woman said proudly. "She's very popular."

Kay nodded quickly, and now that Chanté was looking for it, she could see the desperation written all over her face.

She didn't hear whatever Mia said as they moved away. She didn't see any of what was happening around her; all she could focus on was the sadness in Kay's eyes.

Asif and Marcel rushed down two flights of stairs, searching for Chanté and Sonja. They finally found them in the library. Asif had never known relief like what washed over him when he spotted the thick mass of her curls across the room.

He wrapped his arm around her waist. She jumped at his touch. "Time to go," he whispered and immediately felt her relax.

"Leaving so soon?" Sonja asked, her eyes moving from Asif to Marcel and back again. He could see the question in her eyes, and he nodded once to confirm their completed mission.

She sighed in relief.

"Do you want to come with us?" Chanté asked.

Sonja grimaced. "Raphael likes for me to play hostess. He doesn't like for me to leave."

"Who gives a fuck what he likes?" Marcel spat.

They all turned toward him, but Asif glanced at Sonja. Her grimace went soft and a genuine smile formed on her lips. She brushed her fingers over Marcel's cheek. "If I disappeared tonight, he would be very suspicious."

"But tomorrow," Asif said, reminding her that he hadn't forgotten their deal.

She bent forward and brushed her mouth along the

corner of Marcel's before moving to do the same to Chanté and Asif in turn. "Tomorrow," she said in a breathy sigh before turning and strutting away.

"But—" Chanté started. Asif squeezed her closer.

"She knows what she's doing," he said, turning to Marcel. "Better than most of us. Let's go."

Chanté

+

Asif

TWENTY-FIVE

CHANTÉ FELT numb on the ride back to her hotel. She couldn't get the image of Kay out of her head.

"You okay?" Asif asked.

She jumped in her seat at the sound of his voice and his warm breath ruffling her hair. On any other day, Chanté would have flooded her panties to have him holding her like this, but her desire took a back seat. She turned to look Asif in the eye. "No," she whispered.

"Did something happen?"

She nodded.

"Did Sonja—"

"Not her."

"Who?"

Her mouth was dry. She moved closer and dropped her voice as low as humanly possible. "Mia. She—"

"Not here," he whispered back, pulling her into his chest. Chanté wasn't the one with bruises all over her body she didn't want, but she took comfort in Asif's arms, nonetheless. For a decade, she would have killed for Asif to hold her like this — for him to stick around long enough to have time to hold her like this — and she reveled in it even as she tried to work out a plan that had nothing to do with him.

"My priyekhali," the driver said.

"We're here," Marcel translated from the front seat.

Chanté felt Asif's face in her hair as the car came to a slow stop along the curb. While Marcel paid, Asif stepped from the car and helped Chanté out after him.

They met Marcel on the curb. "Do you need to get out of here or...?" Asif asked.

"I have time," Marcel replied with a shrug. "Besides, you owe me something."

Asif nodded and gestured toward the hotel. "Let's get upstairs," Asif said. "It'll be okay," he whispered against her ear. "I promise."

"You don't make promises," she said in a sad voice.

He smiled against her skin. "But I am. That's how much you mean to me."

She swallowed a sob she'd been holding in her chest for a decade.

They walked into the hotel and boarded the elevator in silence. This wasn't the kind of triumphant return Chanté was used to, but she just couldn't bring herself to celebrate a job well done when they'd had to leave Sonja *and* Kay behind.

ASIF DIDN'T FEEL HIMSELF RELAX UNTIL HE SHUT AND double-locked the penthouse door. She kicked her shoes off and walked straight to the bedroom. He watched her retreat until she reached up to the neck of her dress and he looked away. He needed to stay on track.

He couldn't handle seeing more of Chanté's skin yet.

He turned to Marcel, taking in a deep breath, ready to get down to business, but Marcel was watching Chanté.

Asif cleared his throat loudly, and Marcel jumped. The other man's eyes met his before immediately sliding away. Asif was many things, but never jealous, especially not with Chanté. As far as he was concerned, everyone should see her, and if it were up to him, they would pay for the privilege. She'd taught herself that lesson years ago and had been charging an arm and a leg since.

But he also loved fucking with people. "Do you see something you like?" he asked playfully.

Marcel wrung his hands, the stress evident on his face. He cleared his throat, smiling nervously at the desk across the room. "Let's just finish our business, so I can...leave."

Asif let out a dry laugh. "Sure."

Marcel rolled his eyes. "All I need is a copy of the hard drive and I can get out of your hair."

"Ooh, you know I didn't think about this, but I don't have any tech with me."

"I do. Obviously," Chanté said, walking back into the living room. She'd stripped out of her dress and thrown a t-shirt on. Just a t-shirt.

Asif's mouth went wide at her thick thighs. It wasn't like he hadn't seen her thighs before or spent hours between them in whatever way she would allow, it was just that the sight would never get old.

"Whatcha need? I've got it."

Marcel choked back a groan, which pulled Asif out of his

own glitch. "We need to copy a terabyte of data," Asif said, pulling the chain out from underneath his t-shirt.

She nodded, sitting at the desk next to the couch, unloading a setup with a laptop, secondary monitor, and a bunch of other miscellaneous gadgets Asif couldn't name but recognized from previous missions.

"This came in handy," Asif said, handing over the chain.

"Good. I've been trying to get The Agency to just hand them out to every agent in the field. Easy to collect and pass data without feeling the need to hide it."

"Is it just necklaces and earrings?" Marcel asked.

Chanté plucked the earrings from her ears, as if she'd forgotten they were there. "One time I saw an agent fix a microSD to her hearing aid. It was genius. I thought about putting them in some bedazzled nipple tassels, but I don't know who'd wear those but me."

"Do you—" Marcel started and then tried to discreetly adjust the bulge in his pants before continuing. "Do you just leave your computers out like this? Isn't this against your protocol?"

Chanté shrugged. "I'm an independent contractor. As long as I deliver, no one gets to tell me what to do."

Asif couldn't help but laugh.

"Is that true?" Marcel asked.

"She's very good at her job and we give her a lot of leeway. She's very special," he said, smiling proudly.

Chanté smiled for the first time since they left Raphael's apartment. "Say it again," she sighed.

"Chanté is one of a kind," Asif said, sounding much more earnest than he meant to, but still only betraying a fraction of his feelings for her. "She also encrypts her computers to within an inch of their operating systems," he added as she unfolded her glasses and set them on her adorable button nose.

"And do," she whispered, squinting at the screen.

Asif looked back at Marcel. This time, the man was watching him, and it sent an ice-cold shiver down Asif's spine.

"Don't get any ideas," he said, using all his energy to make those words sound easy, harmless, while instinct kicked in and Asif's brain started formulating ways to kill Marcel the moment he even thought about using Chanté to get to him.

Marcel licked his lips as he raised his hands and took a step back. "I'm only wondering who Mia Malkova is."

Chanté's fingers froze over the keyboard. "How'd you know about her?"

Marcel looked to Asif. "She was in the room with Raphael and Joseph Herman."

"Birds of a feather," she hummed.

Asif nodded and turned to Marcel as Chanté got back to her work. "She's a Russian-American fugitive. She used to launder her father's dirty money through a number of bars, nightclubs, and strip clubs in the U.S., but she disappeared a few years ago."

"I'd kinda hoped she was dead," Chanté mumbled, her fingers flying across her keyboard.

"That would have been nice," Asif agreed.

"Who is her father?" Marcel asked.

"Yuri Malkov."

Marcel squinted before shaking his head. "Never heard of him."

"That's no surprise," Asif said, motioning for Marcel to follow him to the living room. "The Malkovs were a nothing crime family in the grand scheme but had a near-iron fist on the city where they were based."

"What happened?"

"Mia happened." Asif laughed mirthlessly. "She was her father's least favorite child, and that made her greedy and spiteful."

"I could almost understand that part," Chanté offered.

Asif nodded. "She started embezzling from her father's operations and then rinsing it through her own business interests. Not enough to catch her father's attention, but enough to begin planning to usurp the man who raised her. He didn't like her, but of all Yuri's children, she was the most like him."

Marcel nodded. "Not a unique profile."

"Not at all," Asif conceded. "Honestly, she would have remained a mystery to all of us, except for the fact that Mia was much more reckless than her father and she got caught. Well" — he shrugged — "she was about to get caught before she disappeared."

"Obviously this didn't happen, but had you considered that her father retaliated?"

Asif shrugged.

"Nah," Chanté said. "Before his trial, they asked about his daughter's whereabouts, and he said he didn't know."

"And you believed him?"

She uncapped the diamond and plugged it into a USB strip connected to her laptop. "I did, actually. He snitched on two of his sons, why lie to protect her?"

Asif chuckled lightly. "I guess you have a point. How did you know this?" he asked. "No one told me, and it was *my* case."

She shook her head. "Mia was your case. And no one

told me anything, I have a program that searches for any news about half a dozen criminals who've gotten away. I don't really care, but I hate the idea of people who aren't as smart as me getting one over. It makes me irrationally angry. Also, I negotiated a finder's fee from your boss."

"Just when I think I know you." He laughed.

She finally looked up from her screen again. "Me and my pussy have hidden depths," she teased.

Marcel spluttered out a shocked cough.

"How big?" she asked.

Asif huffed out another laugh.

"How much memory again?" she corrected, chuckling to herself.

He laughed for real this time. "A terabyte."

She nodded and plucked a card from the case and slipped it into the card reader. She grabbed her Bluetooth mouse and clicked a few times. "It takes a bit to get through the encryption. I'll tell you how long once the connection stabilizes."

"Thank you," Asif whispered.

"So you've found Malkova, what now?" Marcel asked.

"Nothing," Asif said.

"Excuse me?" Chanté said.

"I mean," Asif started, patting the air. "I'll let my superiors know where she is." He reached into his pants pocket and pulled out a card. "She gave me her card, and now that we know exactly where she is, we can set up a—"

Chanté pulled a card from her own small purse. "I got one of those too."

Asif reached for Chanté's, but she leaned away. "Chanté, don't."

"I'm not doing anything," she said.

"I'll handle it," he said. "I promise."

"If you handling it just means calling in backup who'll take days to get here, then that's unacceptable."

"Why not?"

"Because she was with Kay."

"Who?"

Chanté rolled her eyes. "The dancer who ran away to be with her."

"They're still together?"

"Yes, and she was covered in bruises," Chanté said in a tight voice. She was trying not to scream or dissolve into tears.

"Chanté—"

"Don't," she said, turning back to her computer. Her fingers stretched over the keyboard, but she didn't resume her work. She took a deep breath and lifted her gaze back to his. "You promised."

Marcel cleared his throat, and Asif reluctantly turned his gaze back to the other man.

"I really don't want to cause discord," Marcel said.

"Our entire relationship is discord," Chanté muttered angrily.

Asif's head snapped in her direction. "No, it's not," he shot back.

"Yes, it is. I just take my frustration out on your bank account."

"I don't want to cause further strife," Marcel corrected. "But if you have serious concerns about the safety of your former friend—"

"Coworker," Chanté corrected. "But no one deserves this."

"I agree," Marcel said.

"I can make sure whoever we send will extract her first," Asif said.

"That'll take time," Chanté grumbled.

"*This* is taking time," Asif cried. "What's the difference?"

She pressed her lips shut obstinately. Asif glared back, desperate to get through to her.

Once again, Marcel spoke up and figuratively stepped between them. "How long until the copy is done?" he asked her.

She glared at Asif for a few more seconds before checking her computer. "Two hours."

"Okay," Marcel said carefully. "Then we have two hours to put together a plan to get your fri— coworker away from Mia Malkova."

"I'm fine with that," Chanté ground out, glaring a hole in Asif's face.

Asif leaned forward, both palms on the desk. He was close enough now to smell her perfume. He didn't care about Marcel and he wasn't interested in Mia. As usual, all that mattered was Chanté. He lifted his hand to her hair, smoothing one of her curls between the pads of his fingers.

"I'll stay for you," he said.

She sucked in a sharp breath and her eyes went wide. "You never have before."

Asif had been shot, tortured, even broken his hand punching his way out of a bar fight in Argentina, and nothing hurt more than those four words. "You never asked me to stay before."

She blinked at him and pursed her lips. "Not with words," she whispered.

"Because you think I'll say no?"

She rolled her eyes. "Because I know you'll say no. I know you better than you think."

"And I know *you* better than you think. Ask me with words, Chanté, and you might be surprised this time."

"What's different now?" she whispered, leaning forward. Her eyes were big and bright and full of hope.

He moved his hand to the nape of her neck and answered honestly. "Nothing."

She moved forward. Her lips brushed his. "Will you stay and help me?"

"Yes," he whispered against her lips. "For you."

Chanté

+

Asif

TWENTY-SIX

THEY DIDN'T NEED the two hours.

They moved from the desk to the couch and pulled the threads of a firm plan together with ease. "Are you sure you're allowed to help with this?" Asif asked. "I wouldn't want you to jeopardize your bright future."

Marcel rolled his eyes. "I'll be fine. Besides, if Malkova is doing business with Raphael, the French government will want to know that."

"I'll tell Sonja."

"I'll do that," Marcel said.

"And how will you do that?" Asif asked.

"I recommend three fingers," she whispered.

Chanté enjoyed watching her meaning dawn on Marcel after a while. "Oooh, he's pretty when he's embarrassed," she cooed.

Asif pulled her back into his front and rubbed his hand down her arm. "He is."

"Is sexual innuendo in the training manual at your agency?" Marcel asked, running a hand over his head.

"No, but they believe in honing all your innate skills."

"Innate." The man laughed drily.

"We still have an hour left," Chanté whispered without bothering to look at the computer screen.

Chanté crossed her legs toward Marcel. Her foot was close to bumping his legs but didn't touch him. His eyes were on the crease of her thighs. "What do you— An hour," he said wistfully, tearing his gaze away from her legs.

"Does your agency frown upon fraternization?" Chanté asked.

Asif moved his hand forward onto her breast. She sighed as he started playing with her nipple, but she kept her eyes focused on Marcel.

"It's, er... I don't know."

Asif tweaked her nipples and she moaned, arching her back as her pussy flooded.

"Ignorance can be bliss," Asif said.

"Do you... Have you two done this before?"

Chanté heard him, but she couldn't focus on an answer, so Asif took over. "A time or two."

"And what...does it entail?"

Chanté blinked open her eyes to find Marcel's gaze riveted to them and felt a rush from that alone. Asif seemed to be on the same page because he threw his other arm around her body. His hand landed in her lap and his fingers curled around the hem of her shirt. His palm was cool against her overheated skin. He started pulling the t-shirt over her stomach.

Marcel's eyes widened and his lips parted, so Chanté parted her legs to match.

She planted one foot on the couch and the other on the floor. "Would you like to touch me?" Chanté breathed.

Marcel let out a soft breath and nodded slowly. "Yes." As soon as the word left his lips, he lifted his eyes to Asif. Chanté rolled her eyes.

"You don't need to ask me for permission to touch her," he laughed. "That's not how this works."

"But you will need to ask me before you touch him. That *is* how this works."

Marcel's gaze locked with Chanté's. "Do you want me to touch him?"

She lifted her foot from the floor and grabbed her leg behind the knee. Cool air hit her pussy. She could feel her own arousal leaking from her slit. "Definitely. But we can work up to that if you need to. We can be gentle."

He was already moving to his knees on the floor between her legs. Even as he bent his head down and nudged her clit with his nose, she could see him thinking. See his eyes moving up to Asif — to make sure he was watching.

Chanté didn't have to check. She could hear Asif's heavy breathing. Could feel the steel in his pants against her side. Could feel the way his fingers rolled her nipple between his strong fingers and knew he was as excited as she was.

Marcel flattened his tongue against her pussy, and she cried out. He lifted his head, eyes taking her in nervously. Asif cupped her breast. "Don't stop," he groaned, and Marcel dipped his head again.

His tongue was thorough and curious. He explored every inch of her sex, licking at her, sucking on her until she sank down on the couch and Marcel had to cup her ass with both hands to keep her pussy in the perfect position for him to feast.

The room filled with the sound of him eating her out like his life depended on it.

Meanwhile, Asif pulled her shirt up her body so he could caress and grope her breasts just the way she liked.

He shimmied his way out from underneath her and laid across the couch, kissing her softly, inhaling her moans. "You're ready to come," he said.

She nodded, too overcome to speak. Too close to breathe.

He covered her mouth with his. "Then come," he sighed against her lips, and she did, trapping Marcel's face between her thighs.

They kissed and suckled on her as she shivered through that first orgasm, holding her until she couldn't stand it anymore.

"Enough. Enough. Fuck," she cried into Asif's mouth. They pulled away in degrees but never left her alone. In fact, when Chanté crumpled from the couch, she rolled right into Asif's arms. He pulled her into his lap and rested his back against the couch, holding onto her as their hearts slowed from a gallop to a gentle trot.

Marcel was sitting next to them, panting, face wet from her release. He started to wipe at his face and she mustered the courage to protest. "You should let Asif taste," she sighed contentedly, the rumble of Asif's laughter vibrating against her breasts.

"You don't have—"

Marcel was already moving closer. Chanté shifted out of the way and into the best position to watch as their faces moved together, their lips touched and parted, and Asif welcomed his tongue into his mouth.

Chanté got greedy.

She straddled Asif's waist, pressing her wet pussy against his pants, and sat up, pressing her mouth against Asif's chin and Marcel's cheek. They turned to make room for her in this kiss. Their three tongues slid together. Asif's hips started pumping up into her sex. Marcel's hand moved to grab her ass.

The night was only just beginning.

Chanté wanted to be in charge, and Asif would never stand in the way of that.

When she was tired of them writhing on the floor in front of the couch together, she led them to the bedroom. "Undress each other, please," she demanded prettily, pulling her own t-shirt off unceremoniously.

"You don't want to help?" Asif asked.

Chanté pulled open the top drawer in the bedside table and reached inside. "I want you both inside me at the same time," she sighed. "Does that help?"

Marcel groaned and Asif moved his right palm over the ridge in the other man's pants. "Yep, it helped."

"Great," she said, pulling a fresh box of condoms and a small bottle of lube from the drawer.

"How many condoms did you bring?" he asked, unbuckling Marcel's pants. The other man was kissing Asif's neck and pulling Asif's shirt from his pants.

"I came here to find you, I had to be prepared."

Marcel pulled Asif's shirt over his head. The minute he felt Marcel's warm hands on his skin, Asif didn't want to talk anymore. None of them did.

It was always so exciting what he and Chanté could make happen when they were naked. She pushed Marcel onto his back while Asif rolled both of their condoms in place and kneeled at the foot of the bed. Chanté kissed her way down Marcel's chest and stomach, meeting Asif at the tip of Marcel's shaft. They smiled at one another, snaking their tongues out, each caressing one of his balls.

When Marcel started cursing in French, they both thought he was ready.

Asif stood and nodded to Marcel's groin. "Hop on, sweetheart. I wanna see you take his dick." She was all too happy to comply.

Asif popped open the lube and filled his palm. While Chanté crawled over Marcel's body, he stroked his own shaft with one wet hand and used the other on Marcel. He heard Chanté and Marcel start to kiss and he moved the mushroom head of Marcel's to her opening. He spread the remaining lube on his fingers around her asshole while she lowered herself down his length, wetting his hand in her arousal.

She started to move along his shaft, and Asif moved a wet finger along her perineum and back to her asshole. She came from that first touch, clamping down on Marcel's dick loud enough to make him cry out.

"Please," she groaned, and Asif climbed onto the bed.

He straddled Marcel's hips and pressed at her opening. Chanté was so sensitive, so aroused, she could hardly still her hips long enough to let him be gentle. As soon as he'd worked the tip just inside the tight ring of her ass, she pushed back against him.

"Fuck. Wait," Asif groaned.

"Fuck," Marcel whimpered.

Chanté was squirming between them. Asif had to grab her hips and hold her steady so he could push inside.

"Fuck, I feel you," Marcel groaned.

"Isn't it amazing?" Chanté sighed, completely lost in her own lust.

Asif pushed in a few inches and then back. "Now you," he panted.

Marcel's hands cupped Chanté's ass and he pumped his hips up into her.

Asif arched his back and sighed up at the ceiling. Chanté fell forward onto Marcel's chest.

They took turns pushing in and out of her, settling into a rhythm as Chanté stretched around their shafts. They enjoyed stroking one another through her openings. Their fingers tangled together as they gripped her hard, holding her still, so they could get her off from their persistent strokes.

Soon enough, they didn't have to wait for one another and found a new pleasure fucking into her at the same time and with more force. They fucked into her until they couldn't be gentle anymore. Until their groans were as loud as yells. Until Chanté's orgasms had drenched Marcel's thighs. Until each man filled their condoms and they needed a break.

And then they repositioned and started all over again.

Chanté

+

Asif

TWENTY-SEVEN

CHANTÉ WOKE up with a delicious ache in her...well, everywhere.

The warmth of use spread from between her legs down her thighs. Her glutes were sore enough she almost felt like she'd spent the night giving lap dances to high rollers. She could feel the remnants of Asif and Marcel's touch on her hips and thighs.

She felt amazing and popped up in bed with a smile on her face. Marcel and Asif were passed out on opposite sides of the bed. They'd all been too wrecked to even burrow under the covers. It had been years since she'd felt so good — years since she and Asif had fucked someone together.

Crawling carefully from the bed, she jumped to her feet. She didn't even need coffee. Walking into the open closet, she snatched a terrycloth robe from the hanger and pulled it on. All she wanted was a good, long soak in a hot bath and as much room service as the hotel could send up quickly.

"But first," she sighed, closing the bedroom door softly behind her. She sat back down at her computer.

The copy of Raphael's hard drive was finished — had probably been finished hours ago — and Chanté pulled the copy from the reader. She found an empty SD card holder in her things and packaged it up for Marcel, then started another copy for Asif.

Her fingers were poised to check in on Kenny and Maya, or to ping Caleb just to say 'hey,' but that was only because she was dreading making the call. But if she didn't do it now, she didn't know when she'd have the chance. Normally, that wouldn't have mattered to her, but she wanted to piss Maryam off about as much as she wanted to walk naked down a Russian street in the dead of winter.

She set up a secure connection on her video app and hoped to death she wouldn't answer.

"It's early for you," Maryam rasped in a voice that sounded rougher than normal. She was sitting in a dark room with a warm light radiating off to the side. Her hair was covered in a satin scarf and she looked tired, but relieved. Vaguely, Chanté wondered if the woman was up worrying about them, but realistically, she knew she was probably up watching some rescue mission in Berlin or something.

"I get up early," Chanté replied defensively.

The woman lifted an eyebrow as she took a deep sip of tea.

"Sometimes," Chanté added. "Anyway, I'm calling with an update."

"I would assume so. Unless there's something else you'd like to discuss."

Chanté's face lit up. There was actually so much she'd be willing to discuss with Maryam — her haircare routine, if her husband knew what she did for a living, and any thoughts whatsoever on universal healthcare. But she stopped herself when she noted the light teasing in Maryam's voice and the reminder that she'd somehow known the woman for nearly a decade but knew next to nothing about her — not for lack of trying.

"I helped your agent complete his mission."

"That's wonderful news," she replied drily.

"Yep," Chanté chirped.

"If you like, I can have a team coordinate your transportation. We can have you out of there ASAP if the situation has become dire."

Chanté shrugged. "No, we're good. And not coming back just yet."

Maryam's eyebrow lifted again.

Chanté grabbed the lapels of her robe and held them closed. "It's just I... We..." She looked toward the bedroom door and wondered if she should have waited for Asif to do this. He charmed everyone, maybe he could have charmed Maryam. Or maybe not. If she'd waited for him, he could have borne the brunt of her stare at least, and she started to regret her decision to do this alone.

"There's been a development," Chanté said, trying to sound serious.

"I'm listening," she said coolly.

"Um... I don't know if I'm allowed to mention this mission? It's old, and I don't know if you have clearance?"

Maryam took another slow sip of her tea. When her cup moved away, there was an amused smile playing across her mouth. "Did this mission concern your agent?" she asked.

Chanté tightened her hold on her robe, hoping to stifle the giddiness those last two words made her feel. And then she pressed her lips together and nodded.

"Well, then," Maryam said with a casual shrug. "As it

happens, I have been granted overview status when it comes to your man's missions." A small squeak slipped from Chanté's lips. "Besides, he has been AWOL for weeks, which is a problem on its own, but if you — a trusted asset — are going to join him? Well, there will be a response..." She let that sentence trail off as a smile spread on her face.

Chanté leaned toward the computer screen. "That's a threat, right?" she whispered.

"Does it feel like a threat?" she responded.

Chanté nodded quickly.

"Then impact is all that matters. So, you can tell me what is delaying your return or we can see if that was a threat...or not?"

Chanté swallowed the lump in her throat. Her stomach was clenched in fear, but she was in awe of her at the same time. "Okay, so first of all, this was my choice. Asif is just..." Chanté started to say that he was loyal to her as a memory of him leaning over this desk, looking into her eyes, telling her he would stay flashed in her brain, but that was a fantasy. One she'd crafted to soothe her own fragile heart when it came to him, so she smothered her words and bit back a smile, taking a deep breath before she continued. "Asif won't leave me unprotected in the field, so he agreed to stay."

Maryam let out a low, husky laugh. "That doesn't sound like him."

"Um, anyway, so last night at the party, we ran into Mia Malkova, who was this—"

"I know Malkova," Maryam said, sitting up straight in her chair. Suddenly, the smile disappeared from her face, and the sound of her typing on her computer filtered through their connection. "I'm listening. Please continue," she said without even a glance toward her webcam.

"Um, so…it's been years since Asif or I have seen her, and I don't think we should let this opportunity to finally collect her pass."

Maryam's typing stopped, and now she focused on the camera. "Chanté, my dear, I understand that you don't really know me even after all these years of working together, but I do know you. You are very charming, but a very poor liar."

Chanté sighed. "Okay, fine. I don't give a shit about Mia, but she was with a dancer I used to know, and something didn't feel right about their relationship."

"Like what?"

"Like all the damn bruises over her body," Chanté spat back.

Maryam nodded solemnly. "Does Asif have a plan?" she asked.

"Yes, *we* have come up with a plan," Chanté said, annoyed and only barely able to hide it.

There was that smirk again. "Let me hear it," she demanded.

"Um…"

"If I deem the plan suitable *and* you succeed, I will double your commission."

Chanté lifted her eyebrows, tempted. But she still wasn't sure. She chewed her bottom lip and glanced at the bedroom door.

"And I will continue to hold off on reporting Asif's absence," Maryam added.

Chanté caved and let the plan spill with as much detail as she could remember. A part of her was worried when she started the retelling that the plan would sound more half-baked than normal, but it didn't, and by the time she was done, she felt better than expected.

"And then we get the fuck out of Russia and live happily ever after," she finished with a lighthearted laugh.

"Is that the goal?" Maryam asked. "To live happily ever after?"

Chanté shook her head quickly. "Oh no, I was just joking."

"Why?"

"Huh?"

"The work we do is difficult," she said. "Everyone needs someone to come home to. Or" — she smiled with a shrug — "have in the field to watch your back."

Chanté wasn't just speechless, she stopped breathing. She was already terrified about what Maryam knew about her, but the idea that agents besides Monica, Lane, and Kenny knew how Chanté felt about Asif was nearly overwhelming. All she could do was shake her head. She couldn't bear to explain that Asif didn't want that — he didn't want her, not really.

Maryam watched her through the screen with a silent focus.

While she spoke, Chanté had let go of the death grip she had on her robe, but under the agent's gaze, she grabbed hold of it again. She felt exposed.

Finally, Maryam sighed and sat back in her chair. "I think your plan is acceptable," she said in an official tone. "There is an expected lack of personnel." She stopped here to roll her eyes. "But this is Asif we're talking about."

Chanté relaxed slightly at the shift in this discussion. "We have the French agent."

"Oh, a hearty three people," she laughed, but then swatted the air. "Two days."

"Hmm?" Chanté asked, wide-eyed.

"You and Asif have two days to complete this mission and return."

"That's not a lot of time," Chanté said.

"It is not. Please, don't waste it," she said, disconnecting the call without another word.

"Rude," Chanté breathed, even as she slumped back into her chair. Her body was aching before, but it was much less delicious now.

The bedroom door opened, but Chanté was too tired to jump in surprise.

"Good morning," Asif yawned. He strolled into the room with his curly hair big and wild around his shoulders and completely naked.

This was the second morning she'd woken up with Asif. That had never happened before, and Chanté was too afraid to let herself get used to it. No matter what he said last night. "Good morning to you too."

"How long have you been up?"

She shrugged. "Not long," she said.

"Working?" he asked, glancing at her computer.

"Nope. Just cleaning up." She slid the SD card case in Asif's direction. "Marcel's copy is done. Here's one for you."

"Thanks," Asif said, picking up the case as he moved close to her side.

"I might pack up my stuff just in case we need to make a hasty exit."

"That's smart." Asif leaned his left hip against the desk. In the chair, she was at the perfect height to look his dick directly in the eye, and she was too tired to lift her eyes up.

"Are you hungry?" Asif asked.

Chanté licked her lips, and his dick made a sad lurch.

"For food," he corrected.

She leaned her head back on the chair and finally looked up at him. "I could eat."

He raised his eyebrows. "So could I. But first..." He leaned forward and smiled at her. "Wanna take a bath?"

Her eyes widened. "Together?

"Unless you don't want me to scrub your back."

Now her eyes squinted. "This makes me feel like you have something up your sleeve."

"And you don't?" he asked with a devastating grin.

"I try to avoid sleeves," she laughed.

He reached forward and slipped his hand between the lapels of her robe, pulling it open slightly, just enough to caress her chest. "I understand why you don't trust me," he whispered, his gaze settled on the patch of skin he was caressing. "But I'm not always trying to deceive you."

Chanté felt her body responding. She was exhausted and nervous about the mission, but over the years, she'd discovered that whatever emotions were swirling in her gut, she could always make room for Asif.

"It's been a decade and you still don't get me," she whispered. He lifted his eyes to hers. "I trust you with my life. You're the one who doesn't trust me."

His hand moved to her face. "Then I guess we're both clueless," he said. "Come on, I'll draw you a bath and order some food."

CHANTÉ WAS MAD AT ASIF AND THAT WAS OKAY.

She refused to look at him before her bath, and even

though he'd made sure to order all her favorite dishes, as she sat down to eat, she didn't even acknowledge Asif's presence. And that was okay. He kept reminding himself that it was perfectly fine for her to be mad at him, but he found himself getting angrier and angrier about it.

And that was not okay.

"You sure you have to leave?" Chanté asked Marcel.

No, she didn't just ask him that; she'd been asking him that since Asif had emerged from the shower, every few minutes and loud enough for Asif to hear.

"Yes," Asif called across the room, answering for the other man.

"Um," Marcel said, glancing between Asif and Chanté. "Yes. I need to check in with my contacts." He ducked his head, trying to hide his shy smile. It was adorably endearing, and Asif couldn't even appreciate it because Chanté was mad at him and he was annoyed.

"When will you be back?" Chanté asked.

Asif sucked his teeth loudly and crossed his arms.

Marcel looked nervous again and aimed his answer somewhere between Asif and Chanté, but not directly at either of them. "I have some other loose ends to wrap up with my own endeavors. Since Mia's club is nocturnal, I'll be back in the early evening. But if something comes up" — he turned to Asif here — "you can contact me."

Asif nodded once.

"What if we're not together?" Chanté asked. "Maybe I should have—"

"No," Asif said, cutting her off. Marcel's eyes went wide. "We'll be in touch if something comes up."

Marcel nodded and turned as fast as he could. Chanté rounded on Asif before Marcel was through the door.

He smiled because at least she was looking at him. "You wanna hit me?" he teased.

"I'm not breaking a nail over you," she said.

"What about on me?" he asked.

That caught her off guard, but Chanté was ever resilient. "You'd have to pay me," she said, crossing her arms over her breasts.

He started walking toward her. "We both know I'm not above giving you money," he said. "And with enthusiasm."

She tried not to smile. He'd always loved that spot where her two front teeth bit into her bottom lip and wanted to sink his teeth into those same spots before sucking it into his mouth. He walked in front of her, close enough to touch, but he kept his hands to himself.

"Did I do something to make you mad?" he asked.

"Be more specific," she ground out.

"I'll take that as a yes. Do you want to tell me what I did? Or do you want to just pretend none of this happened? We're so good at pretending," he said, a small smile on his face.

Her face shifted from angry to conflicted, and she sucked her bottom lip into her mouth. She was fighting a war internally, and this was the only time Asif had ever hoped for Chanté to lose.

He'd been playing a dangerous game with Chanté since he met her. Her brain was a beautiful piece of machinery, and even after a decade, he still could hardly fathom a fraction of the schemes she was cooking up in her pretty little head. But Chanté, even at her absolute best, still had a tiny fracture in her thinking that made her second-guess herself. It made her miss something Asif thought was clear as day, even though he wished it wasn't. For a decade, he'd been flying close to the sun, exploiting that fracture in her thinking to hide something he thought was unfortunately obvious. It was a gamble, and he'd been damn lucky, but he could see the exact moment when his luck ran out.

Chanté had the perfect face. Her head was perfectly round, haloed by her big curls. There wasn't a sharp angle anywhere — adorable button nose, full lips, big, round cheeks — and he'd never had enough time to learn those curves with his fingers. She had big, expressive brown eyes that opened wide and filled slowly with tears.

"Do you really not want to be with me at all?" she asked.

Chanté had been sitting with that question for most of her adult life. It haunted her in all the worst ways. Whenever she met someone new and they fell at her feet, all Chanté could wonder was why it had never been that easy for her and Asif. When she had a good night on stage, she wished Asif could see it. And then she hated herself for thinking about him at all. If Chanté's life was a galaxy, she was the sun — obviously — and Asif was her favorite orbiting planet. But that was only in her mind. Asif had refused to stick around long enough to give Chanté a glimpse of what he thought of her. Still, she'd never thought the answer was nothing.

He couldn't look at her. Every time she tried to catch his eyes, they shifted away, and that stung. Even at his most unreliable, he'd never done that.

"Never mind," she said, turning toward the kitchen.

"Chanté." He said her name like it burned his tongue. That more than stung.

She used to love the way Asif said her name. She'd once hacked into the security cameras at a safe house in Argentina to get audio of him crying out to her while they'd fucked wildly against the front door. And then she'd hidden that file in a folder so secure even Caleb didn't know it existed; it was about Asif, and he wouldn't have approved.

But the way he said her name made Chanté think about deleting that folder — over half a decade of digital scraps that meant something to her, but nothing to him.

"Chanté," Asif called her name again. And even though he didn't say it like a burden this time, the panic in his voice didn't make her feel any better.

She didn't know why she came into the kitchen. She didn't cook. She didn't clean. She wasn't hungry. She just didn't want Asif to see her cry.

He stood at the entrance to the kitchen, blocking her exit. She turned away and stared up at the ceiling.

Asif took a loud, long, deep breath. "Let me answer your question."

"You did."

"No, I didn't."

"Non-verbal communication is a thing," she said, getting annoyed.

He sighed again. "Do you remember that outfit you wore at that burlesque club in DC? The one with wings?"

"I've worn a lot of wings," she said, turning around to glare at him. "Be more specific."

"These were red, and they had little crystals on the boning that caught the light while you moved. You had matching gems on your pasties and thong and belly button.

And when you were done with your dance and the lights went out, it was beautiful."

She squinted at him. "You were at that show?"

He licked his lips and shook his head. "I was in Turkey doing something classified, but I paid a junior agent to go and record it for me."

"Why?" Chanté asked, seriously confused.

He smiled sadly at her. "Probably for the same reason you keep giving me watches with tracking devices you think I don't know about," he said, lifting his wrist. He'd taken the tracker out years ago but kept the watch — just like all her gifts — as reminders of her.

"I have no idea what you're talking about," she said in a flat voice.

He stepped into the kitchen, slowly, as if he was afraid she would run away. Besides the fact that there was nowhere for her to go, he'd always been the one running away.

She expected him to get close enough to confuse her with the smell of his cologne, but she didn't expect him to push up against her and press her against the refrigerator. She would have been overcome with emotions about this on a regular day, but after all they'd done last night — all they'd done to each other and Marcel — Chanté was squirming against his body.

"I think about you all the time, Chanté." Asif dipped his head and she tipped hers back, offering her mouth to him without even thinking. As if the last couple of hours never happened — because staying mad at him was impossible. Maybe it would have been easier if she wanted to stay mad at him, but since she never wanted that, she couldn't know for sure.

"No, you don't," she whispered, her eyes skittering away from his gaze.

Asif moved a hand under her chin and tilted her head until she had no choice but to look up at him. Glare up at him.

"If you think about me so much, why do I always feel like I'm running after you?"

"Because you're stubborn."

"What's that got to do with anything?"

He moved his thumb over her chin and brushed her bottom lip.

"How many times do you think I've been shot, Chanté?"

"Like this year? Since I met you? Or throughout your entire career?"

Asif smiled and tilted his head to the side. "All three," he said.

Chanté knew a challenge when she heard one. "Zero, six, twenty," she replied confidently.

He squinted. "How do you know that? Did you hack into my personnel file?"

She rolled her eyes. "I wish. Those are under lockdown." She shrugged. "But I have my sources."

Now it was Asif's turn to roll his eyes. "Kenny," he said, sucking his teeth.

"Amongst others."

"Kierra," Asif said.

"There could be others," Chanté said unconvincingly.

"How much reconnaissance have you done on me?"

"That's none of your business. What is your business is that I wouldn't have had to do any—" She stopped here to correct herself in real time. "I wouldn't have had to do most of that surveillance if you didn't think it was okay to hop in and out of my life like a goddamn leapfrog."

"I shouldn't have been able to do that, Chanté. You're better than that."

"No shit," she spat back. "Obviously, I shouldn't keep letting you spin the block on me, except I love you and I—"

She tilted her head back and blinked up at the ceiling, desperate not to let him see her cry up close.

There was only a sliver of space between their bodies, but Asif got rid of it in a heartbeat, pressing himself firmly against her.

She was on the verge of tears, but Chanté could also feel his hard dick pressing against her stomach trying to beat a hole in her chest.

"I don't give up on people I love," she said, dropping her eyes for a quick glance at his face.

He looked pained. There were only so many moments in their life when they'd ever been on the same page. It was bittersweet that this was one of them.

"My job is dangerous, Chanté."

"No shit." She could feel the pressure of tears building at the back of her eyes.

Asif's breath hitched and then she felt his mouth on hers. "Then why won't you let me protect the person I love?"

It was rare for Chanté, of all people, to be speechless. She didn't have an answer to his very good and earth-shaking question. It was just that, in over a decade, she'd never considered the option.

But she hoped Asif could feel how she felt as she sucked his tongue into her mouth.

Chanté

+

Asif

TWENTY-EIGHT

"JE REVIENDRAI DANS UNE SEMAINE. Je dois attacher quelques fils lâches."

Marcel was standing in the bathroom in his hotel room. He'd taken the hottest shower of his life as soon as he returned and it hadn't managed to wipe the smile from his face. The hot water pounding against his back hadn't eased the little lovely aches all over his body either, but he wasn't looking for that.

"Do you need backup?" his contact, Desta, asked.

"Non," he said quickly. "Mmmm, peut-être. If you don't hear from me in twenty-four hours, find me."

She laughed. "Bien sur. But don't make it hard."

The call disconnected quickly. Instead of dropping the phone to the sink, Marcel opened the SIM slot and plucked the card out, replacing it with another. He turned on the faucet, then snapped the tiny card in half and let it wash down the sink. He turned the water off and looked at his reflection in the harsh, sterile light.

Marcel was a prodigy. The kind of man who could put

on whatever personality and accent necessary to get the job done. He was a chameleon, someone who could play at a worldliness he'd never actually experienced. Until last night.

He turned around and looked at his reflection in the mirror. It was faint, and he could see it mostly because he could feel it — the fading ache of Chanté's teeth in the delicate skin just below his shoulder. Or maybe it was Asif's bite.

Not knowing made his groin tighten and his face warm.

They said some missions changed you, but he'd never thought it would be like this. The big question mark in his head was wondering who he would be when he returned home.

He shook his head, grabbed his phone, and walked back into the bedroom. He had a few hours before he needed to get back to Chanté's hotel room, which was just enough time to reach for one of those loose threads.

He dressed as quickly and carefully as he could. He made sure his dark skin was moisturized. He spritzed his body in a Russian cologne that wouldn't stand out in the crowd but would convey to those who knew that he was as wealthy as he looked. Or at least his cover identity was wealthy. He'd brought a small fortune in designer suits, all dark, stylish, and tailored. Again, just enough to accentuate his features, but not enough to make him stand out any more than he already did. He dressed carefully, each article of clothing covering his skin with slow precision.

His little sister used to tell him that the process of putting on her leotard and preparing her feet for her pointe shoes was how she got her mind in the right frame for a punishing practice. By the time her shoes were tied, she wasn't Aïssatou, she was Anne, the soon-to-be principal ballerina of her company. And by the time Marcel slid his belt buckle closed, he wasn't her protective older brother, or the man between Chanté and Asif, or even his cover.

He was a spy.

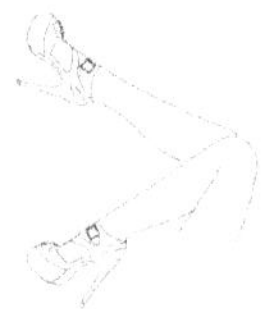

"THESE ARE TOO HIGH, RAPHAEL," SONJA WHINED prettily.

"What is too high when you have legs like these?" he said, motioning toward her.

She was standing on a tiny pedestal in the middle of the boutique, modeling the third pair of heels Raphael had chosen. She wasn't even interested in buying anything; Sonja just enjoyed dressing up sometimes.

"Do you have these in blue?" she asked the attendant slowly. The woman didn't speak English, but she was pretty, and Raphael always chose aesthetics over practicality.

The woman smiled at Sonja and nodded. Sonja blinked back.

Raphael's phone rang, and Sonja sighed in relief. She shifted so Raphael was at her back and then spoke quickly. "Prinesi mne eti siniye tufli."

The girl's face lit up in recognition, and she nodded quickly and scurried away. When Sonja turned toward Raphael, he'd just started to frown. Their gazes locked and she lifted her eyebrows. He rolled his eyes in return, stood from the couch, and walked away. Her eyes tracked him as he moved through the store.

A dark, shadowy figure moved on the other end of the

mirror, somewhere deep in the menswear section. She thought she'd made it up until it moved again.

"Vot oni," the salesgirl said, rushing back into the room.

Sonja's smile had faltered, but she brought it back, and not just to preserve her cover. The woman kneeled down and pulled the shoes from the box, preparing them for Sonja to try on. She carefully stepped from her heels, and the dark figure moved again.

"These would be beautiful in boots," Sonja mused softly in Russian.

The saleswoman looked eagerly up at her, nodding and quickly replying that there were some boots from the same designer.

Sonja pretended to be excited about that and asked to see them. She pretended to think for a few seconds before adding three other shoe styles she might like to see. She wasn't interested in any of them, but she'd buy them — well, Raphael would. It was the least she could do for wasting this girl's time.

As soon as the girl disappeared into the back room, Sonja turned quickly, heading toward the menswear section. She didn't move clandestinely. She didn't have time for that. Some moments required a little recklessness. She made her way through the mid-height display cases, craning her neck to see past the mannequins.

She yelped when the arm wrapped around her waist and yanked her through a door into a dark, cool hallway.

He smelled like warm honey and smoke.

"Good morning," he whispered into her ear before setting her back on her feet.

She faced him, brushing her hair from her vision. Marcel looked good enough to eat. "Hello," she breathed.

"I have a proposition for you," he said, leaning close.

Her sex rippled at those words, leaving her speechless for a long moment. A long moment he didn't rush. "Another? I'm listening," she breathed, licking her lips.

His gaze dipped to her mouth before he gave her his instructions.

Chanté

+

Asif

TWENTY-NINE

EIGHT YEARS AGO...

IT HAD BEEN EARLY in the afternoon when they arrived at Joi's apartment, and now the sun was setting. Chanté was curled up in the passenger seat of Asif's car, leaning against the window, watching the sun dip while Asif steered them unhurriedly through the city streets. She considered suggesting he take the freeway, but after the sex they'd just had, Chanté felt like she was floating. The last thing she wanted was to cut their time short, especially when his hand was a warm, heavy anchor on her thigh.

"You doing alright over there?" he asked in a gentle voice.

"I'm great," she whispered.

He chuckled lightly, squeezing her thigh.

A few minutes or hours later — Chanté hardly knew — she recognized the diner a few blocks from her apartment and sighed.

He squeezed her thigh again.

"You're leaving, aren't you?" Her voice made a small cloud of condensation bloom on the window.

"Yes."

"Joi gave you the info you needed?"

"Yeah. It's enough for me to hand this over to someone else."

"And now you're leaving." She didn't even bother posing it as a question because it was a heartbreaking fact.

His only answer was another squeeze of her leg.

She licked her lips and mustered up the courage to turn her head so she could look at his profile, her own longing already eating a hole in her soul. Asif's face was lit by the setting sun, and Chanté did her best to memorize him from this angle. When he'd disappeared from her life two years ago, she remembered what she could, but every day, she'd felt like she forgot something about him — something she'd loved.

She didn't want to do that again.

"Is it gonna be another two years before I see you?" she asked. She tried to make her voice sound light, unfazed even, but she failed. She sounded like she was on the verge of tears. Because she was.

Asif eased the car to a stop. Behind his head, she could see her and Kenny's local grocery store. She knew he was parked in front of her apartment, but she refused to budge. She wanted an answer, even though she already knew what it was.

Asif squeezed her thigh before moving his hand to the buckle holding her seatbelt in place at the same time as his left hand undid his own seatbelt.

As soon as she was free, Chanté climbed over the center console into Asif's lap. She didn't care about embarrassing herself; she just didn't want to forget him, and she was desperate for him not to forget her.

Asif leaned his seat back, making room for her in his lap. She wanted more than this, but she'd take whatever she could get. "When do you graduate?" he asked as his hands gently cupped her face.

"What do you care?"

He sighed softly and cupped the back of her neck with his right hand. "I think you'd be surprised. But I was asking to make a point."

"The only point I want is the tip of your dick."

He laughed. "You haven't had enough?"

"Never."

His smile dimmed. "Soon. You can graduate and move to a different city. You can forget all about me in a few weeks if you wanted."

"*If* I wanted. I don't."

He pulled her forward, and she inhaled his soft breath. "I wish you did," he mumbled against her bottom lip.

Chanté rolled her eyes and sucked his tongue into her mouth. He didn't kiss her like he wanted to be forgotten. Chanté had kissed a lot of people, but Asif was the only one who'd ever kissed her like he wanted to imprint himself on her soul — and he succeeded.

But the thing that made her tear up while their lips pressed together was the fear that he'd never let her give any of that back.

She could feel him pulling away in increments. Her heart broke by the same measure.

"I'll walk you upstairs."

She licked her lips, the word 'stay' sitting on the very tip of her tongue. The sharp pressure of tears at the back of her eyes hurt. She nodded silently but refused to let go.

Asif didn't rush her. He rubbed her back and hips while

she clung onto him until she didn't think she'd burst into tears, which took a while. By the time they crawled from his car, it was pitch black, and Chanté shivered on the sidewalk. Asif threw his arm over her shoulders and led her to the front of her apartment building.

She started to reach for the keypad to unlock the door, but Asif beat her to it.

She watched him key in her code in confusion. "How do you know that?" she asked as the door unlocked and he pulled it open.

He kissed her forehead, and she could feel his smile on her skin. "A little birdy told me," he lied, pushing her gently ahead of him into the building.

She didn't want to leave the warmth of his arms and was happy when he grabbed onto her again. They clung to one another all the way to her floor. He matched her slow pace from the elevator to her door, but no matter how slow her steps, unless she stopped walking completely, it could only take so long. Still, he didn't rush her.

"Do you have a key to my apartment too?" she asked, pretending as if she wasn't falling apart internally.

He squeezed her to his side. "You'd like that, wouldn't you?"

She wrapped both arms around his waist and slipped her cold hand under the hem, feeling his hot skin against her palm. He hissed at her touch. "I'd like a lot of things you won't give me," she said, dropping her mask completely.

He wrapped both arms around her. "I know, sweetheart. Trust that it's for the best."

"No," she whispered.

He smiled against her forehead, squeezing her one more time before pulling away.

Chanté swayed at the loss of his touch. She felt pathetic, but she leaned into that since she couldn't lean into him anymore.

He reached into his pocket and pulled out the check from all those hours ago. She wanted it, but not as much as she wanted him.

He slipped that piece of paper into her pocket. "Unlock the door. Go to bed. You'll feel better in the morning after you deposit this."

She lifted her gaze to look at him. "Where will you be in the morning?"

He smiled sadly and shrugged. "No idea." He grabbed her face gently with both hands and brushed her cheeks with his thumbs. "But I'll be thinking about you," he added.

"Thinking about me," she said in a small, sad whisper, but she wanted to ask why he wouldn't just stay.

"That's all I can give," he said. Chanté appreciated his willingness to find new ways to let her down as gently as he could.

She nodded and turned her head to kiss the palm of his hand and then his hands fell away. She blinked back tears again as she rummaged in her purse for her keys. He stayed while she unlocked and pushed open the door. She started to turn around, but he stopped her with a strong grip on her arms.

Asif breathed deep inside her curls before shoving his face into the side of her neck. His kiss was firm but fleeting, and it broke her heart.

He moved his mouth to her ear. "Don't ever let anyone give you a penny less than you deserve," he whispered before letting her go.

She stood just inside her door and listened to the sound

of Asif's footsteps fade away. She stayed there until he was gone. Until even the sound of him was a quickly fading memory, hoping he'd come back. He didn't.

When she finally mustered the courage to speak, she called out for Kenny. "Honey, I'm home." Their apartment was pitch black and dead silent. She'd hoped he was just in his room. She didn't want to be alone tonight.

She locked the door behind her and turned on every light in the living room and kitchen. She grabbed a bottle of water from the refrigerator and chugged half of it. She'd already come and cried a lot today and she planned to cry for most of the night. What was the point of being young if she couldn't dramatically fall apart over the unavailable man she was sure was the love of her life?

Chanté

+

Asif

THIRTY

"ONE MORE," Chanté huffed. She was out of breath, covered in sweat — hers and Asif's — and far more. She could have died happy in that moment, but she was greedy.

When it came to Asif, Chanté had to be greedy; she'd learned to hoard bits and pieces of him whenever he was close. Old habits die hard, especially when it felt so good to take all she could from him.

She'd been riding him for so long, her strong thighs were starting to hurt. Such a rare occurrence after years on the pole, but she was still going.

"You keep saying that," Asif moaned, arching his back as she dug her knees into the mattress and bore down on him. His hands were wrapped in the sheets as if they could give him the strength to survive this.

Watching him flail as another orgasm rushed forward only heightened Chanté's excitement. She rolled her hips on top of him, squeezing his length tight inside her. "Shit," she hissed in a low moan. Her muscles locked as one more orgasm wracked through her. Chanté threw her head back and sighed — she was too tired to even cry out anymore.

Chanté's palms were flat on his chest, her long nails scratching at his skin, the bright colors of her nail polish contrasting with his dark black chest hair and brown skin. She'd had enough dreams like this that the thrill of it alone gave her enough energy to bounce on him with just a little more vigor. She might regret this in a few hours when she was trying to balance in her heels, but that was a problem for later.

When her muscles finally relaxed, she dropped her head and smiled down at Asif.

He was blinking up at the ceiling with his own slack-jawed smile spreading his lips.

"One more?" she panted back again.

He opened his mouth, and she felt his stomach rise and fall at the apex of her thighs in silent laughter. It took a few moments for him to catch his breath and drop his chin to his chest.

She raised her eyebrows and smiled back.

Asif unwound his hands from the sheets and smoothed his sweaty palms up her thighs. His pupils were completely blown. His long hair was stuck to his forehead and along his cheeks. He was trembling beneath her. The realization that she'd done this to him — that he was falling apart because of her — made her feel light enough to float.

"One more," he groaned in a voice gone husky with lust. His fingers moved to her hips and dug into her flesh.

Chanté groaned and scooted her knees in close to his sides and pressed her hands into his chest, lifting her ass from his body. She could feel his heart racing underneath her fingertips. Asif's eyes were trained on her. She lowered herself slowly, watching as his eye twitched.

She lifted up again, even slower than the first time. He licked his lips, and she bounced back down his length.

This time when he groaned, the muscles in his neck strained through his skin and his jaw tightened. His fingers dug into her flesh hard enough to bruise. She wanted it to bruise. She wanted to remember this time with him any way she could.

"That all you got?" His laughter cut off with a groan and his stomach tightened.

Chanté lifted an eyebrow. "You look like you might not survive if I give you any more."

This time she heard his laughter and felt it. But it was the smile on his face that really got to her.

Asif lifted his shoulders from the bed and moved his hands around to the small of her back and pulled her forward. Chanté groaned as her back bowed, watching as he covered her right nipple with his mouth and sucked. She started bouncing on top of him, short and quick, just enough to keep them both on the edge.

He finally released her nipple with one last hard suck and kissed his way up her chest. "Of all the ways I thought I'd die, this is the best. Hands down." He licked the base of her throat. "If I had to choose," he whispered. "It would always be you."

Chanté wrapped her arms around Asif's shoulders, and he held her around the waist. She pressed her hips forward and shivered through a short but powerful orgasm. Asif kissed along her jaw.

"If you think I'm gonna let you go that easily," she panted, pushing him back onto the bed.

His hands moved back to her hips and he gripped her waist, helping her to start bouncing on top of him for real this time. They both groaned.

He started to lift his hips up into her, and the sound of their flesh slapping together intensified. The things this room had seen over the last few days were a gift. She'd remember every detail.

Asif pulled her down to his chest. "I've been trying to get you to let me go for a decade," he whispered, then barely swallowed a groan.

"You ready to stop yet?" she panted.

He wrapped a hand around her neck. His eyes started to water. She rode him faster.

"I'm never gonna be ready to put you in danger."

"Good," she moaned. "I'm too pretty to get shot."

"You are," he said, staring deep into her eyes. "You're too pretty to wonder if I'm going to make it home." It took a lot of effort for him to get those words out. She knew his orgasm was coming on fast, and she wanted it. She wanted to feel the sweet crush of his arms around her as he held her close and roared in her ear when he came. She wanted the satisfaction of knowing that they were in this together. She'd always wanted exactly that, and it was close enough she could taste it on her tongue, feel it deep in her pussy, and knew it deep down in her soul. But she also needed to make something plain.

"Then the answer is to take me with you," she added, in gasping, halting breaths. "That way, I can make sure you always make it home to me." Asif opened his mouth to say something, but she covered his lips with hers.

Chanté grabbed onto Asif's shoulders for more leverage and started to pull herself up his shaft before slamming down into his lifted hips again. She knew Asif well enough to know that he would argue. On this, he always seemed to have the energy to fight. But they could do that later. Right now, there were more important things at hand.

Chanté held on tight to his body, and for the first time in all their years together, she fucked Asif the way she'd always wanted — desperately, hungrily, happily.

"Zip me up, please," Chanté sang.

He still couldn't believe she'd managed to wiggle her way into the gold dress, but he'd enjoyed the fuck out of watching her do it.

"Asif," Chanté cried sharply.

"What?" His gaze jumped from her ass to her face.

She was standing in front of the mirror, looking at him over her shoulder.

His eyes only met hers for a second because he'd noticed the bare expanse of her back and needed to see more.

An hour ago, he'd been watching his fingers dig into her soft skin while he fucked into her with every ounce of energy he had. But he'd been dreaming about kissing every inch of her — pretending he didn't have a care in the world. He'd never had a dream like that before.

"After," Chanté said.

Asif's eyes jumped to hers again and he forced a smile on his face. He pushed up to his feet. "Is that a promise?" he teased, walking slowly toward her.

She watched him walk and moved her tongue over her

bottom lip. "Every word I've ever said to you was a promise," she whispered.

His heart throbbed at her words. He'd only ever felt like this about Chanté. His fingers were shaking when they touched the zipper at the small of her back. She lifted her eyes to look up at him, and he couldn't help but smile at the perfection of her brown eyes and the adorable snub nose that immediately caught his attention the night they met.

But he couldn't say it back.

He couldn't tell her he'd ever done anything but lie to her. He couldn't even promise that he'd stop. So, he moved her zipper up her spine while his right index finger led the way.

Chanté's eyes fluttered closed, and her bottom lip popped from between her teeth, wet and plump. His dick was too weak to respond, but he tried. He felt her shudder under his touch, so he slowed down.

A faint smile spread along her mouth just before she turned away. His eyes moved to her reflection. She reached back and moved her hair out of the way of the zipper as Asif reluctantly pulled it closed.

"Promise me one more thing?" he asked, moving his hands over her shoulders.

Her eyes lit up, and she nodded once.

He let himself frown now. "If things go left, you get out of there."

"Don't," Chanté whispered back.

He pressed his face into her curls. They smelled citrusy clean — a familiar scent.

"Even if it means you leave me," Asif said. He could've looked away and spared them both the sadness of all they saw in one another's eyes, but she deserved better than that.

"No," she said.

He pressed a kiss into the depths of her big hair and squeezed her shoulders. "I'll buy you a pair of Swarovski-encrusted heels. Six inches."

Chanté gasped. "Diabolical," she whispered.

He leaned to the right around the halo of her hair and kissed her playfully on her cheek. And then he turned to the mirror. "Promise me."

She rolled her eyes but couldn't help but smile. "Fine," she said. "We look cute."

He wrapped his left arm around her waist. "We do." He squinted at her reflection. "And you look like you don't have any underwear on."

She laughed and shrugged him off. "What the fuck does that look like?" she asked, rounding on him.

He couldn't help but laugh back. "Like you. Am I right?"

"That's honestly none of your business," she shot back, but then shrugged. "For argument's sake," she corrected.

"Of course," he nodded with a mischievous smile. He bent forward to reach for the hem of her skirt. "But let's pretend."

She laughed happily. Like *really* happily. When he left, he'd try to remember this over all the times she'd cried over him.

"You think we have ti—" She didn't even get to finish the question before four quick raps on the hotel door announced Marcel's return. They both frowned at it.

"I'll let him in," she said with a smile.

He nodded and stepped back. She took a couple of steps toward the door before doubling back and jumping into Asif's arms. "After," she laughed and pressed a quick kiss on his mouth.

She tried to turn quickly away, but he held on and kissed her just a bit longer — just a bit harder — before reluctantly letting her go.

He watched her as she ran from the room, waiting until she was far enough away before pulling out his phone.

"Bob's Rent-to-Own," Carlisle yawned.

"You could do better," Asif said.

"I'll take that into advisement. What do you want?"

"Where are you?"

"In town," he said simply.

Asif frowned. "You are?"

"Kenny thought you might need some backup," Carlisle said, "and he didn't want to be the one to come save you."

"Asshole."

"Definitely. What do you need?"

"Hopefully, nothing."

"But in reality?"

"If anything happens to me, get Chanté the hell out of here."

Carlisle laughed. "Kenny already gave me those orders."

"What about me?" Asif asked.

"He said you'd probably be fine."

"Probably?" Asif laughed.

"Yup. See ya," Carlisle said before hanging up.

Asif shook his head. "Hopefully not."

"Hey," Marcel said, leaning into the bedroom. Asif turned to him and slipped his phone into his pocket. "Ready to go?"

Asif put on his best smile and grabbed at his lapels. "Obviously."

The other man laughed but looked him over.

"After!" Chanté screamed from the living room.

Marcel laughed again and turned from the doorway.

Asif glanced at his reflection quickly before following. He took a deep breath before walking into the living room in just enough time to watch Chanté shove something into the bodice of her dress. She bounced on the balls of her feet. Asif groaned at the sight.

She smiled at him. "Making sure it won't fall out," she laughed.

"What even was that?"

"A tracker," she said.

"Good. That way you can't slip away." He leaned against the desk and crossed his hands in front of his lap.

She scrunched her nose. "Sorry, it's not for me. If I can't convince Kay to come with me, I'm going to put this on her." She frowned and squinted her eyes. "Or maybe in her bag? But that's risky. I don't know, I'll figure it out."

Asif had to take a deep breath in and out through his nose. He didn't trust himself to open his mouth.

She shrugged. "I have something for you, though," she said.

He raised his eyes. "Did you decide to stay here?"

"No." She walked across the room to him. Their shoulders brushed. He turned to watch her.

She was rummaging around on the desk, trying not to smile. He always loved the way she blushed under his gaze.

Finally, she turned toward him. He was staring at her face, her long eyelashes, her dark eyeliner, the curve of her nose. He couldn't look away.

Her lashes fluttered as she lost the battle to hide her smile when she finally lifted her gaze to his.

"I want you safe," he whispered.

She sighed. "We talked about this."

"We can talk about it again and you can change your mind."

"No, thank you," she said. "But because I'm a solution-oriented person, I have this," she added, lifting the box in her hands up for his attention.

His gaze dropped and his eyelashes lifted in quick succession. "Do you have something to ask me?" he asked, angling his body toward her and reaching for the box.

"Don't you wish," she whispered.

He smiled and moved the pad of his left index finger over the cool metal of one gold ring. "Maybe I do," he said, looking up at the sound of her sharp gasp. "What am I looking at here?"

Chanté licked her lips and swallowed slowly. "A tracker," she said cheerily.

"Another one?" He shook his head.

"Two, actually," she corrected. She lifted her hand and pointed at the thicker metal ring with one nail. "This one's for you." She moved her nail to the other ring. "And this one's for me."

"How does this work?" he asked, dipping his head closer to hers.

She swallowed again and her eyes dipped to his mouth. "Um... It's..." He stood from the table and turned fully toward her.

They stared into one another's eyes.

"I'm nervous to tell you," she whispered.

"Why?"

She pressed her lips together in a grimace and shrugged sadly. He couldn't count how many times she'd looked at him like this. How many times he'd caused her to look at him like this. "I'm worried if I tell you, you'll run away."

He couldn't blame her for that and he didn't have a response — at least not one that would ease her anxiety. All he could do was nod and not lie to her. "I'm not going to run out of here right now," he said. Her face fell and she grabbed for the box, but he moved it out of her reach. "But if you tell me what this is, I promise not to take it off. Ever."

Her eyes lit up, and her smile was infectious. "Seriously?"

"Seriously."

She licked her lips nervously, but he could also see her gathering the courage to speak. He'd always loved that about her. "So, it's really simple, actually. We put these on, and if one of us goes missing, we can track each other."

"You're the hacker, not me," he said.

She rolled her eyes. "You have access to lots of engineers who could do it for you, although if you want it done quick, call Caleb."

Asif raised his eyebrows. "He hates me."

She nodded. "A lot. But he loves me. He also knows his way around my code. Some of the other agency techs are going to need a little time to get past my firewalls." She seemed proud of that, and he was proud of her.

"Got it. If I lose track of you, I'll contact the only person who'd put a hit out on me for making you cry."

"Don't be dramatic. I can think of at least three other people who'd do that. Kenny, for one," she laughed.

"Good point. Alright," he said, reaching for the ring.

"Wait," she said, putting her hands up. "There's one more thing."

"Did you think of more people who want to kill me?"

"No," she said. "I mean, we could be here all day."

He smiled. "So what?"

"Um, these...rings do something else besides just track."

He raised his eyebrows. "I'm listening."

"Um, it'll be easier to experience it than explain." She tentatively plucked the larger ring from the box and met his gaze, but only for a moment before her eyes shifted away. "Give me your hand. Your...um, left hand."

Asif's eyebrows were practically in his hairline now as he lifted his hand for her to take. Her fingers were warm, dry, and trembling, but she held it together. He, on the other hand, held his breath as Chanté held onto his hand and slowly slipped her tracker down his ring finger.

His eyes were riveted on her face again — her wet lips, the sharp edge of her winged eyeliner, all the details he'd never stayed around long enough to get his fill of.

"That it?" he asked.

Her eyes lifted quickly to his, but before they could shift away again, he moved his fingers under her chin and tipped her head back.

"Is that it, Chanté?"

She shook her head and lifted her hand to his wrist. "Put the other ring on me," she whispered.

Asif's heart was beating so hard against his chest it hurt. For the first time in a long time, he was speechless, but happy to do as she said.

He had to tear his eyes away from her face to look at the box, blinking at the ring for a few seconds before he could see it clearly and pluck it out. Once his fingers wrapped around the ring, though, the matching one on his finger caught his eye, and he froze for a few seconds as his brain tried to take it all in.

"Asif," she whispered.

He nodded and swallowed the lump in his throat and

snapped the box shut. Chanté jumped at the sound. He could hear his blood pumping in his veins.

She offered her hand to him eagerly. He took it just as eagerly. There was no hesitation as he steadied her shaking hand and slipped the ring onto her ring finger. But once it was snugly in place, he didn't let go. Instead, he turned it around her finger, loving the cool contrast to her skin. Fascinated at all it could mean but didn't.

He was just about to ask her what was next when he felt it.

His eyes jumped to her face.

A slow, beautiful, serene smile was spreading across her mouth. "When we're both wearing them, we can feel each other's heartbeat," she said, stepping closer.

He held onto her hand.

"I can track your physical location, which is fine," she said. "But I can know how you feel, too. And that's all I've ever really wanted."

"Chanté—" he started to say.

"Um, I'm still here," Marcel said, breaking the tension between them. "And we need to leave."

Chanté

+

Asif

THIRTY-ONE

"YOU HAVE SUCH AN INTERESTING FACE," Mia said as soon as she met him at the back entrance.

"Is that a compliment?" Asif asked. He knew the answer to his question, but he didn't have to feign confusion because what a weird way to greet someone.

Sure, he'd once been stabbed as a hello, but it hadn't nicked any arteries and at least attempted murder was direct. He fucking hated microaggressions.

"We will see, I guess," Mia said, smiling smugly at him. She lifted her hand slowly, but Asif ducked out of her grasp. He also hated when white women touched his hair without his permission.

"Possibly," he replied.

"How may I help you...?" She let that question dissipate slowly.

It took him a second to realize that she didn't remember his name. "Yusuf," he offered.

Her only response was raised eyebrows.

"We met—"

"I remember that. Why are you here?"

Mia was very lucky that, contrary to popular belief, Asif was very well-trained because he fought the urge to punch her with a smile. "We don't know one another well, so suffice it to say that I never let money go cold." He batted his eyelashes to punctuate his point.

Mia didn't move for an uncomfortably long moment, but Asif was unbothered. He waited until her face lifted as she smiled.

"Then you are definitely in the right place," she said, stepping to her right for Asif to enter the building.

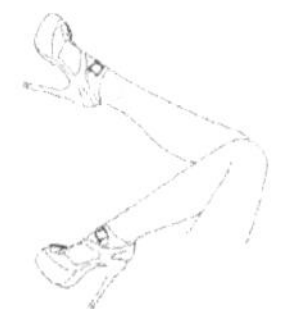

"He'll be fine," Marcel whispered into Chanté's ear as they approached the door of Mia's club.

"I know," she said in a tight voice. She moved her right hand to her left and turned the ring on her finger. It was faint, but she could feel the steady thrum of his pulse. It wasn't as good as having her eyes on him, but it was something. Something that made a faint smile cross her lips. "I know," she whispered again.

Marcel rushed past her to the front door. It was at least eight feet tall, carved wood and metal. Gaudy. Exactly what Chanté expected from someone like Mia.

He grabbed the handle and turned to her. "Ready?" he said.

Chanté turned her ring one more time before meeting his eyes. "Do you ever have a moment where you realize that your life is weird as hell?" she asked.

He smiled. "Yes, but this is all I know. And if it's my normal, can it really be weird?"

She smiled. "The power of positive thinking," she whispered.

Marcel shrugged and offered his arm to Chanté. "Something like that."

She grabbed onto his forearm as he pulled the door open. "In and out," she said. Marcel choked as an embarrassed smile split his lips. "I didn't mean it like that," she cried in exasperation.

Chanté stepped out of the cold, shivering as warm air hit her cool skin.

The reception area was close, intimate, and probably made it easier to check the flow of human traffic. There was a reception desk to the right, with a tall, pale woman with long, dark hair and soft makeup smiling in their direction. Chanté smiled back at the woman as she caught a shadow move just behind the desk. Security. After a decade dancing in clubs, she normally would have taken some relief in that, but since she was here to hopefully bring this entire building down — metaphorically — she simply noted the shadowy presence and moved on.

"Hello," the receptionist said in a sultry voice that was more than pleasing to Chanté's ears.

"Hi," she said in the high-pitched, perky voice that never failed to throw people off solid ground. Most people didn't expect that tone of voice from her and Chanté loved the unexpected. "We're here to see Kay," she said.

The woman frowned as she blinked at her. "Is Kay expecting you?"

Chanté shrugged. "She might be. She might not."

The security guard moved from the shadows.

"Oh. Hello," Chanté called to him.

The guard didn't have a response, but Marcel moved closer to Chanté's back, angling himself at her left side. He wasn't fully between her and the guard, but he could be soon enough. She couldn't imagine why Asif was so resistant to backup. Chanté loved it, especially because she really didn't know what the hell she was doing in the field once people pulled out guns and fists.

"What is your name?" the receptionist asked.

"Chanté," she said and then spelled her name slowly.

The woman looked down at whatever notes she had on the tablet in her hands. Chanté watched a flurry of emotions pass over her face before a fake smile appeared and she lifted her head. "I see your name on the white list," she said. "Our owner asked us to treat you like a VIP when you arrived."

Chanté's face lit up. "Oooh, so exciting."

The receptionist smiled. "Let me get someone to show you to your table."

Chanté nodded. "Kay?" she asked again.

The woman nodded. "She is preparing to perform."

Chanté gasped in surprise. She was putting it on a bit thick, but what did she care if this woman thought she was acting strange? She was. And in her experience, Marcel was right. The barometer for strangeness in strip clubs was heavily skewed, no matter where she was in the world.

"Please, wait here. I will have someone take you to your seat."

Chanté widened her smile and batted her eyes. She could feel Marcel's stress wafting off him, but Chanté was a master at not letting other people's emotions affect her mood. Besides, if all hell broke loose, she didn't plan to break a nail, so what did she have to frown about, really?

She pretended to be admiring the artwork on the wall by the door for the next few minutes while Marcel and the security guard stared at one another like exes who barely survived a bad breakup.

A soft gasp pulled her attention away from another painting of an ugly man. She turned toward the sound and made eye contact with a familiar face. "Inessa," she called.

"Betty," the girl cried back excitedly.

The receptionist looked between Chanté and the other girl before speaking to Inessa in Russian. Chanté didn't know if it was the language or a change in mood, but the woman's voice was no longer husky and alluring but harsh.

"Betty's my stage name," Chanté said quickly in Inessa's defense. "My real name is Chanté."

Inessa's excitement crumpled at the other woman's words before shaking her head quickly. She spoke in Russian before switching to English. "Betty...I mean Chanté is a dancer. She was at the Menagerie just a few days ago." She turned toward Chanté with a renewed smile on her face. "She was amazing."

Chanté's cheeks warmed and she batted at the air as she walked toward her. She grabbed Inessa's hands and squeezed. "I love compliments."

Inessa giggled, and Marcel's deeper chuckle bounced around the stone room. She wasn't sure, but she even thought she heard a gruff rumble from the guard.

"Will you be dancing here?" Chanté asked Inessa. "I still haven't seen your moves."

Inessa shook her head quickly. "I'm not ready." Chanté remembered that feeling, but she hated the way the girl's eyes shifted to her left in the receptionist's direction. She couldn't blame the girl for her lack of confidence, but she could blame the dancers here and at the Menagerie for not making things easier. The girls at The Petal weren't perfect, but they'd made Chanté's transition into dancing better than she could have hoped.

Clearly Inessa didn't have that kind of support, and it made Chanté sad.

"Are you waitressing?" Chanté asked, pulling Inessa's attention back to her.

"Oh. Yes. Yes. Come, I will show you to your table."

Chanté squeezed her hands one more time before letting her go. She turned to indicate to Marcel that he should follow them, and she spared a withering look toward the receptionist before following Inessa down a short hallway, through another heavy, ornate door into a dark room that was as different from The Petal as she could imagine, and yet, she felt right at home.

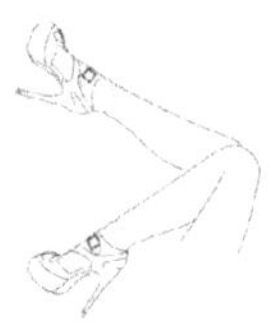

"This DJ ain't too bad," Chanté mumbled to herself, straining her neck trying to see over the top of the crowd toward the DJ booth.

"Please try not to be so conspicuous," Marcel whispered.

"Huh? Oh, sorry. But you don't know how hard it is to find a good DJ."

He frowned at her words. She thought about explaining her predicament, but now wasn't the time. She could explain herself later.

She winked and turned back to the room. The VIP booths were situated along the left wall, giving them as good a view of the lower floor — dotted with small round tables — and the circular stage at the head of the room. Chanté's booth was as close to the stage as it was possible to get without being on it.

It had been years since Chanté had danced at a club where she wasn't a featured guest. Years since she'd had to work the floor to get the real money in private dances. Years since she'd had to share a dressing room with strangers. Years since the money she made dancing paid her bills. Dancing had given her freedom, and as much as she loved it, hacking couldn't compare to the rush of blood she got on stage.

Chanté never felt more beautiful, graceful, or free than when she was spinning around a pole.

But as she sat back in the booth, trying not to seem too excited, she realized that she so rarely got to see clubs like this anymore. She missed her days as a waitress when she would take all her breaks at the bar so she could watch the girls' routines. And then she remembered the night she met Asif.

All roads in Chanté's brain and heart led to Asif.

She moved her right hand back to the ring on her left hand.

The lights dimmed. Chanté's eyes moved to the stage. She gasped softly and held her breath, but no one else even bothered to lower their voice. Chanté was disgusted. As much as she loved stripping, she really hated how much her experience of any given club was based on the crowd, and this crowd sucked.

She watched with clear-eyed focus as Kay stepped on stage.

"Well, this is a wonderful surprise."

Chanté might not have noted that voice if Marcel hadn't

stiffened by her side. She turned her head away from the stage to find Raphael and Sonja standing next to their booth. Chanté let her gaze move down Sonja's body. Even though it couldn't have been more than ten degrees Fahrenheit outside, the other woman was wearing a sparkly gold mini dress with an A-line silhouette. "You were made to wear gold," Chanté gushed.

"You're too kind," Sonja smiled.

"Doesn't mean I'm not right," Chanté said.

Sonja laughed prettily and nodded.

A figure came around Raphael's other side. Chanté only had enough time to register that he looked familiar before he was walking up to the booth, claiming the seat next to her.

"Joseph, right?" she said, bouncing slightly on the seat to back away.

"You remember me?" he said softly.

Chanté didn't love his tone of voice. She shrugged her shoulders. "I have an excellent memory."

"A woman of many talents," Joseph said.

Goosebumps erupted over Chanté's skin, but not in a good way. She felt cold, and a knot formed in her stomach. Chanté knew what danger felt like.

"Do you mind if we join you?" Raphael asked, already pulling a chair out for Sonja to sit.

Chanté nodded politely as Joseph filled her peripheral vision, inching closer.

She made unexpected eye contact with Sonja, and the woman smiled in a way Chanté recognized. Another woman who wanted to be anywhere else but here.

Chanté

+

Asif

THIRTY-TWO

"DO YOU WORK ALONE?" Mia asked.

"Never," Asif said. "But I am new to Russia and always looking for business partners."

Mia was leading him down a plain hallway. Asif hated going into buildings blind, but they hadn't had time for Chanté to dig up any blueprints. Well, they'd had time, they just chose to use it otherwise. All he knew was that he was heading deeper into the building and could encounter anything in these rooms and no one would know.

He reached for the ring on his left hand, twirling it in a circle.

Chanté would know.

Her heartbeat was steady, and that settled Asif's nerves. "What about you?" he asked. "Do you work alone?"

"On some endeavors," she replied quickly. "But as you said, I never want to leave money on the table."

Asif squinted. "Are you American?" he asked.

She stopped and turned fully around. "How did you know?"

Asif feigned excitement. "Your accent? I grew up watching American telly and film. I've always wanted to visit. What brought you to Russia?"

"Family connections," she said with a shrug. "That, and it's easier to do some of the work I want here than at home."

Asif nodded. "That makes sense."

"You've never been to the States?" she asked, narrowing her eyes at him.

Asif's heart rate spiked but only for a few beats before he managed to regain his composure. "No, but I hope to in the next year. I'm just not sure where I should visit first."

"Where were you thinking?" Mia asked.

Asif's face lit up. "Everyone says New York or Los Angeles, but I really want to visit Chicago."

Mia gave him a broad smile. "Excellent choice. I love Chicago. I've thought about opening a club there."

"It seems like we might have a few things in common."

"It seems so," she said. "Come. Let's have a drink and discuss."

They walked a few more feet down the hallway. Mia pushed a door open, and Asif took a deep breath before plunging into the unknown. Thankfully, all he found through the door was a warm, surprisingly cozy office with a small window on one side. The window was cracked, but the room was still warm thanks to a small fireplace in the corner. It wasn't a roaring fire, but for such a small room, Asif found the heat nearly unbearable. He shifted uncomfortably, pulling at the neck of his shirt.

"Have a seat," Mia said, gesturing toward the seat in front of him.

A sharp pulse radiated around his left ring finger. He reached for the ring and focused on Chanté's rapidly beating heart. When he started to sweat, it wasn't because of the fire.

"Is everything alright?" Mia asked.

She was standing just a few steps in front of him, watching him with amusement that could easily shift.

Technically, Asif had a choice, but in the end, it wasn't anything of the sort. "I'm fine," he said. "A drink?"

"Ah, yes." She turned to a large ornate cart. "What would you like?"

As soon as her back was to him, he reached into his pocket. There were a few things Asif kept on him at all times. The watch from Chanté, a SIM card tucked into the lining of his left shoe, and a small but powerful taser pen that looked like a pen light.

It wouldn't kill anyone — unless they had a pacemaker — but for the right target, it would put them down for the count.

Mia was the right target.

Asif let her crumple to the ground in a heap. He thought about arranging her comfortably, but he remembered the look on Chanté's face when describing the bruises on Kay's body. Mia would wake up in a half-hour or so with a stiff neck and bruises and she'd be lucky that was it.

Asif pulled his cell phone from his other pocket. He dialed Carlisle's number and the other man picked up quickly.

"So is Chanté still hung up on you or do you think I have a chance?" Carlisle said by way of greeting.

Asif sighed in frustration, and of course, Carlisle laughed. Sometimes, even Asif was surprised he and his fellow agents ever got anything accomplished. "Where are you?"

"Nearby," he said simply. "Waiting on the call."

"This is the call," Asif ground out.

"Cool. For what?"

"Covert extraction and extradition," Asif said.

"I was hoping for something a little more exciting," Carlisle sighed.

"You would."

"Does that mean you don't need me to rescue Chanté?"

"Yes," Asif ground out, his fingers going to that ring again. "That's exactly what this means."

"Damn. Where are you?"

Asif turned away from Mia's body and walked to the fireplace.

"There's a fireplace in this room."

"I hate to break it to you, but there are three chimneys," Carlisle said.

"No problem." Asif bent down to the hearth and pulled the damper open. He started to stoke the fire. "Check for smoke," Asif said and then disconnected the call. He couldn't wait for Carlisle to get it together.

He needed to know what had Chanté's heartbeat running a marathon. But first, he moved to Mia's desk, opening drawers until he found a loaded gun strapped to the side of the drawer to her left. He shoved it into the back of his pants and rushed from the room.

CHANTÉ DIDN'T REMEMBER MUCH ABOUT KAY AS A person, but once she started dancing, she remembered her well. It had been years since either of them had worked at The Petal — years since The Petal had shut down — but she could still see the telltale touches of the kind of show those customers used to like. Kay moved around the stage like she owned it, she made strong eye contact with people who looked like they might have heavy pockets, and most of all, she still looked strong. The people who trekked their way downtown to visit The Petal didn't want a dancer made of skin and bones. They liked fat asses, muscles, and a good soundtrack, and so did Chanté.

Unfortunately, all Kay's talent and ass were wasted on this crowd.

And even more unfortunately, Joseph was sitting right in Chanté's line of sight, and no matter how many times she inched away from him, patently ignoring his presence, he refused to get the hint.

The men were talking to one another, and Chanté was doing her best not to let the fact that they refused to even engage her or Sonja in their conversation grate her nerves. Just because she didn't want to talk to them didn't mean she wanted to be excluded.

She turned to Sonja, looking to commiserate, but the other woman was staring straight ahead with a placid smile frozen on her face, which made Chanté sigh. She didn't know for sure if the woman was on something, but she'd seen similar kinds of dead-eyed stares over the years and they were always so sad. She turned to the stage just as Kay turned her back to the crowd and pulled her corset open. And then the lights went out. Chanté sighed sadly. She wasn't in the mood for burlesque.

But then a hand snaked onto her thigh and she jumped

in her seat while slapping the hand away. "What the fuck?" she screamed.

"Betty?" Marcel's voice was full of concern behind her. She'd scooted herself fully across the bench into his side.

The lights came on and Chanté was glaring at Joseph full-on while he aimed a lecherous smile back.

"Touch me again and I'll make sure every bone in that hand never heals correctly," she hissed.

"Betty?" Marcel asked again, his voice still soft but a note of warning edging at the margins.

She didn't even glance in Marcel's direction because she honestly didn't trust Joseph enough to take her eyes off him. She hated men like him. Over the course of her career, she'd danced for a number of them. But once she started naming her fee just to show up at a club, she refused to even look their way. Men like Joseph didn't understand the word no.

They thought in terms of power.

In pain.

"Is everything alright?" Raphael called in an annoying tone of voice she connected to rich people devoid of a moral compass — asking a question to which they didn't want an answer. Chanté didn't dance for men like him either.

"Things will be perfectly fine whenever your friend learns some manners. Some morals." She brushed a hand over the part of her leg the man had touched.

She felt dirty. And angry. And somewhere, deep down, there was a small puddle of fear.

She'd been trying so hard not to think about Asif, but she couldn't help but let her thoughts stray to him. Chanté was lucky enough to rarely feel danger, but when she did, it was impossible to drown that sprig of hope that Asif would appear out of nowhere to save her.

"Ah, there's Yusuf," Raphael cried. "Now this is a party."

Chanté tore her eyes away from Joseph. There was a chance her desperate imagination had made that up, but there was always a chance it hadn't.

Her eyes found him immediately in the crowd.

In the warm, dim light, he was perfect. Dark suit, dark eyes, his long dark hair down around his shoulders, gaze entirely focused on her.

He was real.

And he was hers.

She always knew that, but for the first time in all the years they'd known one another, Chanté thought Asif had finally realized that it was true.

Chanté

+

Asif

THIRTY-THREE

"RIGHT ON TIME," Dr. Schuller said as soon as Chanté walked through the classroom door.

"Not late. Not early," she trilled. It had become their thing over the course of the semester. Dr. Schuller was an expert in cyber espionage, and Chanté had arranged her entire semester around getting into his class. They hadn't been sure what to make of one another — him, an old white man who'd been middle-aged before the internet existed, and her walking into class in tall heels with a face full of makeup — but they'd managed to forge a relationship over time. She hadn't officially asked Dr. Schuller to supervise her thesis project, but she could tell he knew it was coming.

He was the only reason she'd managed to drag herself out of bed to come to class when she really just wanted to burrow under the covers and masturbate to memories of Asif. Thankfully, today's class would be short. Dr. Schuller believed in practical training and expected everyone to find and secure a summer internship, and today was just a check-in.

Chanté wasn't actually interested in doing an internship, especially not in the summer when the money at strip clubs would be at its best. But if she could get Dr. Schuller as her advisor, she'd find some rinky-dink internship at a bank or something.

Chanté slipped into a seat in the front row, crossed her legs, and tried not to cry.

"Alright, let's start, shall we?" Dr. Schuller was standing at the front of the class between the chalkboard and the wooden desk, both items of furniture not just from another decade but another century. The man was in his element. "Now, who would like to update us on the internship search?"

Chanté sank down in her chair. She didn't have anything to present, and even if she did, she didn't trust herself to speak more than a few words. Thankfully, there were other people in the course with far less good will with their professor and much more enthusiasm than her. She was happy to ride out the next half-hour or so in a daze, and that's exactly what she did.

She pasted a blank look on her face, pretending to pay attention, but in her mind, she was replaying every moment she'd spent with Asif. Not just over the last couple of days, but since they met. There weren't nearly enough.

"Okay, that's all for today. Good progress. Don't forget to submit your extra credit before midnight. And I'll see you on Thursday."

Chanté blinked back into consciousness when the girl next to her knocked her shoulder with her backpack.

"Sorry," the girl said.

Chanté realized she didn't know the girl's name but smiled brightly. "No problem."

"Chanté," Dr. Schuller called. "Come see me, please."

Normally, Chanté loved when Dr. Schuller called her up after class. It usually meant he was going to tell her a classified story he shouldn't or that he had a bit of code he wanted to share since they both knew she was too advanced for this course. But her sadness was smothering the normal feelings of excitement. Still, she kept the smile on her face, grabbed her bag, and walked up to the desk.

"Hey, Dr. Schuller. Sorry if I was a little out of it today. I haven't been sleeping well," she said preemptively.

He batted at the air and picked up his worn leather briefcase from the desk. He gestured for her to follow him. "You didn't miss anything," he whispered as they walked from the room.

It didn't pull Chanté fully out of her funk, but she did manage to laugh lightly.

"You do look tired," he said, looking at her.

"Winter makes me blue," she said with a shrug.

"Oh, excellent language! Why did we ever stop using 'blue' for sad?"

"Before my time, old man," Chanté laughed.

"True. True," he sighed. "You're all so young."

She heard the wistfulness in his voice. Normally she didn't have a problem letting her professor get all nostalgic, but today wasn't the day. "What's up, Dr. Schuller? I have an appointment with the résumé lab in the Job Center." A lie, but a good one.

"That can wait. But I take that to mean that you haven't secured an internship yet?"

"Technically, no," she said. "But I believe my opportunity is right around the corner."

"The power of positive thinking," he said, nodding. They

were heading in the direction of his office and he ushered her around the next corner, past the stairwell, and down a narrow hallway full of faculty offices.

"But how interesting that my very best student seems to be the only one struggling to find a placement."

Chanté smiled and turned toward the hallway. Someone was sitting in a chair outside of the secretary's office; someone else pushed into the men's bathroom while a woman flipped through a brochure down the hall near Dr. Schuller's door. She took all this in while mentally dragging together the threads of an excuse she should have prepared in advance.

"I think it's less about finding an internship," she started, winging the fuck out of every word. "I just think that, you know, this is a really serious decision, right? And I don't want just *any* internship. I want a *great* internship. You know?"

She turned back to him with an oddly triumphant smile on her face. She thought she pulled that off.

Dr. Schuller's blank face suggested she might have been wrong. "I thought you might say something like that. And I think I might have a *great* opportunity for you."

Chanté was too tired to keep her smile in place. "Oh, I don't know, Dr. Schuller. You said searching for internships is an important skill. And I should, you know, make some contacts or...whatever."

Dr. Schuller laughed and reached into his pocket for his key ring.

"I thought you might say that as well. And you would normally be right. However, this opportunity is one I couldn't, in good conscience, let you pass up. Besides, nothing is guaranteed. You still have to interview."

If she'd been on top of her game, she might have been

able to dig her way out of this, but she was hurtling toward emotional rock bottom, so her best was way out of reach. "Can I think about it?" she asked, cringing softly.

"Of course," Dr. Schuller said, and Chanté exhaled. "You have five more steps to make up your mind."

"Huh?"

Dr. Schuller was looking forward. "You found me okay?" he called down the hallway.

Chanté turned to the hall to find the person who'd been flipping through the brochure watching their approach.

From a new angle and with more focus, Chanté realized the woman was South Asian, older than she might have guessed, and beautiful. Her hair was pulled back in a sleek, low ponytail. She was wearing a long, plain, but perfectly tailored black dress with a matching scarf around her shoulders.

"Of course, I found you easily," the woman said. Her voice was deep, husky even, which seemed like an odd combination considering the softness of her face, which immediately piqued Chanté's interest.

Dr. Schuller and the woman laughed, and Chanté laughed along with them out of nervousness.

"Three. Two. One," Dr. Schuller said as they came to a stop in front of his door. "Time's up, Chanté. What's your answer?"

"To what?"

He shook his head slowly. "The internship. Are you interested?"

"I don't even know what it is," she said, trying to wiggle out of this.

"And you won't know what it is unless you get the job," he said.

"That sounds heavy," she replied. "Do you really think I'm ready for all that?" She widened her eyes and the pitch of her voice, reminding him that she was quite young and immature. It didn't always get her out of sticky situations, but it rarely hurt.

"We do, actually," the woman replied.

Chanté looked at her, eyebrows bunched in confusion. "Who are you?"

"You can't know that either. Not unless you get the job," Dr. Schuller said.

"Wait," Chanté whispered.

"Tick tock," Dr. Schuller said.

"Seriously?" she whispered back.

For the first time in days, Chanté managed to push thoughts of Asif to the margins of her brain.

"What do you say, Chanté?" Dr. Schuller sang, laughing at the rhyme.

"Uh, um..." Chanté looked from Dr. Schuller to the woman and back again. Her brain was short-circuiting as she tried to weigh all the options.

Her professor was clearly enjoying watching her squirm, but the woman was so silent, Chanté might have forgotten she was there.

He shouldn't have mattered in this moment, but Asif was never too far from her mind. He wanted her to succeed. He wanted her to flourish without him.

She wanted him.

"Okay," she said, first to Dr. Schuller and then to the mysterious, nameless woman.

"Aha," Dr. Schuller said. "Good answer. I'll leave you to it."

He turned and started to retrace his steps.

"You're leaving me?" Chanté called after him.

Dr. Schuller turned, walking backward with a pep in his step. "You've got this, Chanté. You don't need any help to shine." He waved and turned, walking away without another word.

Chanté could feel tears building at the back of her eyes. Knowing Dr. Schuller thought so well of her was one thing, but wondering why Asif couldn't see her so clearly was another.

The woman cleared her throat.

Chanté blinked rapidly before turning to face her. She'd moved to Dr. Schuller's office door and was holding it open for her to walk inside.

Chanté took a deep breath, pushed her emotions to the side, plastered on her work smile, and took the first step into the room.

The woman followed her inside, shutting the door firmly behind her. She walked to the other side of Dr. Schuller's desk and sat, motioning for Chanté to do the same.

She had a serene smile on her face, but Chanté had the faint feeling that this woman could kill her if she wanted. She'd never felt that on a job interview before.

"You may call me Maryam," the woman said.

"Is that your real name?" Chanté whispered.

The woman's smile turned down at the corners. She looked mischievous and pulled Chanté into a quick confidence. "That's classified," she whispered.

Chanté squirmed excitedly in her seat. "Oh, I definitely want this job."

"That's great to hear," Maryam said. "Let's get started."

Chanté

+

Asif

THIRTY-FOUR

"GREAT MINDS THINK ALIKE, IT SEEMS," Asif said as he strolled up the steps toward their booth.

He smiled at the group, but his was focus was entirely on Chanté.

She looked pissed and her heartbeat was still pulsating around his ring finger. He tried to communicate an entire interview's worth of questions in his brief glances, but there wasn't enough time. And whatever she was trying to communicate to him in her own gaze, he couldn't read.

Raphael stood from his seat. "What brings you here?"

Asif shrugged. "Just a conversation with Mia," he said because it didn't make sense to lie unnecessarily.

"Excellent. I thought you two would get on."

Asif moved his attention back to Chanté.

"What'd you think of the performance?" he asked, just for a reason not to have to look away.

Chanté licked her lips and he could practically see her brain moving. "Parts of it were beautiful," she said, "but it could have been better."

"Is that a professional critique?" Asif asked.

Chanté blinked up at him with sad eyes, and he nodded quickly in understanding. He was just about to look away when her eyes slid to her left and she pressed her lips together. He nodded once and turned to Marcel, putting a smile on his face.

"I wish I had known you would be here, we could have come together." From the corner of his eye, Asif saw the smile bloom on Chanté's face, and he felt her heart rate begin to slow.

For his part, Marcel smoothed a hand down his shirt and cleared his voice, conveying his unease in his body.

"I feel like there's a story here," Raphael said with a hearty laugh. "I must have it."

Asif felt movement near his left side and turned to see Sonja leaning forward in her seat. Her gaze was focused on Marcel and she had the look of a statue coming to life. He couldn't see her face head-on, but Asif knew what an interested woman looked like.

"I'd like to hear this story as well," she purred.

When Asif turned back to Marcel, the man looked like he wanted to bury himself in the cushions of the couch, but his eyes didn't move from Sonja's face.

"Interesting," he muttered before turning fully to his right.

Joseph was staring at the side of Chanté's face, but as soon as he felt Asif's attention, he turned toward him with a frown.

"It's good to see you again," he said with a smile.

Joseph grimaced, and Asif assumed that was his best attempt at a smile that didn't make him look creepy as fuck.

"Would you like to sit?" he said and started to move toward Chanté.

Asif saw her tense and felt her heartbeat spike through his ring, and he caressed the metal with his thumb. "Actually, I wondered if you were interested in joining me at the bar," Asif said.

Joseph froze and his face went blank. Asif watched with glee as the man's slow, clunky brain processed the invitation. Unsurprisingly, when he finally caught up, his mouth turned down in disgust.

"No. Thank you," he spat out.

"I'll go to the bar with you, Yusuf," Chanté said in a soft, pretty voice he knew was meant to elicit money and nothing else.

He stared at Joseph for a few more seconds before turning toward her and offering her his hand. She stood quickly and reached for his fingers.

Asif's eyes flicked to Marcel, and he nodded quickly.

He hated to leave the man alone in the middle of this group but he trusted him enough to get out of here as soon as possible. He and Chanté had a dancer to save — or kidnap — and hopefully Mia was already on her way to a windowless van.

They were so close to this night being over. So close to Asif depositing Chanté somewhere safe and as far away from him as possible. Or maybe, he thought as she kicked Joseph's foot and nudged him hard with her kneecap until he jumped to his feet and let her out of the booth — maybe he'd take her to a beautiful white sand beach where they could be together for a few days or weeks or months.

She beamed at him once she was by his side.

Maybe forever.

A large boom shocked the room and everyone jumped.

The music stopped and the murmuring sounds of the crowd came to an immediate halt. It was faint, but Asif knew what a raid sounded like, and apparently, a few other people in this room did as well.

Raphael jumped to his feet and cursed in French.

"Calm down," Asif hissed, but then the fucking lights went out, someone in the crowd started screaming, and a blunt object hit the back of Asif's head.

After that, all hell broke loose.

AS SOON AS THE LIGHTS WENT OUT, MARCEL FELT A kind of calm wash over him. He heard the people around him scrambling, yelling, a hard grunt, and then someone falling to the floor. None of these were particularly comforting sounds but he couldn't stop them, so he reserved his energy until he could do something besides stumble in the dark.

"Yusuf. Yusuf?" Sonja's voice was low but stressed.

Marcel leaned in the general direction of her voice. "What's wrong?" he hissed.

"I don't know," she said. "He just fell into me. I'm not sure what happened."

"Chanté?" He called her name, but as soon as he said it, clarity started to dawn on him. He scooted quickly out of the booth just as the lights came on. A heavy door slammed somewhere. Chanté was gone. And so was Joseph.

"Merde," he spat out.

Sonja had pushed her chair out of the way and was kneeling down next to Asif's body. She was cradling his head in her hands, but she shirked away, pulling her right hand back. Bright red blood smeared her palm.

"Joseph?" she hissed.

"Of course, it was." Marcel reached for Asif's head, feeling for his pulse with nimble fingers.

"Are we certain?" Raphael asked, bending forward. "Never mind. We should get out of here."

Sonja turned to glare at her friend. "Yusuf is unconscious," she hissed.

"But we are not," Raphael replied. "Come." He started to move from the booth and then grabbed at Sonja's arm, pulling her to her feet.

Marcel was torn between Sonja and Asif, but mission objective kept him at Asif's side. Marcel reached for a glass of water on the table and poured the full glass onto his face. Asif's body jerked and he groaned, blinking his eyes open.

"Fuck," Asif groaned.

"After," Marcel joked.

Asif squinted one eye open, his mouth set in a frown. "It was funny when she said it."

Marcel helped Asif sit up and waited for him to understand. When he did, he jerked from Marcel's grip and slammed his shoulder against the glass table.

"Fuck," he spat this time.

"Are you okay?" Sonja asked.

"Oh, good, you're awake," Raphael trilled. "Now get up so we can get out of here."

Asif rubbed his shoulder and leaned heavily on Marcel to stand. "Where's Chanté?"

"Who's Chanté?" Raphael asked.

"Betty," Sonja said in exasperation.

"Probably running for safety if she's smart," Raphael said.

Once again, Sonja glared in his direction. "I thought I heard her cry out, but I couldn't be sure with all the chaos," she said to Asif. "I think Joseph took her."

Raphael laughed drily. "Took her where? He's probably—"

Asif pulled a gun from the back of his pants and aimed it directly at Raphael's face without ever looking in the man's direction. "Which way?" he asked Sonja.

It was a subtle shift, this movement from Yusuf — the man he'd been portraying — and the man Asif really was. Marcel could see realization dawn on Sonja's face.

She shook her head. "I'm not sure."

Asif didn't blink as he stared through Sonja. His body was tense. Even though the man seemed only a few breaths away from unconsciousness, he also looked deadly as ever.

Marcel inched close. "He didn't take her through the front," he whispered. His eyes flitted across the room where he confirmed that the doors were still closed. "Is there an exit to the backstage area?" he asked carefully.

Asif did blink now, and he nodded twice. Marcel reached out to steady him as he swayed to his right.

"Is there another door?" Marcel asked.

This time Asif didn't risk blinking, but he did lower his gun. His eyes shifted away from Sonja's face and she exhaled. Marcel watched Asif and Raphael from his peripheral vision as someone finally pulled the door open, which was a mistake.

Someone with a bullhorn yelled something out in Russian. Sonja and Raphael turned in that direction, but Marcel watched Asif.

Finally, after a few moments, Asif laid his hand on Marcel's shoulder heavily and took the first step down from their booth. He was shaky on his feet but steadier with each successive step.

It wasn't a traditional goodbye, but it was more than they'd gotten the last time their paths had crossed.

Sonja had gotten herself into some rough situations over the years, but this was undoubtedly the worst.

"You shouldn't have done that," Raphael said, reaching for her arm again.

He was by no means the worst man she'd ever attached herself to as a means to an end, but a small part of her had expected more of Raphael. She knew better than to believe in a man, however, and as she pulled herself from his grasp, she realized that their time together was over.

"And why not?" she spat back.

"He and I have millions of Euros worth of deals in the works," Raphael ground out. "If you jeopardize that, I'll—"

"You'll what?" Sonja asked.

She was disgusted by him for the first time since they met. Sure, she'd seen him do some things that were, by her barometer, morally questionable, but Sonja had privileged her own comfort over her admittedly lax morals. This, however, was a bridge too far.

She knew Chanté. She liked Chanté. And Yusuf had a

gun. "There should be limits on who you do business with," she said in a slow voice full of anger.

Raphael squinted at her. "I don't believe in any limits that will affect the flow of my money. You know that, and I *thought* you agreed."

She had and it made her skin warm with shame, and not just because Marcel was so close and watching this unfold before him. It had been years since she felt anything bordering on shame.

The voice blaring through the megaphone switched to English. "This is a raid. Do not run. Do not resist. Do not make us shoot you."

Raphael looked stressed. "We can have this conversation later."

"There won't be a later," Marcel said.

Sonja and Marcel turned toward him, just in time for the person holding the megaphone to burst through the crowd. He stopped at the bottom step and looked up at Marcel for a few seconds before ascending.

"Everything alright?" the man asked Marcel in French.

Marcel nodded once and then swung his head in their direction. Sonja stopped breathing. But Marcel's eyes slid past her.

"Raphael Verinac," Marcel said. "You are under arrest."

Sonja took a small step away from her friend — former friend — and hoped her luck would hold out just a little longer.

"For what?" Raphael cried.

Marcel laughed. "So many things. My associate will be happy to give you the list."

He started to bluster, but Marcel's associate was already

stepping onto the platform with handcuffs raised. Sonja took another step back.

Raphael was thinking about running, she could see it in his eyes. She wouldn't run with him, but if he left her behind, she wouldn't take the fall for him either.

But one thing she could say about Raphael was that he was always unpredictable, and tonight was no different. He seemed to weigh his options and decided that surrender was best. He extended his arms for the handcuffs.

The officer spun his finger around, and Raphael stepped in front of Sonja, turning and pushing his arms back to be shackled.

"Call my lawyer," he ground out with a sadistic smile on his face.

Sonja nodded once and wrapped her arms around her stomach, watching as Raphael was led away. She tuned out the chaos of the room as her brain whirred and she tried to figure out what came next.

Marcel stepped across the podium. He didn't crowd her space, but he was close enough that she could smell his cologne again. It shouldn't have, but that smell made her body react. She held herself tighter and tried not to let her basest thoughts get her off track.

"Thank you for helping us," Marcel whispered.

"You," she said, tilting her chin up in a defiance she didn't feel but was adept at mimicking. "I agreed to help you." Her voice was shaking.

"Are you alright?" he asked, dipping his head close.

"No."

"That's alright," he said gently.

"It's not," she spat back.

He had soft, caring eyes. Sonja knew better than anyone she didn't deserve that. She looked away.

"What happens now? To me," she asked.

"We'll need to interview you."

"Okay, I'll give you a number where you can reach me."

Marcel smiled, tilting his head to the side.

She didn't want to, but she laughed, looking away.

"You can come with me," he said, pulling her gaze back to his. She raised her eyebrows, and he stepped closer. "I don't trust you to run away."

"I don't trust you not to arrest me."

She jumped when his hand settled on her arm. His skin was dry, warm, soft. He wrapped his fist around her forearm and applied gentle pressure. The touch made the rest of the room disappear.

"Come with me to Paris, and maybe we will learn to trust one another."

"And if we don't?" she said before licking her lips.

His eyes watched her tongue move and he inched closer still. His chest bumped against her arms, which acted as a barrier.

"But what if we do?" Marcel whispered, almost close enough for their lips to brush.

Chanté

+

Asif

THIRTY-FIVE

ASIF RETRACED his steps through the crowd and back through a door tucked behind the bar.

The hallway lights were fluorescent white and he shut his eyes immediately. He pressed his fingers against his eyelids as a lightning bolt of hot fire shot through his brain.

"Fuck." He knew what a concussion felt like.

Someone knocked him to the side and Asif stumbled into the wall. He cracked one eyelid just enough to see some old men in suits rushing down the hallway. Asif doubted they'd make their way to safety, but he didn't care.

He shut his eyes again and fought the urge to throw up, waiting until he stopped feeling the world spin on its axis. It took less than a minute, but all he could think about was how far away Joseph could drag Chanté in a minute. How much he could do to her in a handful of minutes.

When he could bear to open his eyes for more than a millisecond at a time, he pushed forward, stumbling every few steps but refusing to let his failing body stop him from getting to her. The building was a maze and Asif plunged into the labyrinth of hallways blind. He was halfway toward Mia's office when he realized that he could call Carlisle. He moved his right hand to his pocket, surprised to find that he was still clutching her gun tight in his palm.

His mother would have been proud. She always told new recruits to never let their guns out of sight or grip. If she were here, she might have laughed at final confirmation that he did listen to her.

That he'd never wanted anything more than to be just like her.

Except for right now. Right now, he wanted to find Chanté more than anything.

He switched his firearm from his right to his left hand. He reached in his pocket and pressed the button to call the last number.

"Kinda busy right now," Carlisle said in a tight voice.

"What's up?"

"You tell me. Why the fuck is French intelligence crawling all over the building?"

"Fuck," Asif sighed. He should have known Marcel wasn't hanging around just to help him.

"Exactly. So, it's taking a little time for us to complete this extraction."

Asif's eyes went wide. "You haven't gotten her yet?"

"Haven't even got in the building ye— Oh, we're in. Had to blow a door on the roof."

"Fuck!" Asif yelled, and dark spots appeared in his vision.

"Don't worry. We're on the way," Carlisle said, disconnecting the call.

Frustrated, Asif closed his eyes and tried to listen past the sound of his blood rushing in his veins. It took a minute to slow his thoughts, but when he did, he heard the frantic sounds of heels clicking on concrete and women crying out. It was better than nothing, and Asif turned, running down the hallway toward that cacophony. He rushed into a dead end with hallways jutting off in two directions. One hallway was full of dancers — half-dressed women throwing thick winter coats over their bodies with thin, sheer clothing and heels hanging out of half-closed duffel bags.

He stretched his neck and called out for Kay. A short Asian girl turned to him and he felt a shot of hope that he could understand her. He called to her in English. He didn't know more than a word of Russian, and for the first time in this mission, he regretted the cavalier attitude that brought him here. "Have you seen a man and a woman come through here? She's small, brown, big hair?"

Her face lit up. "Chanté?"

Asif's heart slammed against his chest. "Do you know her?"

She nodded. "She's at the booth—"

Asif shook his head and swayed a little, but not as bad as before. "He— Someone took her. Back here, I think, but it's..." Asif's voice trailed off and he shrugged his arms, a wave of despair washing over him. "I don't know where she is. I can't let anything happen to her."

He could feel the pressure of tears building at the back of his eyes, but he couldn't let them fall. He refused to fall apart when she needed him most.

"She's not here," the girl said, pointing behind him, the implication clear that if Chanté wasn't here, the only place to find her was back toward Mia's office.

Asif nodded and turned in that direction, rushing and praying.

His hand was hot and sweaty and it made her want to gag.

She'd tried to get out of his hold, but Joseph was more than twice her size and crazy, and Chanté wasn't strong enough to fight him off. Well, not under these circumstances, so she went limp. Unfortunately, he was strong enough to hold her with ease, but at least once she stopped fighting, he moved his meaty hand from her mouth. She gulped fresh air and tried to memorize the route he was taking, but every plain white hallway looked the same as the next.

Every time her heels touched the ground, she pressed her toes downward, searching for purchase so she could make a break for it. Meanwhile, Joseph seemed to be searching for something, trying to open every door they passed, but they were all locked.

Fortunately or unfortunately.

Definitely unfortunate, she thought, when finally, one of those doorknobs gave and Joseph pushed the door open.

Chanté stopped playing dead and jerked out of his hold. Surprise worked in her favor. His grip slipped. As soon as her feet hit the floor, her left ankle buckled, but Chanté refused to let that stop her. She took off running back in the direction they came. She could run in heels, even with an ankle that became sorer with every step, but Joseph was faster than she might have expected.

He grabbed her around the waist, punching all the air

from her diaphragm. He pulled her back hard enough that one of her shoes flew off.

"Let me go!" she screamed.

He slammed his fist over her mouth again and it stung like a slap.

But this time she refused to play meek. Chanté scratched at his hand hard enough to break a nail, so she scratched him with the jagged part.

He cried out in pain and jerked his head back.

"Help!" she screamed at the top of her lungs.

"Chanté!" The sound of Asif's voice sounded like heaven.

"Asi—" That was all of his name she managed to get out before Joseph slapped her in the mouth for real. The sharp, metallic tang of blood flooded her tongue.

Joseph pulled her back through the open door, kicking it shut in front of her.

But Asif was close by. Asif was here.

Joseph threw her on the ground. Chanté grunted in pain as her knees hit the hard floor. She barely had time to breathe before his foot slammed into her side.

Tears sprang to Chanté's eyes and immediately spilled down her cheeks. She scrambled away from him, pressing herself against a wall. She looked up to find him smiling down at her, finally revealing himself to be the monster her intuition recognized from the start.

She held her breath until he turned toward the desk.

The room was hot as hell, and she could feel sweat building at her hairline and falling down the side of her face. He walked to the desk and snatched the phone receiver from the cradle. Everything hurt on her next exhale. Her bottom lip, her ankle, her ribs — hell, even her scalp. Terror was riding adrenaline through her veins like a bucking bronco.

She glanced quickly between Joseph's profile and the door. She wouldn't make it. She could try, but she knew she wouldn't.

She reached down and slipped her shoe from her right foot. She might have to run again, and she certainly couldn't do it with her bum ankle and a single six-inch heel.

She wouldn't make it, but she had to try.

She was trying to hype herself up to make the move when a loud groan grabbed hers and Joseph's attention.

She turned toward the sound and found Mia pulling herself up from the floor.

Chanté

+

Asif

THIRTY-SIX

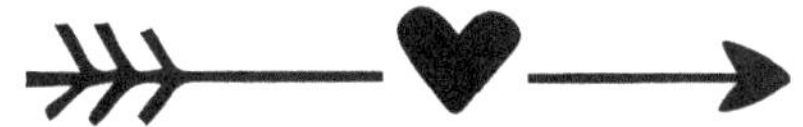

ASIF TOOK off running down the hallway, heading straight toward Mia's office. There were probably other rooms, other places he could be holding her, but he could feel it in his gut that the place to end this was right where it started.

His nausea faded away. He stopped feeling the migraine spreading around his brain. All he could focus on was her. All that ever mattered was Chanté.

Asif rounded the corner to the hallway just as the door flew open and Mia came stumbling out. A dark figure on the other end of the hall peeked into view, but Asif couldn't worry about that. He aimed his gun at her face.

"You bastard!" she screamed at him.

"Chanté!" Asif yelled.

"Asif." She called his name, sounding terrified. But it was the high-pitched cry after that made his stomach lurch into his throat.

He shifted his arm to the right and shot into the wall. Mia flinched and started to back away. He dropped his arm a fraction of an inch and let her go, aiming his attention on the door.

When Mia seemed to understand that she wasn't the focus of Asif's attention, she turned around and ran away.

Straight into Kay.

Asif eyed them warily as he moved toward that door. It was an indefensible position, to be honest. And if Joseph was armed, Asif could be walking straight into a death trap. He pressed forward anyway.

It took him a second to realize that Mia and Kay were still embracing down the hall, and by the time he saw it, Mia was falling to the ground. Kay's hand and the front of her dress were covered in a spray of blood. She looked frozen.

Asif's eyes were wide, but he didn't stop.

Joseph came barreling through the doorway, tackling Asif and slamming him back into the wall. He grabbed Asif's hands and tried to break his hold on the gun, but he wouldn't let it go. His grip would break eventually, but not until his fingers were mangled.

The next time Joseph slammed his fists against the wall, Asif reared back and headbutted the man in the forehead. It wasn't the smartest move, considering his existing head trauma, but saving his life so he could save hers would always be worth whatever damage he suffered.

Joseph stumbled back, and Asif took advantage of the brief space to kick him in the chest. He darted to the left and started to lift his gun again, but Joseph wouldn't go down without a fight and launched himself at Asif once more. Asif had just enough time to dart from his grasp, losing the opportunity to take a shot in the process.

But the gun wasn't useless. Asif slammed the butt of the gun at Joseph's head, but the other man moved just in time and Asif only made contact with his shoulder. Joseph grunted and then slammed his fist into Asif's side.

Vaguely, he heard Chanté's cry, and he made the mistake of turning in the direction of her voice. She limped into the hallway.

"Get ou—" Joseph's big, meaty fist slammed against Asif's face and he fell to the floor. Joseph quickly kicked the gun from Asif's broken hand. Stunned, Asif tried to scramble back. "Get out of here, Chanté."

"Get out of here!"

He screamed at her while Joseph stalked toward him. Asif was scrambling toward the gun, and she thought about making a play for it as well when the sound of wheezing breaths pulled her attention to the other side of the hallway.

"Kay, oh my god," she breathed. "Ca—" She stopped mid-word when she saw Mia lying on the floor with a knife handle protruding from her chest.

"Even better," Chanté said, running, limping toward her. Kay only moved when Chanté got close. Her eyes widened in shock, but they didn't have time to talk about this. "She'll bleed out faster this way," Chanté huffed, bending forward and snatching the knife from Mia's body.

The woman cried out in pain, not that Chanté gave a shit.

A door slammed open and a white man in black tactical gear appeared at the base of the hallway. Chanté recognized him but couldn't remember his name and they didn't have time for introductions.

"Down," he barked at them. "Get down!"

"Wh—" Kay started, but Chanté cut her off. She'd learned the hard way to just do what they said in a gun, fist, or knife fight. She dropped the knife and grabbed Kay, turning to Asif.

Joseph was standing above him, clenching his fists. The sadistic fuck was toying with Asif.

So when the bullet pierced his skull and blood, bone, and brains splattered from his forehead, Chanté didn't just feel relief, she felt elated.

Asif scrambled back as Joseph's corpse pitched forward.

"What the fuck?" Chanté breathed at the person standing at the other end of the hallway, hand raised and gun still aimed at where Joseph had once been standing. She blinked rapidly as the figure started moving forward.

"What are you doing here?" Asif asked, panting, his voice full of gratitude.

"Saving your life, it seems." The familiar deep, husky voice sounded as it always did, but Chanté still couldn't make sense of what she was seeing. She'd never seen Maryam in tactical gear. It hardly made sense.

"Ah, fuck. We got a stuck pig," Carlisle called. Chanté jumped as he pushed her and Kay out of the way.

Kay reacted and tried to push Carlisle from Mia's body. "Let her die!" she screamed.

A lot had happened in the last few moments, but Kay's scream gave Chanté goosebumps. She reached for Kay, holding her tight in her arms. "It's okay," she said, shushing her gently. "It's okay. It's over."

The woman struggled for a few seconds but surprisingly

quickly, she collapsed into quiet again, leaning her head onto Chanté's shoulder.

Carlisle had pulled a first-aid kit from somewhere and was pressing down onto Mia's wound. He glanced up at Chanté and Kay. His eyes were soft at the edges as he took in Kay's exhausted form.

"She's in a lot of pain," he said softly. "We'll keep her that way as long as we can. I promise."

"Thank you," Chanté whispered back because Kay didn't have the energy to speak.

Carlisle nodded and went back to work. Chanté held onto Kay but turned her attention back to Maryam and Asif.

The woman was kneeling down next to Asif. She'd grabbed his chin and was looking him over. "You look like you have a concussion," she said.

Asif collapsed onto his back and laughed drily. "Wouldn't be the first time."

"It wouldn't," she said, pressing her hand against Asif's chest. "Are you alright?" Maryam asked.

Asif tilted his head and his eyes moved until they settled on Chanté. "That depends," he said to Maryam. "Are you alright?" he asked Chanté.

She nodded quickly. "I'm fine," she said even though she felt like one big, throbbing bruise.

"Thank you," Maryam said.

Chanté looked at her and raised her eyebrows. "Huh? Me?"

Maryam smiled softly, patting her hand against Asif's chest. "You. Thank you for finding him and thank you for all the times you've saved my son's life."

Chanté's eyes went wide. "Son?" She dropped her gaze to Asif.

He had the nerve to smile at her, making a cut on his bottom lip split and start bleeding again. "I've been meaning to tell you that," he laughed.

"The fuck does that mean? You've been meaning to tell me you had your mother recruit me into The Agency and what, you just forgot?"

"What?" Asif said. "I didn't—"

Maryam patted his chest one more time and then stood. "It seems we have a lot to discuss." She laughed for a second before turning serious and pressing the receiver at her ear. "Get us an exit, Mr. Sanchez. I refuse to die in a strip club in Saint Petersburg."

Chanté

+

Asif

THIRTY-SEVEN

THE VERSION of Chanté who lived in Asif's head was circling a pole on that dark stage again. Watching him. Smirking at him. Waiting for him.

"Wake the fuck up. I'm bored," Chanté whispered.

Asif focused his brain on her mouth, but this version of Chanté never spoke. She didn't laugh, either. In the torturous but imaginary version of Chanté he allowed himself, Chanté was forever out of reach.

He felt warm breath against his ear and then soft skin on his earlobe.

"You better not die," she whispered. "I'll resurrect you and kill you."

Asif felt himself smile, so he knew he wasn't dead yet.

He opened his eyes slowly and found himself staring at a plain white ceiling, which was quickly eclipsed by Chanté's face.

Her smiling face. "Finally. You've been unconscious for sixteen hours."

Asif opened his mouth to speak, but his lips and tongue

were dry. He swallowed, but it was like choking down stale bread.

"Oh, hold on."

Her face disappeared, and he turned in her direction, desperately searching for her. He got a glimpse of the room around them and recognized a hotel, but not as nice as Chanté's penthouse. Chanté was perched on the side of the bed, pouring water from a carafe into a glass. He let his eyes wander over her cheek and down her neck. She was wearing a tank top, and as soon as his eyes got below her neckline, he started to chart the familiar contours of her skin, but it wasn't familiar.

He froze at the first bruise. His heart was racing by the second and third. But when she started to turn back toward him and winced, Asif tried to sit up in a panic.

"Don't move," she said. "You're hurt."

"You're hurt," he croaked, shredding his dry throat.

"I'm fine," Chanté said, but she winced through that, so he didn't believe her. Once her grimace passed, she rolled her eyes. "Okay, I'm not fine. But neither are you."

It was a struggle to pull himself up to sitting, and by the time he did, he wanted to lie down and go back to sleep, but he couldn't do that yet. He pressed his back against the headboard and closed his eyes as a wave of pain shot through his body.

He took a deep breath, and the cool glass pressed against his lips.

"Drink," she whispered.

He opened his eyes. She was staring at him with soft eyes and dark circles — every ounce of vulnerability on display for him. He held her gaze and did as she said, and that, at least, put a smile back on her face.

It took some time, but he finally drank all the water she offered. "Better?" she asked.

He licked his dry lips. "Better. Where are you hurt?" She started to smile, but he cut her off with a hand on her thigh. He wanted to grab onto her, but he was too afraid to make it worse. And Asif couldn't bear to hurt her anymore. "Where?" he asked again. "Please."

She fidgeted with the glass in her hand and dropped her head. One of her curls fell over her face and Asif couldn't help himself. He lifted his free hand over his body, grunting in pain, but he refused to let that stop him from touching her.

"You wanna know what I thought the first time I saw you?" he whispered, smoothing his hand down her hair.

She lifted her head quickly. The light was dancing in her eyes. "Yes."

He squeezed her thigh gently. Softly. "Then tell me where you're hurt."

She rolled her eyes and licked her lips. "Fine. I have a sore ankle, not broken or sprained, just sore. Bruised ribs, which is lucky because he kicked me hard as fuck."

"He what—" Asif lurched forward and winced in pain.

She pressed him back onto the headboard. "You also have bruised ribs, by the way."

"Thanks, I would never have realized what the throbbing in my side was."

She shrugged prettily at him. "You're welcome."

"Is that it?"

She shrugged again, this time more disinterestedly. "Besides some scrapes and bruises and maybe some PTSD... Pretty much."

Asif already felt terrible, but as she listed each injury, he felt like a Mack truck was running over him. There were tears in his eyes. "I'm sorry."

She frowned at him. "For what?"

"For this. All of this. I shouldn't—"

"You didn't," she said with a shrug.

"I—"

"Please shut up," Chanté said with a smile.

Asif closed his mouth and blinked up at her.

Chanté gasped excitedly. "You mean all I had to do to get you to listen to me was bruise a few ribs?"

"Chanté," he said seriously.

She covered his mouth quickly and shook her head. She plucked the glass from his hand and set it back on the bedside table before carefully climbing onto the bed next to him. He moved his arm so she could settle into his side, which made her smile.

"Even though my delusional ass thinks you're the center of the world..." She opened her mouth and then closed it, blinking quickly as she thought through that. "Center of the world *next* to me," she added in clarification.

Asif's smile dragged along the inside of her palm.

"Anyway, it's not true. I love you. I'm obsessed with you, but everything isn't about you." Her mouth dipped into a sad smile. "Everything isn't your fault."

Her eyes were tired and rimmed red. Asif pulled her closer. He kissed her hand before it fell away from his mouth.

"Now, tell me what you thought about me the first time you saw me," she said with a smile.

He smoothed his bruised knuckles over her bruised cheek. "I thought you were beautiful, and then I bent the entirety of my world and my mission just to be with you."

"And then you left," she whispered.

"Because you're in nothing but danger when I'm around."

"I am, but I can take care of myself."

"Chanté," he sighed again.

"And when I *can't* take care of myself, apparently your entire family can pick up the slack."

"Not my entire family," he said.

"You and your mom can protect me and your dad while we hang out at the farmers' market."

Asif rolled his eyes. "Or you could just— Wait, how do you know my dad likes to hang out at the farmers' market?"

Two knocks interrupted their conversation just before the door opened.

"We thought we heard voices," his mother said, walking into the room.

"But we were nervous to open the door," his father chuckled as he followed her inside.

"Baba? What are you doing here?"

Chanté started to stand from the bed, but Asif's father shook his head, shushing her. "Stay. Stay. You both need to rest." He bracketed the sides of her head and bent forward, pressing his mouth against her forehead.

The way he'd always kissed Asif's forehead.

The man patted Chanté's cheeks before moving to the side. He was in pain, but Asif still leaned forward so his father could repeat the action on him. Asif closed his eyes to accept his father's kiss. He felt Chanté shuffle on the bed to give him and his father room. When they pulled back, Asif looked up at the man who'd raised him. When his mother was half a world away undermining a coup, it was his father who drove him to school in the morning, who showed up at all his basketball games, who made dinner every night.

It was his father who kept Asif and their home together.

"I have no problem with your mother flying all over the world without me. But when it comes to you, wild horses couldn't keep me away."

Asif leaned his face against his father's hand, pressing his cheek into his soft palm.

His mother cleared her throat. His father patted his cheek once and stepped back, standing next to his wife. The last time the two of them had stood side-by-side next to one another, they'd been grounding him for accidentally jumping a car — he just wanted to see if he could.

"For the next five minutes, everything we say in this room will be completely candid and then we'll never speak directly of this again."

"Honestly, you're amazing," Chanté whispered, staring up at Asif's mother in awe.

"Thank you. Now, Asif, I know you've been under the impression that your father has spent the last thirty years truly believing that I was just the world's busiest CFO and the bruises and bullet wounds were normal."

"I— I mean, when you put it like that..."

"Yes. When I remind you that your father is smart and capable in his own right."

His father brushed at the air and blushed.

"How odd that you assumed your father stayed home to care for you while working from home. Doing what job, I wonder?"

Asif immediately opened his mouth to tell her exactly what his father did for a living — because of course, he knew — except he didn't. His gaze slid to his father. "Baba?"

"You have somehow spent all of your life imagining that I loved you so little I would leave you and your father alone and unprotected while I worked."

Asif shook his head. "I didn't—"

"You did," his father corrected him gently.

"And you loved yourself so little that you've spent your entire career courting trouble." She frowned at him. "And running away from happiness." At this point, her eyes slid to Chanté for a second before returning.

"As The Agency Director, all my agents' lives matter. But as your mother, no one is more important to me than you. Although Chanté is better at following my orders,'" she said, a small smile playing on her lips.

Asif's eyebrows shot into his forehead. "Is there another Chanté? One I don't know about? Because she never listens to me."

"I listen," Chanté said. "I just don't agree ninety-four percent of the time."

"She also steals from me," Asif said, never taking his eyes from his mother.

She shrugged. "That's your own fault. You asked me to pay her a bonus after you met."

Chanté gasped. "You did?"

"You opened the door for her to have access to your accounts. Who can blame her for being curious? And what a gift that she had the skill to take that curiosity and make it a career." His mother laughed almost involuntarily. As if it snuck up on her, but nothing snuck up on his mother. "In fact," she said, laughing, reaching back for her husband, who offered his hand for support. "The entire organization has you to thank for all the help Chanté has offered us over the years."

When he glanced at Chanté, she was practically glowing.

Asif looked to his father for support, but he, too, was smiling proudly. By the time his gaze made it back to his mother, she'd managed to compose herself. Now, she was looking down at him with soft but serious eyes.

"I sent you to surveil Raphael and you did far more than that. The Agency thanks you for your service, but there will have to be consequences for going rogue."

Asif started to speak, but his mother raised a hand, cutting him off silently. "You were the one who asked to be treated like any other agent. Had you not ultimately succeeded in this mission, including capturing Yuri Malkov's daughter, *and* repaired our relationship with French intelligence, you would be unemployed."

"Come on," he said, smiling. Unfortunately, he was too tired to be truly charming, and his mother was largely immune to him anyway.

"Someone who was not my son might have been burned days ago. Thankfully, Chanté was able to help you save your career."

"Does it come with a bonus?" she muttered.

His mother smiled. "Six-month suspension," she told Asif.

"Six months?"

"And you must pass a physical to return," she said.

"What—"

"*And* as a consequence of your actions, you will be banned from going into the field alone for one year after you return."

"Mom. Wait." Asif tried to stand from the bed, but everyone reacted quickly, shaking their head. Chanté was closer, and Asif was so weak that she managed to push him back against the headboard with one hand. He was exhausted. "I can't work like that."

"I disagree," his mother said. "You did a fantastic job with your little team this time."

"Those were special circumstances."

His mother started to speak, but Chanté got there before her.

"They don't have to be," she muttered.

Asif could feel her staring a hole in the side of his face, and when he turned to her, she had that same soft look in her eyes — the one she had all those years ago at the door of her apartment. The one he tried never to dream about because it would break his heart.

"I agree," his mother said. "A real partnership is a sacred thing. Your father and I want that for you more than anything else. But you have six months to think on it."

He heard the rustling of her sari as she took the few steps toward the bed. His eyes were still on Chanté as his mother bent forward to kiss him on the crown of his head. And then she moved two steps over to do the same to Chanté. Although this time, when she pulled back, she whispered soft words into Chanté's hairline.

"What does that mean?" she asked.

"Ask my son," she said before turning away and sweeping from the room. His father winked at them before walking through the door and pulling it softly closed behind him.

"Your mom didn't fire me in Urdu, did she? 'Cause that would suck," Chanté said as soon as they were alone. She forced herself to laugh because the room was too quiet for her liking. And from prior experience, this was the moment when Asif left. It didn't matter that he would have to hobble out of here; she wouldn't put it past him to try.

"She didn't fire you," he said in a voice thick with emotion.

"Are you okay?"

"Yes. No. I—"

Chanté crawled up the bed to get closer. Selfishly and carefully, she placed her hand over his heart. It was galloping against his chest. It wasn't the same feeling as the rings; it was better.

"It's okay," Chanté whispered. "You can feel your feelings."

He shook his head and rested against the headboard. "If I feel my feelings, I won't let you leave."

She had no chill. She didn't want it. All she wanted since she was twenty was Asif. "Then definitely feel your feelings."

He smiled and licked his lips again before turning to look at her. Slowly, he repeated his mother's words in Urdu.

"Why'd she call me Betty? Am I going back in the field?"

He sighed softly. "She didn't call you Betty," he said. "Although I guess that explains your terrible cover name."

"It wasn't—"

He grabbed her waist and squeezed. "It was. But she called you 'beti,'" he said, emphasizing that last word. "Daughter. She said, 'rest well, daughter.'"

Chanté gasped. "For real?"

"For real."

"Is your mom tryna set us up?"

Asif laughed. "Seems like she's been trying to set us up for the last eight years."

Chanté leaned forward. "So, I'm definitely her favorite, right?"

Asif's laugh was dry, pained, but still beautiful.

He moved a hand to her face, and she pressed her cheek into his palm. It was warm and a little clammy, but she didn't care. She'd never cared. "You might be all of ours favorite."

Okay, she'd actually reserved an ounce of chill and now she tossed it from the window. "Maybe?"

"Definitely."

Her eyes started to fill with tears, and she watched as Asif's did the same. "So now what?"

His other hand moved to cup her left cheek. "Apparently, I have six months with nothing to do."

"I heard," she whispered.

"Would you—"

"Yes," she said quickly.

A tear fell from the corner of his eye. She watched it travel a quick path down the side of his face and disappear into his beard. "Would you like to spend the next six months together?"

"Definitely," she said and then carefully leaned into his side, resting her chin on his shoulder. For the first time in a decade, Chanté settled into the silence between them, finally not worried that he'd disappear in a blink of an eye.

But they weren't really the silent type. "I have a list of places I want to fuck you," she said.

Asif laughed. "Of course, you do. And I have a bank account reserved for buying you expensive clothes I want to take off of you."

Chanté turned and pressed her face into the crook of his neck. She licked his skin and he groaned. "We're going to have so much fun together."

Asif looked down at her. "You mean you haven't been having fun before now?" he asked, laughing.

"Shut up," she said, kissing his bobbing Adam's apple.

"I love you," he whispered into her hair.

Chanté

+

Asif

EPILOGUE

CLEVELAND

"How's it feel to be back?" Asif asked as he walked behind her. She turned her head to watch him, shivering in anticipation.

"We just got here. I don't *feel* anything."

He chuckled softly at the neediness in her voice. The desperation. Asif moved forward a few steps, just close enough for her to feel his warmth. And when she did, the trembling only got stronger.

"Look forward," he said.

He couldn't see her face, so he closed his eyes and listened to her body — the soft rasp of her panting breaths, the soft rustle of her skirt as she shifted her thighs together, and eventually, the soft sigh of agreement.

He took another step and bent forward at the waist so he could press his nose into her hair. He'd never get enough of her — of being close enough to smell her, touch her, taste her every day.

He took two steps back to enjoy the view.

Chanté wanted to buy a place in Cleveland. Asif wanted to be with her. So there they were, viewing a high-rise penthouse and enjoying the view of Key Tower. The sun was just about to set and the floor-to-ceiling windows in the living room gave them the best panoramic view of the sky fading from a dark blue to an icy white.

But that was her view. His was better.

It had barely been a month since they'd left Russia and they'd been playing with fire ever since. Chanté wanted to cover the door at a club in Spain so she could dance for him and they could fuck in front of the crowd, they did it. He wanted to hire a designer to take her measurements and design lingerie to Asif's very specifications, they did it. And they did the designer. Twice. They wanted to watch the sunrise from a beach in Phuket, holding one another's hands in silent awe, they did it and made tentative plans to do it again in a year. And maybe every year after that.

And now they were in a high-rise apartment, in the city where they met, and Chanté had on a dress that wouldn't have been decent any part of the year, but it was the dead of winter and her outfit was even less appropriate than normal. They'd found the crystal-covered dress in a vintage store in southern France. Chanté saw it glint through the window and said it had called to her. It exposed her back and arms and so much of her thick legs. She was completely naked underneath.

"Asif," she whispered in a shaky breath.

Sometimes when she called out to him in that soft whine, he forgot whatever game they were playing and got on his knees for her, burying his tongue deep inside her pussy until he was full. But he was strong enough to hold himself together this time. He placed a hand in the middle of her back and pressed her slowly forward. Her six-inch heels made gentle thuds on the hardwood floor. They were just as impractical as the weather, so much so that he'd just let Chanté hop on his back and carried her from the car rather than let her fall on the icy street. She'd laughed at a gust of wind blowing up her dress. Asif couldn't think of a single thing he'd change.

They were a few steps away from the window when Asif moved his fingers under the thick curtain of her curly hair to the clasp of her dress. She gasped as the top of her dress fell off and then moaned when her breasts touched the window.

He moved his hand from her back to her waist and held her in place. He didn't want to press the entire drop of her breasts against the window, he wanted to rest just her nipples against the glass as a tease.

"How's it feel to be back?" he asked again. She set the tips of her long black nails against the window and turned her head to touch her cheek.

"Fantastic," she moaned.

"How's the glass feel?" he asked.

"Cold," she moaned, as if realizing the state she was in had heightened the wave she was riding.

"If we moved in here, I'd have to get all this glass changed to something that would give us privacy and protection."

She whimpered sadly, and Asif's heart tripled in size. How was it possible she was so perfect for him? He bent forward and kissed her shoulder. "What we gain in privacy, we'll lose with hedonism," he whispered over her skin.

Chanté opened her mouth to pant, releasing some tension and a delicate cloud of condensation on the window. Yeah, they'd definitely need something thicker than this if this was the place they chose. "Please," she finally managed to push past her lips as she moved her feet further apart.

Thankfully, Asif was already ahead of her, hands pulling his belt open. "Do you have a condom?" he asked.

Chanté flattened her palms on the window and pressed away. Asif froze, one hand stuffed down his pants, wrapped around his dick, the other patting his back pocket.

She looked over her left shoulder to scowl at him. "I'm not wearing enough clothes to hide a quarter. Where the hell do you think I was going to put a condom?"

"Fuck."

"Why don't you have condoms with all those pockets?" she asked.

"I did. I had a whole stash in my pocket when we left this morning. We used them all."

That brought a smile to her face. He wondered if she was remembering when they pulled over to fuck in a half-abandoned strip mall, or in a private room at Joi's new strip club, or their quickie two properties ago. Either way, they were out of condoms at the most inopportune time.

"Okay, forget it. We don't need it. It's the end of my cycle anyway."

Asif's eyes went wide. "That's something teenagers say right before an accidental pregnancy."

"You think teenagers learn about ovulation cycles?" Chanté asked.

"Good point. Still, a baby's not in the cards for us yet."
She smiled. "Yet?"

"Shhh. Don't get sidetracked. I've got a plan."

She pouted at him, and he pulled her back against him quickly. She tipped her chin up and he covered her mouth with his. He kissed her quick and hard before pressing her fully against the window. He ran his hands down her arms, grabbed her wrists, and moved her hands behind her back. He ripped his zipper down and pulled his dick out, bending his knees to position his shaft inside her hold.

He hissed. Her hands were ice cold and his dick was burning up. Clearly, she liked the contrast as well because it made her laugh. And then she started stroking. He shifted his hips to help her along.

"Spit on it," she moaned.

"Fuck," he groaned. "Fuck." And then he did as she asked.

His shaft moved easier through her hold and he started shifting his hips forward and back. Once they'd established a rhythm, he moved a hand on the back of her right thigh, up to the folds of her sex. She was hot and wet as he slipped two fingers right inside her.

They didn't skip a beat in getting one another off. They were learning the rhythms of one another's bodies and pretending as if this vacation was their everyday. He worried the next five months of his suspension would fly by, but when it ended, he knew they would have made the absolute most of every moment.

"You're so wet, sweetheart," he groaned.

"Dirtier," Chanté panted.

He laughed. "When the weather's clear, I wanna take you on that balcony and fuck you for the entire neighborhood to see."

She didn't need to tell him that worked for her — he felt it when her pussy clenched around him.

There were still half a dozen other properties left to visit and surely, they wouldn't fuck in all of them, but he was open to trying.

His body shook as his cell phone vibrated in his pocket. "Fuck, I'm close," he gasped.

Chanté tugged him forward so the tip of his dick was pressing into her ass. The implication was clear — that dimpled bit of her round ass was where Chanté wanted him to come.

"Yeah. Yeah." His phone vibrated again. Asif pulled it from his pocket. "What?" he groaned.

"Are you dying?" Kenny asked.

Asif had to swallow hard before he could answer. "In a way. Why are you calling me?"

"Who is it?" Chanté moaned.

"Kenny," he said, but his voice drifted off right at the end in a breathy sigh.

"Hey, Ken Doll," Chanté yelled.

"Hear that?" Asif asked.

"Tell her I said hi and she should leave you."

"He said hey," Asif told Chanté. "Now, what do you want?"

"You," Kenny said.

That made Asif's balls tighten. "Oh shit."

Kenny sighed. "Not like that. I need you to get to Cincinnati asap."

"No can do," he ground out. "Suspended." He was losing the battle with making words.

"I got your suspension suspended. This is important."

"Everything we do is important."

"This is a favor to a friend. It's a four-hour drive. I'll meet you at the DEA Cincinnati office at noon. Tell Chanté to bring her gear." Kenny hung up without a goodbye, which was rude and for the best.

Asif bent forward over her back and started groaning.

Her fists were pulling him quickly toward his orgasm, but he didn't want to come alone. He pulled his wet fingers from her pussy and started to circle her clit.

Chanté arched her back and pressed her breasts against the cold glass while they used their hands to get one another off.

He moved his hand to her throat and squeezed as she bucked her ass into his balls and an orgasm ran through her.

"We have to go to work after this," he whispered, fucking into her hands.

She looked up at him with big, innocent eyes. He felt her jerk against his hold as she tried to nod.

"Remember that you're the only thing that matters to me," he said in a strained voice, seconds from coming. "Remember that I only want you to be safe. I don't care what happens to me as long as you're safe."

She squeezed his shaft, and he could barely think. All he could do was hump against her, fuck her hold. "I love you so much," she whispered.

And that was all it took to push Asif over the edge.

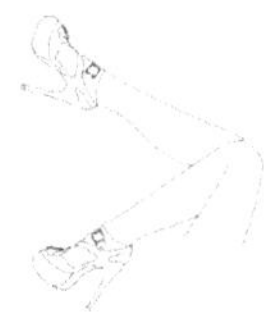

Alvaro Ruiz was a disgraced man.

He hadn't yet had his day in court, but no one who knew anything about his case was under any illusion that his trial, whenever it came, would end without significant jail time. His lawyer was currently working on a plea deal — something that might get him one decade behind bars rather than several — but Alvaro was still undecided about whether he'd take it. On the one hand, it might be nice to delude himself with the promise of future freedom, but freedom to do what? He'd torched his life, and by the time he would be released, he'd well and truly be an old man.

He already felt like an old man. Who knew what a few years in federal prison would do to him? Especially when they were keeping him in solitary. They said it was for his own safety and maybe it was, but the tradeoff between getting hemmed up in a communal shower and staring at the water-stained ceiling of his cell for ninety-nine percent of every day was negligible as far as he could tell. Hell, soon enough, he might decide that the potential danger of a knife to his kidney was worth it — he was almost there.

"Fuck you!"

Alvaro didn't know who yelled and he didn't care.

There was no quiet in prison, not even in solitary. In the months since he'd been arrested, Alvaro had become familiar with the cacophony of this place — metal doors opening and closing with a bang, sirens, all day fucking sirens, shouting, the drip of a leak somewhere. The sound drove some people mad. The sound reminded them that in prison, peace was their ultimate sacrifice.

Fortunately, Alvaro hadn't known peace in nearly a decade. Sure, the lumpy cot, thin blankets, and disgusting food made this experience worse than the life he'd been living, but he'd been living in hell long before he was arrested. Long before he'd decided to betray his oath, even.

He heard the metal clang of the food slot in his door open and turned his head to his right.

"You up?"

All Alvaro's money was currently tied up in two things, paying his attorney and paying CO Baldwin to make sure his food wasn't poisoned. He wasn't made of money, though, so both of those services would end eventually. But not yet.

"I'm up," Alvaro replied, pushing up to sit on the edge of his bed.

"Got something for you," he said.

It was barely five in the morning. Too early for breakfast, but never too early for danger.

"Like what?" Alvaro asked, watching that slot closely.

The man chuckled — an annoying habit Alvaro tolerated because he had no choice. A small envelope appeared through the door.

"What's that?" Alvaro asked warily.

"Come get it and find out. And hurry up, I need to keep moving."

Patience was another luxury no one in prison could afford. In his former lives, Alvaro didn't make impulsive decisions. He thought about everything slowly, gave each decision in his life serious consideration, weighing the risks and benefits, but he couldn't do that anymore.

He jumped from his cot and ignored the stiffness in his right leg as he limped across his small cell. The floor was cold under his thin socks. He grabbed the envelope from Baldwin's hand but made sure not to snatch. It didn't matter how much money he was sending this man to supplement his corruption, every CO he'd ever met was three steps from being an inmate themselves.

"Who's it from?" Alvaro said.

"No idea," Baldwin said and shut the slot.

Alvaro stared at the door and listened as the man's heavy footsteps faded away. He rolled his eyes and turned back to his cot. He sat and took a deep breath before deciding to just lie back down. It was too early to get up and there wasn't anything to do once he did. Why bother rushing through one more day in prison?

His cell was a dim gray, but he lifted the envelope into the small shoot of light filtering through his narrow window. It wasn't enough to see by, but he didn't need a halogen lamp to recognize the handwriting there.

He sat quickly, unable to believe what he was seeing. He had to scoot to the foot of the bed and lifted the envelope fully into the light, staring at it for a while before he mustered up the courage to open it. Inside was a thick piece of square cardstock with one word written carefully in her familiar, elegant script.

Mine.

ALSO BY KATRINA JACKSON

<u>Welcome to Sea Port</u>

From Scratch

Inheritance

Small Town Secrets

Her Christmas Cookie

<u>The Spies Who Loved Her</u>

Pink Slip

Private Eye

Bang & Burn

New Year, New We

His Only Valentine

Bright Lights

Honey Pot

<u>Erotic Accommodations</u>

Room for Three?

Neighborly

<u>Love At Last</u>

Every New Year

One More Valentine

<u>Heist Holidays</u>

Grand Theft N.Y.E.

<u>The Family</u>

Beautiful and Dirty

The Hitman

The Enforcer

Dolci

The Don

Dolore

-

<u>Bay Area Blues</u>

Layover

Back in the Day

<u>Curriculum Vitae</u>

Office Hours

Sabbatical

<u>Mosley Coven</u>

The Night Gate (website exclusive)

A Flicker to a Flame

Invocation

-

<u>**Standalone stories**</u>

Encore

The Tenant

Sex Toy Soldier

Looking

And When You Leave Me

Small Mercies